Sin & Spirit

Also by K.F. Breene

Sin & Spirit

By K.F. Breene

Contact info:
www.kfbreene.com
books@kfbreene.com

Chapter 1

ALEXIS

I WOKE UP gasping for air.

The dreams had started after Valens's death.

The details varied from dream to dream, but a few particulars remained the same. Each time, my soul was torn out of my body, dragged across the Line, and made to walk beside a shadowy creature into the bowels of the spirit world. Into a weightless place without substance, where time didn't exist, my body wasn't welcome, and my mind felt like it was swimming.

Even though I wasn't corporeal in the dreams, it always felt like I was holding hands with my companion. Their touch lent me a comfort I couldn't describe. It hinted at an intimacy I didn't share with anyone, save Kieran. That strange, unwanted sense of connection was what made me fight to the surface of wakefulness, trying to get back to the guy who held my heart. The guy whose soul I was connected to in an unbreakable bond.

I would somersault, end over end, until I slammed

back into my body.

When it first started, I used to wake Kieran with my thrashing. Sometimes I'd need to hold him afterward. To reassure myself that *he* was real, not the shadow being.

Although I was afraid to even think it, much less tell anyone, half of me wondered if they weren't dreams at all. They felt strangely like the few times I'd been helped within the spirit world, tearing down Valens or learning about securing a soul in its spirit box. Similar…but not the same. The differences were enough to make me question if my subconscious was creating the dreams in remembrance.

Kieran didn't budge this time, though, and I didn't want to wake him. I trudged down to the kitchen puffy-eyed and half-asleep, trying to shake myself out of it.

As the cold tiles shocked into my bare feet, I registered Zorn's soul in the house, intense and bright. He was nearly at the doorway leading to the formal dining room and the sitting room beyond it.

I frowned in the dim moonlight filtering in from the windows. What was Zorn doing back here? He'd left after dinner.

I nearly stopped to wait for him, feeling him moving in my direction. But I continued on to the refrigerator instead, desperately needing something to quench my cotton mouth. I had no idea why he'd returned, and frankly, I didn't really care. My house had become the hub of the Six and Bria, Kieran's close-knit staff. The family atmosphere appealed to them, and I enjoyed having them around. Not in the middle of the night, per se, but whatever. Zorn was strange. You had to take the good with the bad.

I grabbed hold of the fridge handle as Daisy's soul caught my awareness. It wasn't where it belonged—in her bedroom upstairs. Instead, she was skulking quickly through the sitting room, maybe sneaking up on Zorn, or possibly laying some sort of trap for Mordecai to unknowingly stumble into tomorrow morning. She'd really taken to Zorn's training, and she, unfortunately, practiced her budding craft on us. A bucket of water splashing down over me as I left my bedroom was not awesome. A knife flung at my head from some sort of spring as I flicked on the coffee pot was downright terrible. I'd had to threaten her life to get her to stop. Since I was her kind-of parent who owned the roof over her head, she had to listen to me. But poor Mordecai hadn't been so lucky. At least his shifter magic allowed him to one-up her in their combat training. That helped even the score.

Bright light from the fridge made me squint as I grabbed out a bottle of water. A flash of movement caught my eye. A tiny scuff announced Zorn rolling across the open area and ducking behind the island.

Fridge door still open, I turned to see what he was doing when he popped up. His right hand was pulled back, ready to throw.

A knife!

Before I could shout *no*, a blur of movement came from the side. A projectile sped at Zorn as he was letting go of the knife. A book followed almost immediately, but the trajectory was different—it cut at a diagonal, through the empty air between Zorn and me.

I jolted, ready to duck, when the book knocked the knife out of the air!

"Holy—" My eyes widened in surprise at the excellent throw—and the fact that Zorn had hurled a knife at me—as Daisy exploded into the kitchen, dressed in black and holding a long dagger.

Zorn pushed toward Daisy, black paint on his face. Apparently he had a stash of daggers on him, because he already had another one in hand. Whatever Daisy had thrown hadn't stuck in his body anywhere. She was clearly trying to remedy that as she moved forward with her dagger and struck. But it was a shallow, weak attempt. He blocked easily and quickly countered.

"Okay, come on, you guys. I'm tired. Can't you do this somewhere else?" I whined, shutting the fridge door.

But Daisy was already slashing at him with her other hand, having pulled a knife from the heavens knew where. She'd set him up.

He smacked his forearm against hers at the last moment to block the thrust. She slid her arm off, knife pointed down, slicing his skin.

Zorn didn't even suck in a pained or startled breath.

I leaned heavily against the island, tired, annoyed, and, honestly, a little fascinated. I never got to see them train anymore. These days I was always busy at the cursed government building, trying to find my place in this new life with Kieran. I wanted to contribute in some way, and the only alternative was wasting my days away as a socialite. No thanks. I didn't really even know what that was.

Zorn stepped diagonally to the side, and a drop of liquid caught the moonlight as it fell to the ground. He healed faster than normal, thanks to his blood bond with Kieran, but it wasn't immediate. He'd better clean the floor when they were done. He jabbed his blade at Daisy's side.

She twisted away at the last moment, the strike too close for comfort. For *my* comfort, anyway. While he might heal quickly, Daisy was human. She possessed no such ability. Summoned by my anxiety, the Line pulsed in the room, a slash of black within a nest of bruise-like colors, the entranceway to the spirit world. Spirit blanketed the walls, covered the floor. It spread across the windows and wove into the ghost-repellent magic encasing the house. Power filled my body, ready for use.

I held it at bay, not wanting to interfere. Zorn knew what he was doing. He wouldn't hurt her more than she could tolerate.

Daisy brought her arms around, knocking Zorn's hands away. Her blade passed across Zorn's wrist. He gritted his teeth and spun, lashing out in retaliation.

She was already moving, crouching and bending, as graceful as a dancer. Her small stature didn't hinder her from holding her own with six-foot-tall, well-built Zorn. If anything, it made her quicker. Harder to pin down.

I wondered why he didn't just tackle her and be done with it. Mordecai certainly would have. Though Mordecai had been stabbed too many times to count. Thank heavens powerful shifters healed at lightning-fast rates.

Zorn swiped her right hand, opening up a line of red. Daisy did suck in a pained breath. Then the hilt of a throwing knife blossomed in Zorn's side.

"Oh shi—" I backed away from the island. If knives were flying, I didn't want to accidentally get a ricochet in the face.

Zorn's arms moved faster. So much so that his limbs seemed to almost liquify. Two steps and he was next to her, his blade cutting the air millimeters from her arm. Next he slashed inches from her chest. She barely moved out of the way, playing defense now. Another slash and Zorn finally managed to nick her upper arm, angling the knife so it didn't plunge down deep.

More power trickled into me. I gritted my teeth, fighting the desire to come to her aid and end this fight the easy way. *My* way.

She didn't stop, merely changed stance. Someone flung another knife, but I didn't see where it landed.

My attention was on a moving object behind them. Getting to a better vantage point, I could see Frank sprinting across the lawn in what I could only assume was terror.

What could make a ghost run like that?

"Wait. You guys. Stop." I hastened toward the window, nearly getting a blade between the ribs for my efforts. I had a blood bond with Kieran, too, and healed just as quickly as Zorn, but I wasn't nearly so stoic about pain. "Stop!"

With my magic I punched their spirit boxes, the hard crust surrounding their most precious possessions: their souls.

Zorn danced back a few steps, wiping at his chest, but Daisy didn't let it slow her down an iota. She surged after Zorn and stabbed down with her blade, getting him in the shoulder. She could've had his heart, but he wouldn't have come back from that one.

"I said wait!" I slashed through her middle this time.

She grunted and bent, staggering to the side. Guilt squeezed me, but I ignored it. She might not be blood-related, but she was still my kid. I hated hurting her. "Your fault," I mumbled. I also didn't like taking blame.

I jumped over a tight-lipped Zorn, ran around the table, and made it to the window just as Frank disappeared into the trees lining the cliff at the end of the street. Spirit lit up the world. Power pulsed around me, through me. I turned my head to see what Frank had been running from.

A creature stood on my grass, roughly a human form. Blacker than midnight, it looked like a person-shaped hole punched through the fabric of the world. It stood ten feet tall, with shoulders wider than a shovel was long. Its robust chest cinched down into too-thin hips before exploding out into two enormous thighs. The thing was absurdly disproportionate.

Positioned in front of the house, it tilted its blank face up to look at the second-story windows. It started forward, stepping like it was walking on the grass, but its form hovered a foot off the ground.

I back-pedaled, my eyes feeling as big as saucers, my heart choking me.

"What's happening?" Daisy asked, already by my side with her knives.

The creature reached the window, and Zorn stepped in front of me, cutting off my view.

"Damn it, Zorn—" I shoved him out of the way as the creature reached out a hand. My breath stuck in my throat.

Its hand curled into a fist, gripping the web of repellent magic coating the house, then tore it away with one quick yank. "Oh crap." The words sounded more like a wheeze. My heart felt like it was punching holes through my ribcage.

Frozen in terror and indecision, I just stood there, struck dumb.

"What's happening?" Daisy asked again, shaking me, trying to get me to snap out of it.

I needed to snap out of it.

The creature bent, then stared through the bared window, its curtains hanging to the sides. As the resident Demigod's main squeeze, I'd never had a problem with Peeping Toms. Kieran was not brutal like Valens, but he also wasn't entirely rational where my safety was concerned. If I was threatened, he got crazy in a hurry. People were smart enough to realize this.

This was not a person. And if it was, it clearly wasn't a person under Kieran's influence.

Shivers washed down my skin as the creature stared directly at me. It didn't have a face, so I couldn't see any eyes, but I *knew* I was its focus. I actually felt it studying me, peering down into my body and analyzing my soul. I stood, frozen, teeth clamped shut with an aching jaw, entirely vulnerable.

Snap out of it!

I reached for power, yanking it from the Line. Wind from the spirit world blew my hair back as I shoved my hands forward. My magic slammed into the creature, hard and rough. I kept pushing, shoving it toward the spirit world whence I knew it came.

The creature jolted backward. Its shock vibrated through me. Its delighted surprise. It seemed...proud, somehow.

That jolt was all I got. The creature bent over and buried its fists in my grass, resisting my magical thrust.

More shivers arrested me. I didn't know how I could decipher its feelings, and I certainly didn't understand why it would delight in my attack. But I did know this thing was powerful as all hell to withstand me.

A rumble shook the foundation of the house. The sea crashed against the cliffs beneath us.

Kieran was awake, and the Demigod knew his territory had been breached.

I entwined my magic with air, a gift from the soul link with Kieran, and whipped the creature. I dug into its chest, grasping for a soul and not finding one. I used spirit and air to tear at the shadowy form. To rip at it. To punch a hole through it.

It shook its head, fighting my efforts. It had more

power than I did, even in this strange, non-human form. Or maybe because of the non-human form?

Kieran stalked into the kitchen like a commander joining the front line, muscles rippling along his bare torso. His fuzzy slippers did not take away from his ferocity. How could they, with his infallible confidence and the malice burning brightly in his hard eyes? Power built around him, the ocean now roaring not far from the house. Storm clouds gathered overhead, laden with heavy rain, and swirling fog engulfed the street. His power rolled across the grass where the creature knelt. The windows shook in their frames and the ground continued to tremor.

I sensed a pulse of uncertainty from the creature. It appeared to be having second thoughts now that Kieran was on scene. His power trumped mine, without question. It looked up, the plane of its face level with mine, its eyeless gaze digging down into my soul again.

And then it stood, faster than thought, and zipped beyond the fabric of the veil. Just like that, it was gone, disappearing into a place I didn't know how to follow. Not that I would have tried. For a moment, all I could do was stare.

The Line still throbbed around me. Kieran came to a stop by my side, followed by Jack, whose turn it was to stay in the spare room for the night.

A huge wolf loped into the kitchen to join us.

"Always late to the party," Daisy muttered. Mordecai replied with a snort. If Daisy had been afraid of the threat she couldn't see, her voice didn't show it.

I was terrified.

"What was it?" Jack asked, gripping a gun in one hand and a knife in the other. He was a Kraken—he had to fight with non-magical weapons outside of the water.

Kieran shook his head and looked down at me. Something in his eyes set me on edge.

"I don't know," I said softly. I tried to explain the creature I had seen. "It tore down my repellent magic like it was nothing. It withstood my attempt to shove it back into the spirit world. I used everything I had, and it…"

"Had the power of a Demigod," Kieran finished for me. "Given I can see ghosts, thanks to our soul link, but couldn't see this and you could, it could only mean one thing."

"One of those Hades bastards is paying house calls." Daisy put her fisted hands on her hips, now gripping a knife tightly in each. She'd clearly intended to help fight. We needed to have a talk about that.

When my limbs stopped shaking.

"They can…travel through the spirit world," I said, clearly late to the party in piecing it all together. "Someone was checking up on me."

"That someone got a surprise, I'll wager," Zorn said.

"He didn't stay long."

"I couldn't see it, but I could feel the pulse of a Demigod's magic. Must be the Hades Demigods' power of invisibility." Kieran wrapped an arm around me and directed me to a seat at the island. "Looks like they aren't invisible to us all."

I heard the pride in his voice, but it was misapplied. "It doesn't matter that I can see them. I can't do a damn thing to stop them. You saw what happened. It didn't go anywhere until you showed up. Could it be…" I took a deep breath. "Could it be my father?"

Kieran had taken my DNA and compared it with other Hades Demigods, the only people that could sire a Spirit Walker as powerful as me. He'd found out that Magnus, a powerfully cunning Demigod who killed his kids, was my biological father. It had not been a welcome revelation, and after the battle with Valens, my identity was no longer hidden. Sooner or later, I would have daddy issues.

Kieran kneaded my shoulders, his touch welcome, and glanced at Jack, who moved to the coffee pot. "I can't say for sure. It's a possibility. But I have power to rival theirs," Kieran said. "If you can see them, we can work together to combat them. Together we are impervious to their greatest asset."

The note of pride was back, and I wished he would just cut it out. Because yeah, if we were in the same place when that thing came back, or another one came to check me out, we'd be okay, sure. But he couldn't always be by my side, and any experienced Demigod would be smart enough to know it. Next time, they'd get me when I was by myself and vulnerable. Next time they might not leave so quickly, or be thwarted so easily.

Next time, they might not be just checking up on me.

Chapter 2

ALEXIS

"WHAT ARE YOU wearing?" Bria asked the next morning as she walked toward me between the rows of cars at the back of the magical government building. Although I now came here daily, I still preferred to park at a distance and take a slow, under-the-radar approach. I'd religiously avoided this place for most of my life, at my mother's direction, and old habits died hard.

Bria's platinum-blonde hair fell straight down to dust her shoulders. Her ripped T-shirt featuring some sort of big hair band from yesteryear fit in perfectly with her dog-collar necklace.

I rubbed my tired eyes, then swore at myself before licking the pad of my finger and wiping it under my left eye. I wasn't used to wearing makeup, but when I went into the belly of the beast, it was a must. Too bad I constantly forgot I had it on. Some days I looked like a raccoon before someone politely told me to visit a mirror.

After doing a self-check of my smart, conservative, beige dress, something I hoped would keep me off the worst-dressed list in the tabloids this week for the first time in two months, I smoothed my not-quite-straightened hair. I'd gotten bored halfway through taming it earlier that morning. "What? I'm business casual."

She came to a stop in front of me, cocked a hip, and gave me a flat stare. "What did Daisy have to say?"

Daisy had found her stride in fashion thanks to Kieran, who'd given her free rein to shop with his unbelievably deep pockets. I shrugged. "She's a teenager. What does she know about dressing like a twenty-something career woman?"

Bria's eyebrows slowly lifted.

I sighed. "Fine. She said I looked frumpy, and I needed to lead the fashion world with a unique sense of style rather than follow the herd of sheeple. Especially when that herd makes me look like an old maid."

"And she is right on all counts."

In frustration, I waved my hand up and down in front of her. "Why would I take your advice? You look crazy."

"That's because I *am* crazy. My style matches my personality. People know exactly who I am, and how few fucks I give. That works for me. You need to give in and realize that if you ever want to be spoken of favorably in those stupid gossip magazines that follow you and Kieran around, you need to find your own style. And you need to flaunt it with confidence. You looked better in your poor girl's clothes than you do in that expensive clusterfuck you're wearing. If you keep dressing like this"—she waved her hand in front of me—"you'll be miserable because you're trying to impress people who don't want to be impressed."

I slouched in defeat, because I didn't want to bother finding my own style. I didn't care about makeup and hair and clothes. Sure, I enjoyed shopping and dressing up to go out, but the last thing I wanted to do each morning was waste an hour primping. I said as much.

Bria rolled her eyes before jerking her head for us to get walking. "Then hire someone to do all that. The great thing about being shacked up with a Demigod— maybe the only great thing…" She gave me a *look*. Even though she'd admitted Kieran was a good guy and a great leader, she'd never quite forgiven me for falling in love with a Demigod. They were notoriously possessive, and so powerful they could be inescapable, something Valens had taken to an extreme with Kieran's mother. "…is that now you can outsource. If being his lady means you have to look the part—and, unfortunately, it does, just like he needs to look the part of a Demigod— hire someone to take care of it. Drink your coffee and eat a croissant while someone picks out your clothes, does your hair, and paints your face. Make this new life work for you how *you* want. Make his bankroll your bitch. Honey, you deserve it."

I waved it away. When you grew up assured you'd be poor your whole life, you kept wishes and daydreams to broad strokes. A bigger house, a dashing suitor, and water that stayed hot long enough for a shower. This seemed frivolous and wasteful, and even though I did like gifts and handouts, I didn't like the idea of asking for help on such a superficial level.

The things we learned about ourselves…

We emerged from the rows of cars and stepped onto the walkway leading to the front entrance. Even from here, there was a stunning view of the sparkling ocean beyond the building.

"What the hell was Zorn doing creeping around the house last night?" I asked. Given that Bria was sexually involved with the stoic djinn, she was as likely to know as anyone. I certainly hadn't thought to ask Zorn himself after the whole shadow-creature episode.

"Oh, that. He'd made a threat on your life to Daisy, without telling her when or where he would strike. Her job was to keep you safe. He was pleased with her response, though he'll probably give you a lecture about being more aware of your surroundings. He shouldn't have gotten that throw off."

I rolled my eyes as we reached the large glass doors.

"If I hadn't known who he was, he wouldn't have. I knew he was there. Friends don't punch friends in the spirit box unless there's a good reason. Like when a shadowy Demigod creature shows up on your front lawn."

I pulled open one of the heavy glass doors and stepped aside so she could go through, then followed her. A large lobby spread out in front of us with a reception desk off to the left. The blue-skinned woman sitting there glanced up, then did a double take when her gaze landed on me. Several other people started staring, too, as they passed through the lobby.

My face heated. I barely stopped myself from fidgeting self-consciously as we veered off to the large staircase against the far right wall. What Daisy and Bria had said about my outfit took over my thoughts. Sure enough, someone paused, turned, and raised her phone, taking a pic. I pretended not to notice as we reached the stairs.

"Good," Bria said, not sparing anyone else a glance. "He figured that since you didn't call him out…"

"It was the middle of the night. I was tired." I bent my head, letting my hair fall in front of it as another person lifted their phone, tracking us as we ascended the stairs. "I wasn't in the mood to care what he was doing. Until he threw the knife at me, that is."

"Lift your chin," she murmured. "Don't let them see

how uncomfortable you are. That'll only make them bolder."

I gritted my teeth and followed her advice.

"That's what I told him," she continued. "He thinks everyone is as suspicious as he is. It's annoying. Anyway—"

"I probably should've checked to make sure both kids were in bed when I first woke up. I didn't notice Daisy skulking around the house until after I felt Zorn's soul."

"Don't tell him that. You'll get a lecture. Anyway, check it out. I have a friend that owes me several dozen favors. This chick was always getting herself in near-death experiences. It was a real fun time getting her out of them until she took a cushy job with a Demigod's inner circle. Sabin's a lesser Demigod without a pot to piss in. No one is threatening him. Anyway, she has a friend that knows a guy whose uncle does security for Demigod Zander. Turns out, they kept some of the last Soul Stealer's stuff. You know, just in case they want to call him back someday. They haven't, of course—they're too terrified. With a well-placed bribe, I was able to get this."

According to Kieran, the last Spirit Walker had been an assassin—someone who'd used his ability in service to the former pope. Demigod Zander had caught him and killed him, apparently a much more common fate in modern times than the Spirit Walkers of legend, who crossed battle fields with their magic and decided wars. Did I really want an assassin to train me, assuming he'd actually do it? I could theoretically force him to do my will, sure, but I didn't like controlling spirits, and I suspected it would be harder to control a fellow Spirit Walker.

She glanced around as we reached the top of the staircase before pulling a black velvet bag out of her pocket. Holding it close to her body, somewhat between us, she extracted a badly worn gold pocket watch with a winder on top. Little cranks and wheels decorated the cover, the design dulled with time. A tarnished chain pooled on her palm with at least three links that had been soldered together at one point or another. It was clear the watch had been heavily used.

"It still works," she said, flipping the cover open to reveal the watch face with a second hand ticking away and a peepshow of gears turning in the middle. "Old trusty. He never had to worry about a battery failing him. He could slip into the spirit world, and when he came back out, he could count on the watch telling him how long he'd been there. Or, if it had stopped ticking, he could monitor time that way, too."

"So you definitely think I can leave my body behind and walk the spirit world without dying?" I asked quietly. We'd spent the last few months searching for information about my magic but hadn't turned up much. Those who knew about it either existed before electronic records or didn't want to share. Probably both, given the secret assassin nature of the last Spirit Walker.

Whom Bria wanted me to call back from the Line.

"No, I'm not sure." She tried to pass the pocket watch, but I yanked my hands away. I didn't want the "tap-tap no backs" rule to apply here. I wasn't sure I wanted anything to do with this. "It's still mostly a working theory."

"Super," I said sarcastically.

"The watch is promising, though. The Demigods of Hades all have assistants to tell them how long they've been wandering in the spirit world. So I've heard, anyway. A body can only live so long when the soul is not present."

"But if they don't know the time until they get back, what good is a watch?"

"No idea."

"And how am I supposed to avoid staying away too long when time doesn't exist in the spirit plane?"

"Not a clue."

I blew out a breath, nodding hello to Mia as I passed the little alcove decorated with a large metal tree crawling up the wall and spreading across the ceiling. She was a ghost with a powerful telekinetic ability and a strong sense of loyalty. She'd helped us take down Valens, and although many of the other ghosts who'd assisted us had drifted across the Line, she'd returned to the little alcove that had become her home. She wanted to stay on hand in case I needed her again. It was a sweet sentiment that made me feel a little guilty. Sure, trouble seemed to follow me around lately, but I really wasn't worth hanging around for. Not when she had to do it as a spirit no one else could see or hear.

I elbowed Bria's hand, and the pocket watch, away. "When did you get that, anyway?" I asked her.

"Not that long ago. As soon as I realized what you were, I started trying to figure out how to get something of the old Soul Stealer's. I don't plan ahead often, but when I do…"

I waited for her to continue as we turned a corner into a dimly lit hallway in the middle of the building. The offices here were for low-level support staff who'd barely graduated from magical training and had just enough clout for their own office.

I grinned to myself as we neared my little mole hole. Kieran had said that if I took a "proper job" in the government, I'd get a "proper" office, which would probably be large and bright and luxurious with a great view—Kieran liked to pamper me in any way he could. But I didn't want to take my place beside him in the government. At least, I didn't think I did. Right now I was mostly concerned with helping people by setting up various charities. As a former poor person, I figured that was a good way to give back—by using someone else's money. Mama didn't raise no fool. This tiny hideout was hidden away from prying eyes, and I liked it just fine. The only thing I'd really found to do so far was charity work.

Bria didn't finish her thought, if there was an end to it. She still held out the pocket watch as if eager to be rid of it.

I fit the key into the lock of a plain white door with two tarnished silver number threes nailed to the middle. Joy, who was comically ill-suited for her name, trudged past me with half-shut eyes and a protruding lower lip, her empty coffee mug in hand. I didn't know what she did here, but I did know she hated it.

"Good morning," I said as I turned the key.

"Hmph," Joy replied, not sparing me a glance.

The tumbler didn't click over.

I hesitated. "It's unlocked."

Bria pushed in closer. "Are you sure you locked it when you left last time?"

"Yes. I always lock it. I don't want anyone snooping."

Bria bent and swiped a small knife out of an ankle holster. "Anyone who snoops for a profession won't be bothered by that lock. Someone probably picked it. The question is, are they still in there?" She hefted her knife. If they were, they'd clearly get a slice of steel for their efforts.

"Don't cut any gossip columnists. I have it bad enough where they are concerned." I let spirit infiltrate the room beyond the closed door, expecting to feel my protective magic on the other side.

My blood turned to ice.

My repellent magic wasn't there. Someone had ripped it away.

I froze, relaying what I sensed.

"Is the room empty?" she asked in a whisper. She didn't shove in front of me and take control, an extremely telling non-action. Generally she liked danger. But if the intruder was a Demigod, we were in over our heads. She wasn't the only one hesitating.

"Of physical people," I said, "but I couldn't feel the soul of that Demigod last night, so I'm not sure. Should we get Kieran? I can't take on anything above a level five on my own."

She blew out a breath. "There's a reason the Demigod snuck into Kieran's territory in the middle of the night. And a reason he took off after Kieran got up. He wanted to check you out, risk-free. Demigods aren't stupid. They like to get an idea of the risk before they engage. If it's the same one as last night, he won't want to hang around in the government building. Kieran might only have a small team blood-tied with him, but he's got a loyal army on premises. No Demigod would want to mess with that. I doubt anyone is in there. And if they are, they'll bugger off as soon as you show your face. You know, given you can see them and raise the alarm."

"You sure?"

"Nope. But I surely hope so."

I ran my lip through my teeth, deciding. I really didn't want to bother Kieran. He had a mountain of work at all times, dozens of people vying for his attention, and I was already seen as his mostly ridiculous luggage. Or so the tabloids said. I didn't want to add to that and paint myself as hysterical for no reason.

And if there was a reason? Why, then I could just run and raise the alarm, like Bria had said.

Steeling my courage, I turned the handle, pushed the door open, and stepped back as though a viper waited just inside.

Darkness layered with spirit greeted me, illuminating the contents of the windowless room. I could see my desk hugging the right wall, as if afraid of my chair pushed up against it. A desk light was perched on the side, right below a hanging light that, oddly enough, had been placed in the corner. Filing cabinets leaned forward on the slightly uneven ground, strange in an office, away from the far wall, which I knew held a picture of a white cat, sitting on the sand in front of an azure ocean-scape, a weird picture left over from the last resident. A plant loomed in the corner, thankfully fake, or it would be dead. No one waited in the small space, living or dead.

"Clear," I said into the slightly musty funk. Not for the first time, it struck me that the last resident had probably stowed a cat or two in here.

Bria pushed in beside me, reaching for the light switch and flicking it on. The mustard-yellow walls seemed to match the smell. The room was as empty as the spirit had shown.

"Which Demigod do you think it was?" I asked. "Kieran didn't answer when I asked last night. Do you think it's my father? Do you think he's figured out I'm his?"

"I don't even think Henry knows," Bria answered.

Henry was the member of the Six I knew least. He was always out in the field, as the guys called it. As a Reflector, he could push people's magic back onto them, which wasn't very helpful with many types of magic, like if someone was a shifter. Stronger magics, like mine, could work around it.

His value wasn't in his magic, however. He was a highly intelligent charmer, able to get information most people couldn't, and had a knack for being in the right place at the right time. Whatever he learned went into that big brain of his, which helped him deduce and decode highly classified and extremely useful information. Or so the guys constantly said in something close to awe.

I pulled out the drawers in my desk, checking to see if anything was missing. Unfortunately, the cat pens and little kitten postcards were still there, the desk not properly cleaned out after the last resident's departure, like the office itself. I really should've seen to it, but I wasn't going to be here long.

"The thing is…" Bria stood against the only bare part of wall in the whole office, where a window showing blue skies and palm trees had been inexpertly painted. "Three of the four Demigods of Hades are males. One is so old he doesn't count. He's politically retired and basically just waiting to die. One is married, but everyone knows Demigod Aaron screws everything that's willing. He's the sire of the last Soul Stealer."

I paused. "I thought the last one worked for the pope? And wasn't he middle-aged when he died? Which was fifty years or so ago."

"He did, and yeah, that's right. Why is that confused look on your face?"

"Well…" I straightened up. "Why would a Demigod's son work for the pope, who is non-magical and believes in the Catholic God instead of the legendary magical gods of myth? And I thought Demigod Aaron was mortal. Why does he look so young if his middle-aged son died fifty years ago?"

"Oh, I see." She nodded. "You're living with your head in the sand, as normal."

I frowned at her and moved to the filing cabinet. Only half of one drawer was mine, and I'd had to displace info on cat shelters to clear it out. I didn't want to know what was in the rest of the cabinets.

"Aaron didn't know about him until after Demigod Zander killed him and traced his lineage. DNA testing—it's informative. Anyway, unlike you, that dude didn't evade the magical testing machine, which led to routine training. The pope, who has as many spies as a Demigod, heard about the kid first, brought him onto the payroll, erased his previous records, and probably brainwashed him somehow. He took the guy's training in a different direction, and *voila*, he had an incredibly efficient, high-level assassin."

"But how did the pope get him training? Obviously not through the Hades Demigods if they didn't know about him."

"That's the million-dollar question. I don't know. He clearly knew the right sort of people, unlike Kieran. And in answer to your question, Demigod Aaron is mortal, which you should know means he still lives for, like, five hundred years or whatever. That dude is still in his prime baby-making years, which leads me to why he might have paid you a visit. He might think you're his. He's got a history of illegitimate children, after all."

"Illegitimate children? How about he's got a history of walking away from his responsibilities and should be castrated."

"Wow. Yeah, sure, I'd be down to help with that. I've never liked that jackass. He hit on me once. That was a big nope. He's a pig and looks like a little troll with a fat gut. On the other hand, he's a Demigod, and powering up children isn't always a bad thing. Some of his…dropped responsibilities have gone on to do great things, even if they did end up with daddy issues. Regardless, he must know by now that he and Magnus were at the same San Francisco summit twenty-five or so years ago. The timing is close enough to raise eyebrows. I mean, obviously, right? That's where Magnus must've met your mom. She was on record as working that summit."

I turned away from the file cabinet slowly. "What's this now? My mom is on record?"

Bria gave me a flat stare. "You work in the government building and you haven't snooped into your mom's past?" After a silent pause, she shook her head. "You are, quite possibly, the least curious person I have ever met in my whole life."

It hadn't even occurred to me. I had no idea why, other than I couldn't imagine her with a life other than the one I had lived with her. "What was her magic? She never actually told me."

"Level—"

A knock at the open door cut Bria off. Red stood in the doorway, all six feet, two inches of her. Her flaming red hair fanned out from her head and a splash of freckles covered her nose and cheeks.

She was one of Kieran's assistants, although she did less assisting and more scaring people away from his office. The joke was that she was Medusa's heir, only she didn't turn people to stone, she made them wet themselves before buggering off. I didn't know anything about her magic, but she did a damn fine job of shooing away all the drooling pretty ladies who wanted to take my place in Kieran's bed.

"Miss Price, the Demigod requests your presence," she said, more formal than normal.

"Oh shoot." I plucked out the nearest file—a prop to sell my utter busyness. I knew Kieran's game. This was another attempt to convince me to govern with him. I preferred my anonymity and the few small projects I'd kickstarted. "I have a charity meeting in…like…nowish." Which was true enough. "That's the only reason I'm here. At the government building, I mean."

"That explains the strange dress, yes," Red said, and I couldn't help a glance down at myself. It was plain, but

I didn't think it was strange… "The charity for medical aid to help the magical needy was rubber-stamped by the Demigod himself this morning." She stared at me for a silent beat. "That means he approved it."

"Yikes. Someone came down with a case of the assholes this morning," Bria muttered, walking over to look out the fake window.

"With his name on the project, all the red tape you had undoubtedly hoped would take up a lot of your time will be torn away," Red said. "Which means you have plenty of newfound time to see him. Now."

My heart swelled at Kieran's unblinking support of my endeavors. I'd thought all magical people living in the magical zones got medical, but it turned out a lot of Demigods didn't notice the weaker or struggling magical people in their territory, thinking of them little better than Chesters. Valens had supported the "only the strong will survive" system. Not Kieran. He was using his position to help those in need. It made me proud to be on his team.

It also annoyed the crap out of me, because the timing wasn't ideal. He could've had a note sent to me before I picked out this—clearly ill-chosen—dress. But if he'd sent a note, I wouldn't have come. Instead, he'd rubber-stamped the charity. I could still refuse his summons, sure, but given what he'd done to help me (and others), I would feel like a jerk walking away.

Which he knew.

As if hearing my thoughts, Bria nodded. "He's good."

Red stretched her lips wide to show her teeth, a comical and slightly horrible rendition of a smile. "I have something for you to change into. If you'll come with me?"

"But wait…" I looked around wildly for a reason I couldn't possibly go.

I knew the guy wanted to share his leadership with me, which was super cute and rare for a Demigod, but really, I was a poor girl at heart. What the hell did I know about business or leading a territory? I had to have a couple of teenagers help me lead my life.

All of which I'd tried to tell him before he dragged me into the last meeting. That had been a shitshow. Something about the laundry system in the building. I hadn't even known there *was* a laundry system in the government building, let alone why. Then they'd started talking about quadrants, another thing I didn't know anything about, and I was done. I'd excused myself to the bathroom and run off.

The tabloid picture of me sprinting across the parking lot, holding my red pumps, had not been my finest moment.

"I'd like to do the paperwork," I hedged, dancing my fingers across files that weren't mine. "Also, I might need to do something in the way of a charity for homeless animals, because the lack of shelters in this city is discouraging, even in the non-magical zone."

"The paperwork is in progress and…" Red hesitated. She was very rarely thrown for a loop, but I could get to anybody. I took it as a point of pride. "I'm sure you can circle back to the homeless animal issue, though we don't have many furry stray pets in the magical area."

"But…" I tapped a file folder. "We don't?"

"No. Various magical creatures hunt stray pets for sport. It keeps our streets stray-free. If you knew anything about your home—the magical area, I mean—you'd know that."

"A case of the assholes with a hint of dickface," Bria said, running a finger across my desk.

I grimaced at Red. That was…gross.

"Now, if you'll come with me?" Red turned sideways, gesturing for me to get moving. She wasn't a lady with a lot of patience.

Bria crossed her arms over her chest. She didn't offer me any help.

"Any excuse you could possibly come up with has a rebuttal, Miss Price, I guarantee it," Red said. "Please, save us both the trouble and come with me. Demigod Kieran and his guest are waiting for you. I have a dress I think you'll really like."

"Should I keep the car running for when you escape?" Bria asked. She was joking, so I didn't give her the affirmative on the tip of my tongue.

"Demigod Kieran would like you to come, too," Red told Bria.

Bria's smile dripped off her face. "Ah, crap, really? What did I do to deserve this?"

I laughed at Bria, my tension easing a little. Kieran would know better than to bring Bria into a professional meeting—she couldn't be trusted to stay civil, especially when dumb or redundant questions were asked—which meant I had some hope of lasting the whole thing.

"Come on." Red nodded, and we glumly followed her to Kieran's huge office upstairs, the one he'd taken over after Valens's things were moved out. A bathroom was tucked away in the corner, and on the door hung a gorgeous cream silk dress that looked much too fine for the likes of me. Even the new likes of me, with the Demigod's mark and the upgraded social status. I'd probably stain it before I even left the office. "Why don't you hop into that and we'll head out. Bria—"

"Nah." Bria waved Red away, standing near the door. "I'm good."

"This is a meeting with two Demigods. Don't make me hook a leash to that collar and drag you to the dressing room."

Bria laughed, delighted. "You're tall, you're strong, hell, you're even mean, but there is no way you are going to drag me anywhere, let alone dress me up like a show pony. I go like this, or I don't go. Pretty simple."

"Demigod Kieran might fire you."

"He's more than welcome to. It won't get rid of me, and he knows it."

"And what if I kick you around this office and dress the bloody mess that results?"

"Dress yourself however you want. And if that bloody mess you're talking about doesn't stay in the world of the living, I'll knock your spirit back into it, dress you up like a circus clown to go with your hair, and let you dance around the office. How'd that be?"

I rolled my eyes at their standoff, flitted into the bathroom, and quickly donned the fabulous dress. I had no doubt Kieran had picked this out. He loved simple elegance—he said it allowed my natural beauty to shine.

Heat pricked the back of my eyes as I checked my plain face in the mirror—I probably should've put on a little more makeup this morning. I only had a light dusting. And my hair was already wild. Freaking beauty standards—I didn't know how to fit in, let alone compete, with the elegant elite. They all seemed so suave and manicured. I didn't know how they did it.

Outsourcing.

I gritted my teeth and let myself out of the bathroom. Kieran made sure I didn't want for anything, but still, a beauty team was a little much.

Bria had not changed by the time I got out. Red's flat expression said she would like to force the issue but valued her job too highly to have a throw-down with another member of Kieran's staff.

"Ready," I said.

Red stared at Bria a little longer before walking over to Kieran's large desk. She picked up two long, nearly flat black boxes and brought them to a little table at the back of the room. With the largest box in hand, she turned to scowl at me. Only when I crossed the room to stand in front of her did she lift the cover, revealing the largest, most beautiful gemstone necklace I'd ever seen. Two draped layers of sapphires and diamonds, set off with little black opals. Light sparkled across it like the sun across the water.

"Dating a Demigod is usually the worst idea imaginable, but sometimes it does have perks," Bria said quietly, looking on.

"Now that I can agree with," Red murmured.

I turned so Red could fasten the necklace around my neck. The weight took my breath away.

"This is too much," I struggled to say.

Red held up a mirror so I could get a look. Now I wished I'd had a few more fucks to give this morning, because a little more effort on my face and hair was needed to live up to the expectation of a necklace this fine.

"It represents our combined magic in the soul connection, doesn't it?" I said softly, the heat prickling my eyes earlier now overflowing into a tear.

Bria whistled, coming to look. "It must. He's one of the more romantic Demigods I've seen. He probably got it from his mother. Lord knows he didn't get it from Valens. That's a beauty."

Red handed off the mirror to Bria so she could pick up the smaller package. A bracelet to match the necklace.

"He thought this would set off the look," Red said, fastening it to my wrist.

I blew out a breath and fanned my face to dry the tears. "I've never owned—I never, in a million years, thought I could ever own anything like this. That I would dress like this. That I would be standing here, with someone helping me put on thousands of dollars' worth of jewelry—"

"Hundreds of thousands of dollars," Bria cut in.

"This is a big dream. The biggest dream. And I didn't even have to marry a turd and sacrifice my happiness for this. I didn't have to gold-dig. I fell in love naturally—"

"Debatable."

"—and still ended up in a fairytale."

Red and Bria both chuckled, and Red dropped the mirror.

"What?" I asked, wiping another tear away.

Red shook her head and headed to the bathroom, probably to take the mirror back.

"Time to get your head on straight, Alexis," Bria said. "This isn't a fairytale. This is the lull before the storm. We need to finish up your training so that by the time Kieran is thrown into the snake pit of Demigods, you're able to get his back. He loves you, true, and these gifts are undoubtedly from his heart, but he's also strapping you with armor. This necklace and dress will show what he's worth. What you're worth. A Demigod's wealth is an extension of their power, and they buy expensive things so everyone knows they can. Kieran lives a life of prestige, sure, but his kind are constantly at war. *Constantly.* You'd best wrap your head around that sooner rather than later. This is a great moment, and definitely savor it, but you need to remember you're not safe anywhere. This necklace ultimately won't help that. Don't let it distract you from what will happen next."

I swallowed. "What's happening next?"

"You're meeting a stranger Demigod that will undoubtedly be sizing you up. Time to play your part."

Chapter 3

KIERAN

T HE DEMIGOD OF Ontario sat opposite Kieran at the large conference table with six of her staff members fanned out around her, all seated. Kieran's Six were fanned around the room, standing. Nancy had claimed what she probably thought was the head of the table, leaving Kieran at the "foot." Her position spoke volumes. When one Demigod visited another in his or her domain, the visitor was essentially declaring themselves lesser. A Demigod of equal or greater power would have suggested a neutral location. However, Nancy's place at the table told a different story.

He suspected she'd requested this meeting on someone else's behalf. She'd been told to suss things out. She was clearly inferior to her benefactor, but her choice of seating was her way of telling Kieran she did not feel inferior to him.

She and her benefactor had likely believed all this would go over his head, given his age and relative lack of experience. They hadn't given Valens enough credit for training his son.

So who was her benefactor?

Kieran reviewed her known alliances in the nearly silent room while they waited for Lexi to arrive. Nancy had made it quite clear she had no interest in idle chitchat, which had further driven home her pompous self-regard. But it was impossible to home in on any one ally. Being a mid-lister in the magical political world, above stronger level fives but nearly at the bottom of the Demigod hierarchy, she'd bowed and bent her way to obscurity in the Magical Summits, never standing firm on any issue. Never giving alliances a chance to blossom and fruit. Her vote, at this point, could be bought by the highest bidder. Heavens knew, with the way she was mishandling Ontario, she needed it. Anyone could be her benefactor. Anyone at all.

The person who had sent her surely knew that. Kieran was potentially dealing with a powerhouse, which could be any of the three active Demigods of Hades. Magnus might know Alexis was his just as easily as Aaron might think she was his. The third, Lydia, knew she hadn't sired her, but that wouldn't stop her from making a play to get someone so powerful in her Demigod line. Kieran needed to find out who it was, and where their interests lay.

The door swung open, admitting Red with the grim look she was known for. A warrior in assistant's clothing. That fact would likely be lost on Nancy.

"Miss Price, sir," she said, stepping aside.

Alexis glided into the room with slightly mussed hair. The cream dress he'd chosen for her swirled elegantly around her legs and plunged low at the neck, showcasing her perfect breasts and the sparkling diamond and sapphire necklace that dipped between them. The matching bracelet encircled her dainty wrist. He'd had the jewelry made to denote both of their magics, and he wished he could've watched her open the boxes. But he couldn't have given them to her this morning or she would've known he'd reorganized her schedule to make sure she attended this meeting.

The mark he'd given her—announcing her as his chosen partner—enhanced her natural loveliness until she just about glowed from within.

He stood, speechless. Everyone else but Nancy stood with him, and he barely contained his surprise. This was an acknowledgement of status. Nancy clearly thought Alexis was more important than the staff she'd brought, all experienced level fives, and had prepped them beforehand.

A suspicion began to take form.

"Alexis, welcome," Kieran managed, stepping away from his seat and holding out his hand.

Boman, at Kieran's immediate left, stepped around him to pull out a chair for her.

"Greetings," she said, then her face scrunched up and turned red. He couldn't contain his smile. "Hi, I mean. Hello."

"Miss Alexis Price, I presume?" Nancy said, resting her elbows on the table and smiling pleasantly.

Bria waltzed in behind Alexis and peeled off to stand at the wall. If she felt underdressed in a room full of people dressed in tailored suits and high fashion, she didn't show it.

"Yes. Hi—llo. Hello." Alexis bustled toward Nancy, her movements graceful despite her flustered state. That was from her physical training, something Nancy surely hadn't done in over a hundred years.

She bent to take Nancy's hand, obviously confused as to why Nancy had stayed seated. He purposely hadn't told her anything about the constant, covert one-upmanship of Demigods. It had been a risk, but now he was damned glad. Alexis's slip of unchecked confusion made it seem like she thought Nancy didn't have enough status to continue sitting. Not while Kieran was standing, at any rate.

The way Nancy's lips curved downward said she'd caught the meaning.

"This is Demigod Nancy of Ontario," Kieran said to cover the moment. "She's gracing us with her presence. You'll remember, of course, that Nancy is a Demigod of Hermes."

"Ah. Yes, of course." Alexis took her seat, allowing the rest of the table to sit after her. Her blank face said she didn't have a clue what Hermes was known for. She was the most unknowledgeable magical person he'd ever met. At the moment, it was hilarious, but it would be a problem if they were ever in a more powerful person's presence. He'd need to help her work on that.

"Her line knows their way around the spirit world," he went on.

"Oh, awesome," she said, nodding, a sparkle in her eyes. "So you share that with the Hades Demigods, then."

Thunderclouds rolled across Nancy's face.

"Forgive her, Your Excellency," Bria said with a placating smile. "I'm not sure if you've heard, but her mother raised her in the dual-society zone to protect her. Thank God, am I right? But she wasn't given much of a magical education. I'll just give her a little history so we're all on the same page, shall I?" Without waiting for the go-ahead, Bria edged down the wall so she could better see Alexis. "Hermes isn't as strong as the top three gods—Zeus, Poseidon, and Hades. So while she is topnotch at zipping through the spirit world on an errand of some kind, she doesn't have as much control or power as someone from Hades's line." Bria shrugged, and Kieran knew she understood every ounce of the shade she was throwing Nancy's way. "But wow would she be useful training you up. All you need is a nudge, after all, and she could definitely provide that."

"Bria, that's enough," Kieran said. She walked a fine line. He could handle Nancy if she took offense and retaliated, but he didn't want to burn that bridge. One day he wanted the option to buy her swing vote.

"Of course, sir. Sorry, sir." Feigning chastisement, Bria straightened up and closed her mouth.

"I apologize, Demigod Nancy," Kieran said. "Bria has done a remarkable job with Alexis's training so far, being a level-five Necromancer, but she hasn't worked under a Demigod before. She's rusty on the correct way of doing things."

Nancy's lips were tight and her expression pinched. "Yes, of course. And…Alexis is a Spirit Walker, correct? I haven't been hearing tall tales?"

"She is, yes. The genuine article." Kieran bent his head in a slight bow. Alexis mimicked it awkwardly, and he nearly busted up laughing.

"I see. And do we have…proof?" Nancy pushed. Bria smirked.

"Alexis?" Kieran said, wondering how she'd deliver the proof. The normal protocol would be to pick the weakest member of the present staff and deliver a quick, sharp punch of power to get the point across.

Alexis didn't know protocol. On purpose.

Her face turned red again and she tilted toward

Kieran. "Are you sure?"

"Yes. Demigod Nancy wants assurance of what you can do. I think we can give her that, don't you?"

Bria's smile widened. She knew what was coming.

A heady blast of power filled the room, a quick slice through everyone's midsections. Kieran's people clenched their teeth and clamped down, bearing it. They'd had practice. Nancy's people didn't fare so well.

Screams and wails filled the space. Two people flung themselves back from the table, falling over their chairs and scrambling to their feet. Bria jogged to the door, flinging it open in time for one of the two, a young man, to run out in a blind panic.

That was the staff member to lean on for intel. He would be the easiest to crack.

Kieran glanced at Henry and saw he had already read the situation.

Nancy's face had gone white. She must have thought her power as a Demigod of Hermes would protect her from Alexis's magic.

"That's enough, Alexis," Kieran said softly, school-ing his expression to one of mild impatience. It would make Alexis seem like a rogue warrior, barely kept on a leash. Dramatics were good for a first encounter with a mediocre-status Demigod. A player had to play the game.

Alexis's power drained away, leaving sniveling or

shocked silence in its wake. Nancy stared at him with wide eyes.

"Should we continue?" he asked in an easy tone.

She gulped and nodded quickly. "Y-yes, of course. Her power has been verified. She is as you say, Demigod Kieran."

Just like that, Kieran had the upper hand. Now all Kieran had to do was charm her into revealing her secrets. His father had taught him well, and his mother's magic gave him a…potent arsenal.

✕　✕　✕

MAGNUS

"DEMIGOD MAGNUS, IT was… She was…" Nancy's voice drifted away, letting silence hang on the phone line.

"She was genuine," Magnus said, adjusting the draping of his silk robe as he crossed a leg over his knee. Lamplight glowed softly around him in the interior chamber of his bedroom. He sat on his couch with a bookmarked novel on the cushion next to him. Her meeting with the child Demigod had taken a break while the Spirit Walker was released, giving her a few moments for a quick call.

"Yes," Nancy breathed out, proving why she was mostly useless in all things political. She got worked up much too easily.

"Spirit Walker, level five," Magnus prompted, as

though there were any other level for such a power.

"Yes. The feeling of it... It's like it reached down into my very center and exposed me to the elements. Like I was entirely vulnerable to her whims. You can't protect yourself, even if you tried, with that magic. No one could."

Magnus sighed softly and leaned back, fighting annoyance. Of course he could protect himself. The girl was a level five, not a Demigod. Her power might compare to his within the spirit realm, but it had limitations. The child Demigod had taken down his father with the Spirit Walker's help, not the other way around. She was a tool. A dangerous, exceptional, rare-beyond-belief tool, but a tool all the same. She was still only a level five.

"What of the child?" Magnus asked, clearly needing to steer the conversation.

"Kieran?"

So she was using his first name, no title. That meant one of three things: she was intrigued by him, starting to respect him, or had already taken him to her bed. She wasn't one to shrug away a pretty face, and not many Demigods said no to another of their kind, regardless of whether they'd foolishly bestowed their mark on someone.

"Yes," Magnus replied.

"He is as you expected. New to the job but competent. The write-ups on him are accurate—people greet him with smiles. They respect him, and that respect is not based on fear, from what I could tell. He seems to have things well in hand."

"Did he give you any indication of his political leanings?"

"No. He was…vague." She rushed to fill the following silence. "But that was just because he's still learning the ropes. He said so. He wants to more aptly understand the issues at hand before he throws his hat in the ring. I think he'll be a solid ally, I really do. He's…competent."

Magnus could hear the lust ringing through her words. Not to mention she sounded like a cheerleader.

So she hadn't gotten Kieran in bed yet, but she was well and truly charmed. In only half a day. The child was good. He clearly had gifts aplenty from his slippery, fork-tongued father. That was annoying. It would've been so much easier had he been incompetent, leaving that little Spirit Walker wide open for the taking.

"Kieran is looking for training for the girl," Nancy went on. "She has come quite far, as you can imagine, but she doesn't know anything about walking in the spirit world. She only knows as much as a Necromancer could teach her, plus what she's figured out for herself. He asked if I had someone on staff that would take that honored role…"

Magnus nearly laughed. *Honored role?* Oh yes, the little upstart had a decided way with women. That must've been how he'd gotten the nuisance from Sydney to help him with his father.

"I told him I didn't have the resources with me on this trip," Nancy continued, "but that I would think about it. He offered a trade, although he wasn't specific. I got the feeling it was a future favor, and that could be…useful, given his father's placement in the order of Demigods."

Magnus shook his head and looked at the ceiling. The kid didn't have a platform or any alliances. He was stepping into the Demigod arena with a stolen territory. At this moment, he was nothing. It was the girl everyone wanted, but anyone with half a brain knew either Magnus or Aaron had sired her. They wouldn't stick their noses in until it was clear who they'd make an enemy of, basically, when they moved in to snatch her. That was the only thing giving Magnus a little time to figure out his next move.

It was amazing Nancy had been able to hold her territory for this long. She was as dumb as rocks.

"Give the child someone with a rudimentary knowledge of spirit. Someone that can help just enough to maintain their position, but not so much that they further weaponize her."

"And the trade?"

He did laugh this time. "Trade for sex, if it pleases you. Otherwise, do this in good faith. A Demigod that puts a mark on his mistress for love is as naive as they come. He'll think you're maneuvering for a future alliance." The gullible made his life so much easier.

In the meantime, he'd send in one of his best, but not in the spirit realm. No, no. He would manage the girl by himself. He needed someone to infiltrate the upstart's camp. His operation. The very men who were sent to guard him. He needed someone who could move around undetected by even the Spirit Walker. And when the time came, he needed someone good enough to take out the child upstart when he least expected it so Magnus could have full access to the girl.

"There's one more thing," Nancy said. She paused.

"Go on," he barked.

"It wasn't just her magic I felt in that room. Within my chest, yes, but not swelling around me. She had traces of his magic mixed in with hers, I'm almost positive. They say she took his blood offering, but I've never heard of it affecting a person's magic in such a way. Is that something particular to Hades magic?"

He tapped his fingers against his knee. "No. And you're sure about this?"

"Yes. Almost positive."

He paused as his annoyance returned. "Thank you for the information. Send me your choices of tutors.

That'll be all."

He hung up as she bleated out a question.

Mixing magic was something to do with her type of magic, yes. Something to do with Hades and spirit. But it had nothing to do with sharing blood. No, it came from the sharing of souls.

Memories swirled around him, of a time when he'd been as naive as the upstart. When he'd felt the first sting of love and thought it meant forever. He'd forged a soul connection with the woman, almost by accident. Their magics had entwined, and they'd reveled in sharing each other from within.

Then his greedy son from an ex-lover had set out to tear him down. Tried to take everything that was his, including his lover. When his soul mate had refused the boy's advances, he'd killed her and her unborn child.

The fires of hell had raged that day, and they'd never been quelled. Not fully. Not even when Magnus had encountered the second sting of love some hundreds of years later. That wild, natural beauty who'd surprised him by quickening his frozen heart. But try as he might, he still couldn't forget what had happened to him. He'd sworn it would never happen again.

And now here he was.

If we don't learn from our pasts, what are we?

Chapter 4

ALEXIS

SOMETHING METALLIC THUNKED down on the kitchen island beneath Bria's cupped hand. Her focus on me was intense as she leaned forward, invading my space. "You heard Nancy—she doesn't have anyone she can spare. You're on your own."

Oh, she was pushing the pocket watch on me again.

I pushed back from the island, still wearing Kieran's necklace and daydreaming like a lovesick teenager about how I would thank him. So far the options were seduction followed by fervent suction.

Unfortunately, the shadows were just starting to elongate in the afternoon sun—I had a few hours before I'd even get to see him. After I'd reduced the Demigod's people to mild hysteria, Kieran had given everyone a much-needed break. He'd walked me out to my car, kissed me warmly, told me he loved me, and asked me to wish him luck. It meant he was going to try to get one over on his visitor. I had complete faith in him. One thing he'd inherited from his father was the ability to manipulate. But while everyone had suspected it of Valens, Kieran was still an unknown. None of the experienced Demigods expected him to be smarter than them. It was easier for him to get away with things.

If he wanted Demigod Nancy to send someone to train me, she would.

"First of all, you basically forced Kieran to ask her—"

"I just hinted, is all," Bria interrupted.

"—and second, I'd just slammed them all with very scary magic. The fact she didn't sprint for the hills was a miracle in itself. Any answers she gave after that probably weren't the result of careful meditation."

"What are we talking about?"

Daisy strolled in sucking a lollipop. Her hair was pulled back in a messy ponytail, and she had on a pair of black sweats and a white shirt over a sports bra. It was her post-training look, even though she'd been off for a couple hours. Given she apparently planned on single-handedly bankrupting Kieran using the credit card he'd given her, this was not usual. Also, we were long overdue for a talk about using other people for their material possessions. We weren't scraping by anymore. Things had changed. I'd always thought the saying "more money, more problems" was stupid, but here we were.

Bria pulled her hand away from the watch. "I was just telling Alexis that, seeing as Demigod Nancy doesn't want to lend someone to train her, she needs to bring the last Soul Stealer's spirit back across the Line to help her."

"Like I said, give Kieran time. He'll work on Nancy, just you wait," I replied.

"Why don't you want to call up that last guy?" Daisy asked, taking a chair next to Bria.

"Because he is damn powerful, and I might not be able to control him," I answered.

"That's not it." Bria leaned back and crossed her arms. "It's because you're worried that you'll be forced to control him, and you don't want to."

"Well, it is a bit unsavory," I admitted. "It's not really fair to interrupt his peaceful existence, drag him back to the world of the living, where his life was probably hell, and then force him to do my bidding."

Bria spread out her hands. "That's how it's done."

"He was a murderer, right?" Daisy asked.

"He was killed for his crimes," I responded, knowing where she was going with this.

"Killed, yeah, but was he punished?" she asked.

I lifted my eyebrows. "Punished by death, yes. Being killed was the punishment. It happened. Case closed."

"Um, really?" She gave me a condescending look. "Last I heard, Spirit Walkers could traverse the land of spirits. He would've been comfortable there. So if they killed him, they basically just set his spirit free."

"Number one, we're not sure about that. And number two…traverse?" I frowned at her. "Which one of the Six told you that elevating your vocabulary would help you win arguments?"

A crease formed between Daisy's eyebrows. Bria raised her hand.

"I wasn't going to rat you out," Daisy murmured.

"That's why I got much love," Bria replied. "But keep at it. It does work, trust me."

I rolled my eyes and stood. "Kieran will talk Nancy around if anyone can. We don't need to go for the nuclear option."

"Are you willing to share him like that?" Bria crossed her arms over her chest.

I paused at the refrigerator. "What do you mean?"

"If Nancy batted her eyelashes any harder, her eyes would've gone rolling out of her face. She wants in his pants. And he wants a tutor for you. Sounds like a good pillow-talk sesh to me."

Anger boiled up in me, uncontrollable. The Line throbbed, immediately present. A gale from the spirit world blew my hair.

Daisy grimaced. "Best not to poke that beehive," she whispered. "Kieran knows I'll light his bed on fire if he screws with Lexi. With him in it."

Bria didn't look away from me, and her hard expression didn't crack. "I'll help you strike the match.

SIN & SPIRIT

And okay, yes, I was being dramatic. I don't think Kieran would actually insert Tab A into Slot B. Or C, depending on how kinky Nancy is. But you have to understand, Lexi, Demigods operate by different rules. They all have more money, magic, and power than they know what to do with…and they have each other, which is the only thing really preventing them from blowing the walls off. Kieran might not technically cheat, but he'll feign intimacy to get what he wants. In this particular case, he'll flirt. He might even run his fingertips in a place you'd rather he didn't." Bria put her hands up, probably correctly interpreting the look on my face. "I'm just saying, until he has another means of getting what he wants, through power and position, maybe just do this on your own so he doesn't need to get that tutor, know what I mean?"

Daisy hooked her thumb at Bria. "That's all bullshit. Sorry for the swear, but honestly, kids my age swear. It's not a big deal. Anyway, the guy's mom was a Selkie. Why would he have to run his fingers anywhere if he has sexy magic? But even if that Demigod did give you a tutor, could you trust them? And how much could they actually teach you? Hermes is nothing but a messenger. He goes where he's told. Sure, it's through the spirit world, but he doesn't get to wander around or anything. Someone else's will is in control. That's not the sort of tutor you need. You need the free spirit kind, like that murderer who has bad taste in pocket watches." She jerked her head at the watch resting on the clean surface of the island.

Bria shook her finger at Daisy. "Yes! Big words, or good research. Way to hit the books, kid." She turned back to me. "The kid has a solid point. Plus, learning how to murder in stealth—"

"I am *not* going to learn how to murder in stealth," I barked.

"You have to ease her into things like that," Daisy whispered out of the side of her mouth. "Gradually. We'll get there."

"I can hear you." I shook my head as the sound of a mini-explosion, like a series of pop guns, invaded the kitchen. "What was—"

From somewhere in the house, Mordecai let out a high-pitched yell, followed by a guttural bellow of frustrated rage. A grin slowly worked across Daisy's lips.

"Daisy, what did you do?" I demanded.

"Daisy!" Loud thumping preceded Mordecai stomping into the archway between the kitchen and the formal dining room, his chest bare and splotched in what looked like blue ink. His beige slacks were splattered as well. His white shoes probably ruined. Blue drips ran down his face. "This has gotten out of hand!" he hollered.

I pointed at the partial tracks of blue following him to his current location. "You better not have gotten ink or whatever that is all over this house, young man, or I will kick you around the front yard."

His mouth dropped open and he pointed at Daisy. "She did this!"

"Where's your proof?" Daisy asked, crossing her arms.

He pulled his hand back so he could point again, a splotch of blue flinging onto the floor. "Your smug smile is the proof! The way you're always doing this to me is the proof! You... It... *I don't need proof!*"

I sighed and angled Mordecai around so he wouldn't get ink all over my fabulous cream dress. The partial tracks led to the sitting room, where four upright rectangles of clear plastic, like walls, enclosed a puddle of blue ink at their center, the floor also covered in plastic. It looked like a tent with no roof.

"Well...why did you go in there?" I asked Mordecai in confusion.

"I didn't go in there." His volume was still too high, but I couldn't really blame him. "I was just walking through, like I always do, and the sides sprang up around me."

"How?" Bria asked, working her way around the plastic sides.

"I rigged it like a mine field," Daisy said, delighted.

"When he stepped on the trigger, the mechanical boxes"—she gestured at the nearest small, mostly flat box, painted nearly the same color as the carpet, and from which a pole and two cords, connected to a pole on top, was strung the plastic—"basically launched the pole up and dragged the cords with it. The plastic is attached to the cords. They are so fast that I knew he would just stop and assess for a moment, trapping himself inside. That's what he always does—thinks before he acts. Easy."

"I think because I have a brain and should not be ruled by my animal," Mordecai yelled. The ink was now drying on his person.

"Right. And until you get to the lessons where you actually think and react at the same time, I guess we're at an impasse."

"Daisy," I scolded, "just because you and he are being trained differently doesn't mean you should take advantage of it."

"Why?" She blinked those luminous eyes at me, and given he was magical and she wasn't, and he was a shifter boy with enhanced strength and she was normal teen girl fighting to grow stronger, and given he had an enormous upper hand…

Well, I just let it go. Fair was fair, after all.

"Mordecai, get those footprints cleaned up," I said.

"Why me?" he whined. "It was Daisy's fault!"

"Because you should've known better than to track ink all over the house. And Daisy—"

"I got it, I got it." She jogged off to the downstairs bathroom and returned with a couple of large plastic bags. "Jesus, Mordecai, light a match."

"I came down here so no one would be bothered!" He was back to hollering. "Next time I'll just do it in your bathroom."

Daisy snickered. "Go ahead. See what happens."

Mordecai's face looked like a thundercloud.

I shook my head, my mood soured, and turned back the way I'd come.

"Where are you going?" Bria asked.

"To change. I really hope this spirit actually wants to train me, because I'm clearly not very good at forcing people to do as they're told."

"Hurry up, kids," Bria said with a determined ring to her voice. "We might need all the help we can get."

Chapter 5

ALEXIS

"DEMIGOD KIERAN WAS pretty sure we'd get some good news from Demigod Nancy on the tutoring front," Boman said an hour later, standing with Bria and me in the backyard as the sun melted into the horizon.

"Was that before or after he released you and Jack from his office to give them a little alone time?" I blurted, then gritted my teeth and wished I could reel the words back in.

"It wasn't like that, Alexis," said Jack, who'd pulled a chair to the side of the yard where the grass met the trees and brought out his book. He was technically off-duty and hated all things spirit, but he'd chosen to hang around lest I do something stupid and get myself killed. Daisy and Mordecai sat next to him, knowing this was a big deal and wanting to be here for it. "Well, I mean, for him. She is mad for him, but he's playing her for a fool. She's not the brightest crayon in the box. Kieran is all but certain someone is pulling her strings."

"And my guess is he's hoping she'll pull his string as well." Frank chuckled, a little removed from our party but no less intrusive. "Don't worry, Alexis honey, men just need a little room to sow their wild oats. Once he gets it out of his system, he'll be fine—"

I flung my hand and Frank went flying, tumbling across the grass and through the fence. Hopefully he'd get lost and not be able to find his way back.

"Daisy had some really good points. I'm not so sure you can trust whatever tutor she offers up," Bria said, spreading out a brightly colored square of fabric at my feet. She dug in her backpack for more Necromancer supplies, including stinky incenses, candles, and even a strangely off-pitch bell I absolutely hated. She was pulling out all the stops for this one.

I traced my thumb across the surface of the pocket watch in my hand, wishing Kieran would call. Or maybe text. I trusted him implicitly. I did. But everyone had gotten into my head, and I just wanted to see his face. To read his eyes. To hear that my misgivings were ridiculous and I had nothing to worry about.

"Even if Demigod Nancy offered someone up, it wouldn't be the right someone," I said softly. "I need one of my own kind, or a Demigod of Hades. Daisy was right: I need to learn to wander, not have my destination controlled."

"No worries, we've got this." Bria sat back on her

haunches with her hands at her hips, looking over her setup. "Even the most powerful spirits lose their might when they lose their bodies." She touched the center of her chest. "I'm a strong level five with my tools and enhancements, trained to control spirits." She put her finger up, as though pointing at the sky. "Lexi is nearly beyond a level five with Kieran's bump, in a league of her own, and a natural at controlling ornery spirits. Together we can handle this, no problem."

"Except he's a spirit who knows his craft. For all we know, he might be able to yank Lexi's soul out before she can defend herself," Boman said, shifting his weight uneasily.

"I have enough safeguards to block him if he goes for my soul," I lied, wishing it were true. I didn't have any safeguards. I didn't even know how I'd know an attack was coming. Hopefully Bria's equipment would help.

"We're good." Bria slid her thumb over a lighter and held the flame to a stub of incense. "You ready, Lexi?"

"I still think we should talk to Kieran about this first," Boman said, scratching his chest and looking at Jack. "This could be bad news, setting this kind of spirit loose."

"We tried to talk to Kieran, remember?" Bria's voice was hard. "He was still in a meeting with Nancy and could not be disturbed."

"We should have Lexi call, just real quick," Boman said.

"I did. His cell phone went straight to voicemail and I got the same response from his assistant." I rolled my shoulders, trying to work out the worry. It wasn't like him to ignore my calls. "It's fine. We have two level fives, my boost, and plenty of combined knowledge. I don't even know why we're worrying about this."

"But you could use Kieran's power to help," Jack said.

"Never mind. Leave it." My voice was a whip crack. It was now or never. If I waited any longer, I'd lose my nerve. That's what I was telling myself, anyway.

I slipped into a light trance, welcoming the Line to drift into view, nearly beside me. Its power throbbed in my middle. Around me. I sank deeper, feeling the pocket watch in my hand. Tracing the grooves on the top, and remembering the look of it inside. I let the feeling vibrate beyond the Line. Beyond the veil. Deep into the spirit world, drifting, following the call of the owner. Still firmly rooted in the world of the living, I couldn't help but wonder how different it would feel to step out of my body entirely, like in those dreams.

My consciousness bumped up against something in the vast emptiness. A smooth something. It felt like a wall. Behind it, I could feel another consciousness move. Spin. Wake up?

Suddenly, something rammed against the other side of the smooth thing. Thrashed against it, like a prisoner trying to get out of a cell. Perhaps it wasn't a wall but a door, because it trembled and then pushed open a crack. Vileness oozed out toward me. Deviancy. Corrosion. It sucked at me, hooks scrabbling for purchase, trying to pull me in with it.

Trying to use me to pull itself out.

I jerked back, and then I was falling. Or running? Back-pedaling, trying to get away. Trying to leave that place.

I slammed into reality and staggered backward, a divot in the grass catching my foot. I was falling again, but this time strong arms wrapped around me. Kept me from hitting the ground.

"Alexis? Alexis!" Boman set me on the grass gently, leaning over me with worried eyes. "Alexis, are you okay?"

"He's here!" Bria shouted.

Boman turned, shielding me with his body. I pushed out from under him and backed away, eyes wide, shivering with the remembered feeling of the vile ooze from behind that door. I'd never felt anything like it.

A shape had materialized in the smoke of Bria's incense. The broad shoulders and defined arms pegged him as a man. He walked across the plane of the Line with a swagger, not drifting aimlessly like most of the spirits I'd called. This spirit was accustomed to crossing into the world of the living.

The dizziness of the spirit world melted away, revealing a very handsome man in his late twenties with dirty blond hair, chiseled features, and half-hooded eyes with a hint of bags underneath, making him look worn out from intense partying. Under the dark eyebrows and black lashes were the clearest blue eyes I'd ever seen. All he needed was a cigarette dangling from his full lips and grease in his hair and he'd be James Dean.

In life, this guy was supposedly a middle-aged man and probably run-down. In spirit, he could be anything he wanted. The guy had good taste, I'd give him that.

He waved his hand in front of his face, as though reacting negatively to the incense. It struck me as odd, though I honestly couldn't remember if a spirit had ever done that before. Of course, Bria usually didn't help me when I called someone, so most of the time there wasn't any incense.

"Now, Alexis, that's just not right." My shoulders tightened of their own accord at the sound of Frank's voice. He'd made it back. "Tit for tat isn't how these things are supposed to go. You can't just call a man in to get back at Kieran. Listen, I told you, men like—"

I shoved Frank away for the second time, careful not to take my eyes off the new spirit when I did so. As

Frank torpedoed out of the yard, the new spirit gave a sexy sort of smirk and a husky little laugh. "He's all right. He didn't mean any harm."

Bria murmured from where she crouched, raising a bell. A single toll filled the yard, the sound much louder than it should've been for such a small item.

The spirit's form wobbled. His brow furrowed for a moment and he glanced down at Bria. Adrenaline surged in my body, but before I could decide what to do, he was looking at me again. The sexy smirk was back.

He jerked his head, indicating Bria. "A Necromancer, right? She's strong. That little trick would've brought a lesser spirit to heel nicely. But for me, it was just a prod. She's telling me to mind my manners." His eyes sparkled devilishly. "Is that what you want from me? Me to mind my manners?"

I stared at him stupidly. He was a helluva lot more confident and...*present* than any other spirit I'd dragged back. It was almost like he hadn't been there long.

Except it had been fifty years.

"You have my pocket watch," he said, hooking a thumb into his jeans pocket. He didn't take his eyes off me, and it was doing weird things to my belly.

"Haven't you heard the saying 'can't take it with you'?" I asked, bending to retrieve the watch from the grass where I'd dropped it.

"You got him by the soul, Lexi?" Jack asked, leaning forward in his chair.

"They care about you." The man jerked his head at the guys. "They think of you like family."

"They are like family."

"They're worried for your safety."

I barely kept from gulping. Tingles worked through my limbs. I tried to play it cool, like the new spirit was doing. "They don't realize I'm not in any danger."

His sexy smirk changed ever so slightly, like he knew a secret that I didn't, and it was tickling him to no end.

Vertigo overcame me. The floor dropped away, but I didn't move. The sky spun. My stomach swirled, and suddenly something was grabbing me. Digging into my chest. Scrabbling to get at my most precious commodity. My soul.

Power blistered through me, mine and Kieran's and the Line's, slamming into the spirit and shoving him back to his hidey-hole. But before I could disengage, I was ripped away with him, dragged deep, deep into the spirit world. It felt like I'd lost my body. Like I'd lost my sense of self. My whole awareness consisted of a presence, my own and another.

It seemed eerily familiar.

Something pulsed in my spectral body. A familiarity

that grasped my very soul. A lifeline.

Panicked, I clutched it with everything I had. My connection to the soul who was dragging me severed, broken in two and swished away into the ether. Floating, terrified, I stopped in the nothingness, deadly alone.

Chapter 6

KIERAN

TERROR RAN THROUGH Kieran's body. Not his terror, Alexis's.

He sat forward on the couch, spilling his drink and then dropping the glass entirely. She had winked out of his mind's eye, like the other times she'd somehow drifted into the spirit world.

"What's the matter?" Nancy asked, her shoes on the floor and her legs curled up under her, nearly facing him on the couch.

He pushed to standing and grabbed his phone out of his pocket. While he waited for it to power up, he jogged to the door and pulled it open, seeing Maureen sitting at her desk and Thane sitting at Red's. Red must've gone home.

"Did anyone call for me?" he asked in a rush.

Thane stood from Red's chair, his face a mask of concern. Zorn bent around the far corner, from which he'd been watching Nancy's people down the hall. The rest of his guys in this building would be running toward his office, having felt his alarm.

"*Did anyone call for me?*" he demanded again, impatience gnawing at him with each moment Alexis stayed off his radar.

"What *is* the matter?" Nancy walked up behind him, fixing her clothes as though she'd just put them back on.

He clenched his jaw in annoyance. She was doing that for show. Trying to give everyone the wrong idea. It wasn't for manipulative reasons, either. She wasn't smart enough for that. This was just...what, desperation? Whatever it was, it wasn't important right now.

"Yes, sir," Maureen said, her limbs shaking as she pushed up to standing. "M-Mister Jackson called and asked if—"

"Did Boman call? Bria or Alexis? Jack?"

"Oh yes. S-sorry, sir. Yes, Boman called for you earlier—said to call him back as soon as you could. And Alexis did, yes, but she didn't leave—"

Kieran peeled away, his heart thumping. His phone screen was just populating, and he tapped on the phone icon at once.

A strange tug within his center took his breath away. He reached out to brace himself against the doorframe. It pulled uncomfortably, as though someone had attached a string behind his ribcage and was dangling on the other end of it, threatening to pull his center out through his sternum. His knees weakened with the intensity of the feeling.

The possible implications screamed through his mind. There were three Demigods who could get to her at any time. *Any* time. They could overpower her—or kill her, if it was Magnus—if he wasn't there to get her back. Was one of them there now?

He shook his head to clear it as Thane and Zorn started to move Nancy's people out.

"Hey!" Nancy said, pushing past him. "What is this?"

"Sorry, Nancy, forgive me." Forcing his impatience and worry away for a moment, Kieran turned and gave Nancy one moment of solid playboy focus. The kind women lost their knees over. The kind Alexis always crinkled her nose at. Not one ounce of it was genuine. "Something came up. Call my assistant tomorrow and let's set up a dinner, yes?"

He gave her a beaming, sultry smile and tickled her with his mother's passionate magic. Two seconds and she was starry-eyed. Too easy.

He let Thane usher her out as Henry showed up, out of breath. Donovan was on his heels.

"Get a hold of Boman or Bria, right now," Kieran said to his guys. "Jack should be nearby. Make sure he is on scene."

"Yes, sir." Donovan put the phone to his ear as

Kieran pushed into his office. Henry came through the door after him and closed it behind them.

"What's happening?" he asked.

Sweat breaking out on his forehead, Kieran listened to Alexis's message from earlier. There were two. One was gushy and excited, and he knew it was her response to the necklace. She couldn't wait to see him. The other was…*off*. She asked similar questions, but her mood had changed considerably. He couldn't tell if it was fear riding her words, or unease.

"Replace Maureen," he said as he tapped Alexis's name to call her. "If she can't hear when something is gravely wrong with my most important attachment in the world, then she has no place answering my phone."

Emotions softly filtered through the soul link. He couldn't make them out. They seemed fuzzy, as though hidden behind a veil. He could only discern that she was in a heightened state, as if in great turmoil.

He choked with fear. He'd never heard of a Hades Demigod being able to drag a living person into the spirit world, but they were secretive at best. He had no idea what they were capable of. He shouldn't have let Alexis out of his sight after what happened last night.

"Find out if Donovan got through," Kieran barked, pacing now, willing Alexis to answer her phone. *Anyone* to answer her phone. It went to voicemail. "Fuck!"

He ended the call, then called her again as he turned

toward the door. When Henry opened it, Thane was on the other side, just reaching to grab the handle. His expression was flat. He was concerned, too.

"No one is answering," Thane said. "Not even Jack or the kids. I tried them all."

"Bria either," Zorn said, his body tense.

Kieran was running before he'd registered it. His guys were at his back, passing Nancy's team in the mostly empty halls. After six, most everyone had gone home.

Mia appeared right next to Kieran, surprising him enough that he staggered.

"A spirit was trespassing here," Mia said, running with him without moving her legs. "One that kinda kept blinking out. I saw him when you were in the meeting with that woman. I tried to follow him, but I kept losing him in the crowd of real people."

"What did he look like?" Kieran asked as he reached the wide stairs with various landings and leading down to the lobby.

"Like a ninja. With a cover over his face and swords and everything."

"What about his eyes? What color were his eyes?" Kieran took the stairs two at a time.

"I don't know. He never looked my way."

"Did you see Alexis today?" He got a nod. "Did anything seem the matter?"

He pushed through the large double doors. She glided through the glass.

"No—"

Lights and colors dazzled Kieran as though he were suddenly in a sparkly space vacuum. His stomach flipped and his feet slammed into the ground. He fell to his knees as Mia moved away from him. They were facing the large glass doors again, from the middle of the lobby. She'd teleported him back inside.

From his position, he could see his guys, still outside. Thane reached around his body slowly and plucked a throwing star from his arm. He shivered before rolling his shoulders, and Kieran knew Thane was fighting the urge to go Berserk. Something was out there.

Zorn puffed out of sight, into his gas form, and Donovan turned to the right, looking for their attacker. Kieran could feel his confusion through the blood bond. Henry was nowhere to be seen.

Kieran pushed to standing. "What's going on?"

"Someone threw a knife at you," Mia said, and her spirit winked out. The next moment, Thane appeared next to Kieran. He thunked down onto to his knees, frozen, and fell face-first onto the ground. He lay there for a moment, stiff as a board. The urge to change forms was clearly clawing at him. The fact that he was fighting the urge meant his magic would do them no good.

"He's the dangerous one when he loses control, right?" Mia asked, bracing herself above Thane, her arms out.

Donovan turned quickly, pushing his way in through one of the glass doors. Henry bleeped back into sight on the outside. He turned slowly and stared into the lobby with a blank expression. He was thinking through a problem.

"Someone is—Look out!" Donovan staggered away to the side. A man, his face half obscured by a black mask, appeared out of thin air with a knife in hand, poised to throw.

Before Kieran could duck, the lights swirled and the air sucked at him. The next moment he landed halfway down the flight of stairs. His feet hit the edges of the step, his balance throwing him forward. He tumbled, butt over noggin, finally skidding to a stop on his face with his legs jackknifing above him.

Out of breath, he popped up in time to see Henry push through the glass and grab the guy in black. Henry stopped moving immediately, but Thane was already running to create a wall between the man and Kieran.

"See?" Mia said, her image flickering, clearly low on power. "Ninja."

The man in black had disappeared into thin air.

"Stay still," Henry yelled at Thane. "Stop moving.

He can't use his magic without movement."

"What is going on? Oh my God, Kieran!" Nancy hurried down the stairs, her staff running behind and then in front of her, realizing something was wrong and wanting to secure her.

It almost looked like the man in black jumped out of Thane. Literally jumped out of his body, going from half translucent, like Mia, to a solid person. He charged at the steps. But before he got to Kieran, ready to end this, he disappeared again.

"Halt," Nancy yelled, slowing to a stop.

The man popped out of her, pounded up a few stairs, and disappeared as someone reached for him. Next he hopped out of one of Nancy's guard, trailing at the back of the group. He was sprinting down the upstairs hallway in a matter of seconds.

"Do you want me to follow?" Mia asked Kieran.

"Zorn, can you hunt him down?" Kieran said.

Zorn appeared next to Kieran for a moment, startling everyone, and then was gone. That was a yes. He wasn't a spirit, but he was equally invisible to those who didn't know the trick of finding his presence. It wasn't only Hades magic that allowed a person to hide in plain sight.

"He could tuck into moving bodies and exit…when he wanted, I guess," Henry said, cataloging the magic. This had been his first time dealing with this type of magic, and it had clearly thrown him for a loop. Kieran was confident that next time there would be no such issue. "You saw him disappear—he could hide himself in others, as long as they were moving."

"What was his purpose?" Kieran asked. "Me?"

Henry looked at him for a second, and Nancy slowly resumed her descent.

"Yes. Demigod Aaron has one of those," Nancy said softly, and her gaze pinged around her staff. Kieran understood that look. This had just gotten bigger than her, which meant she wasn't here because of Demigod Aaron. She belonged to one of the other players. "I forget what the magic is called. The slang is Body Jumper. He's one of Aaron's best. You were able to withstand him. I'm impressed. Not many have."

Thane huffed out a laugh. He probably didn't realize she was serious.

She put a hand on Kieran's forearm and leaned in to kiss his cheek. "Be careful. Clearly Demigod Aaron wants you dead. He probably thinks the girl is his. Even if she's not, he'll want her for his cabinet. Because of her, you have some serious enemies. You're in their way. It'd be safer for you if you cut her loose." She lifted a hand to his cheek. "Think about it."

He didn't register her leaving. The strange feeling in his middle turned into a yank. He sucked in his breath and braced a palm against his middle.

K . F . B R E E N E

"What is it?" Thane asked, his almond-shaped eyes inches from Kieran's face.

"Back off," Kieran said, wheezing as the yank became a consistent pull. Alexis's emotions throbbed with hope and desperation. Although their connection was still fuzzy, those emotions were unmistakable.

"Should I go with Zorn?" Henry asked as Nancy and crew exited the lobby.

"No." Kieran took up a jog, shadowed by Mia. He didn't know what was happening, but Alexis clearly wasn't out of the woods yet. "Stick with me."

He hazarded a glance to the right of the doors, where the knife would've come from. The way was obscured by Nancy and her crew. He had no idea how close of a call it had been. A knife usually wouldn't keep him down for long, if at all, but a well-placed knife to the throat was a different matter. Mia almost certainly hadn't saved his life, but she'd tried to. This wasn't the first time she'd proven her loyalty to one of his squad, but it was a first for him directly, the son of the man who had put her here.

"Thanks," he told her, running for his car. "I have a house for you to haunt, if you don't want to stay here. If you want a place to call home."

Drifting beside him, she smiled. "No, thank you. You need me here." She nodded, and then she was gone.

"What—Oh, the ghost was still here?" Thane asked, looking around with wide eyes.

"Which one?" Donovan asked.

"What do you mean, which one?" Henry said, everyone keeping pace. They all parked in the same area. "The one that teleports, you idiot. Do you think Demigod Kieran and Thane both picked up a new trick?"

"Well, I don't really know, do I, since I was possessed for a moment there?" Donovan responded.

"You weren't possessed, you were ridden like a pony," Henry replied. "You still had your wits. Your excuse for wits, anyway."

The tug intensified, bringing Kieran to a staggering halt. He bent over, trying to ignore the feeling. It wasn't painful, and if he really focused, the throb within it was actually pleasant. Comforting. It felt like Alexis. But everything about the feeling said his soul was being pulled out of his body, which made him want to react violently.

Still, he held on, fighting against the urge to try to sever the connection. Opening himself to it, as he had so many times with Alexis herself.

A moment later, Alexis slammed back into his awareness, as though she'd rammed right into his soul. A plethora of emotions hit him at once, strong and vibrant. Fear and uncertainty, wariness…relief.

He laughed with his own relief, still bent with his

hands on his knees.

"What is it?" Thane bent too close again, his beard nearly brushing Kieran's face.

"Thane, back off, for fuck's sake." Kieran shoved at Thane as he straightened up. He took a deep breath. "She's back. Whatever happened, she's back, and she's relieved." He resumed his jog. "What would've hit me back there?"

"Throwing star, but it would've hit your collarbone," Thane said. "I got it in the arm. He followed up with a big throwing knife, but by then you would've ducked it easily, even with a wound."

"A great many would've been too slow, though," Henry said as they slowed, reaching the cars. "They think you're common."

The other guys snickered.

"Alexis is common," Kieran said with a weight in his gut. The soul link normalized, but whatever had happened had shaken her. She needed him. "Where surprise attacks are concerned, she's common. She hasn't trained for any of this. The few skirmishes and the one battle she was in won't help her here. In those, she met the enemy face to face. She knew they were coming, where from, and what weapons they were using. This is a different sort of fight, one she's never even contemplated." He hooked his fingertips under the door handle, breathing out slowly. "Let's hope they keep going for me."

"If Hades' people are trying to kill you, that means they're doing it so they can snatch her," Thane said softly.

"I know," Kieran said, and sat in the car.

His greatest fear had always been that she would fall into the wrong hands. They'd take the Alexis he knew and loved and turn her into the nightmare she most feared. Valens had never gotten close, but that was because Kieran had kept her a secret.

She wasn't a secret anymore.

Chapter 7

ALEXIS

I STOOD IN Kieran's sitting room by myself, letting the crash of the distant waves wash over me. The moon hung heavy in the dark sky, suspended above the ocean as if on a string. Trees waved gently in the breeze. Quiet had settled all around me, cocooning me. I'd purposely forbidden the guys from following me over here. They'd put up a fuss, but ultimately agreed to stay with the kids.

The afternoon had shaken me to my very foundation. I'd been utterly helpless, suspended in a place I was positive I would've died in if I hadn't felt that cord leading me back to Kieran. Back to reality. He was my anchor, I now knew. Something about that soul link kept me with him, even in the spirit realm.

Soon after I'd crawled my way out and spilled out onto the bright, beautiful green grass underneath the glorious blue sky—of course, my body had been there all along—I'd learned that Kieran had broken up his meeting for me. He'd had to chase Nancy away, possibly tarnishing their business, all because I couldn't take care of myself.

I kept disrupting his life. He took it all in stride, or at least he seemed to, but the cold, hard truth was that I was a hindrance. I couldn't help him lead like he wished I could. My accidental frumpiness had made me a public laughingstock. I couldn't even make it up in smarts, because I wasn't particularly educated or insightful. To top it off, I didn't have knowledge of my magic. My one greatest asset could have excused all the others, if only I could make it work. I'd nearly died today trying to figure it out. How fucking helpful was that?

Tears had drained all the moisture from my body. Or so it seemed. I'd only bothered to clean myself up because I felt him getting closer.

The front door opened, and I knew Kieran had left his shiny red Ferrari in the driveway. He clearly wanted to enter the house like he was the guest and I the resident. Which was ridiculous, since he'd bought both this house and mine, just across the street.

"We've made a mistake," I said curtly when I heard him entering the room. I already knew I was going to handle this badly, riddled with fear as I was, but I owed it to him to make this right.

He slowed to a stop, giving me space.

"*I've* made a mistake," I amended myself. "This isn't the life for me. I love you with everything I have, but we're from two different worlds. I can't be the woman you need."

"Is that right?" he said.

"We both know it's right. And if you're still confused as to why, just grab any tabloid you see and it'll list all the reasons for you. In bullet points. On a monthly cycle. Apparently no one gets tired of reading about my faults."

"Pointing out a powerful woman's supposed faults makes those who are lesser feel better about themselves. They try to tear her down so she'll feel as little as they are. But you cannot tear down a star. You cannot dull greatness."

Tears clouded my vision. *It sure feels like they can.*

"Okay, fine," I said, "let's go about it this way—"

"Sure. I love a good pivot."

I gritted my teeth, anger now flirting with my resolve. "What do I bring to this relationship?" Sadness and fear and vulnerability and uncertainty ran through me in crushing waves. I hated this. I hated doing this. I hated the position in which I'd gotten myself. "Besides helping with your dad, what am I bringing to the table?"

Skin slid across fabric. He was probably putting his hands in his pockets. These wouldn't be comfortable questions.

I filled the silence.

"Today was the first time a Demigod visited since

you took over, and I botched the whole thing. Bria told me how I should have proved my magic. She seemed to think it was funny, which is always a bad sign. Then, as if that wasn't bad enough, I got myself into a fix and made you chase the Demigod away. I need a daycare, not a powerful boyfriend."

"Alexis, none of that was your fault. You didn't know any better."

"Yes, exactly. I didn't know any better. But I should have. Isn't that why you spent the rest of the afternoon locked in a room with a pretty Demigod and a do-not-disturb sign on the door?"

I grimaced at my cutting tone, and the fact that I'd mentioned it in the first place. That wasn't what I was doing here. It wasn't the problem.

But even as I opened my mouth to take it back, pain welled up, hot and heavy.

I shouldn't have needed Kieran earlier—I should've been able to handle things on my own—but the truth was that I *had* needed him. And the fact that I hadn't been able to connect with him because he'd been entertaining a powerful, beautiful woman *alone*, something he never did in business, had knifed a feminine, vulnerable part of me. A part that wondered how I'd landed a gorgeous Demigod at the pinnacle of power in the first place.

A part that would now set matters to rights for him,

no matter how much it hurt.

"Is that what this is about?" he asked softly.

I took a deep breath, trying to stay above the pettiness of jealousy. "No. It's not about that. It's just… What happens when you meet the next Demigod? Or when I botch another important deal…" My voice caught and I gritted my teeth again.

"I can feel you suffering, Alexis, so as much as I would like to help you laugh about all this, I'll reassure you instead. I know how that must've looked, and I probably should've talked to you about it first, but I assumed I'd still be reachable. That do-not-disturb sign never applies to you. Not ever. You should've been put through when you called earlier. I wrongly thought my assistant knew that. That was my fault, and for that, I deeply apologize. But baby, even if I had gotten carried away, you would've felt it through the soul link. Or the blood link. You have various ways of checking up on me, and we both know if I ever did something foolish, your wards would burn my house down while you showed up at my office in person to kill me."

I wiped away a tear before it dripped off my chin.

"Today was business," he said. "I used her emotions to manipulate her. This time, her emotions were centered on lust, so I gave her the charm and intimacy she craved. Faux intimacy, in my case. For someone else, I might need to be excessively brutal. Yet another leader may be swayed by deals and trading. To manipulate properly, I need to be what they expect me to be. I need to use their expectations against them. My father made sure I was trained for this. He trained me to be unemotional when I played this game. It's not pretty, but I'm extremely good at it. Which I doubt you understand, because you're the only one who has ever seen through my bullshit. You're the only one I can't manipulate to get what I want. With you, I have to be genuine. I have to earn it."

I closed my eyes, feeling the distant tide pull at me. Feeling Kieran pull at me.

"It isn't pretty, no, but it is your job," I said. "And I don't have a clue how to help you do your job. I don't have a clue how to fit into your life, Kieran. I…" My lips trembled and tears tracked down my cheeks. "I wish I did, honest to God. But I'm a hindrance, and I know it. It has been well documented that I am a j-joke."

"Alexis Price, you are anything but a joke," Kieran said in a hard tone.

Sobs bubbled up, my embarrassment from the last few months spilling over.

"Look, I know who I'm not. I'm not refined. I'm not classy. I'm not from money and I don't know the first thing about pretending to be." My voice rose. "I mean, what Demigod's girlfriend, or even fuck buddy, can't dress herself? I don't fit into your life outside of this house, Kieran, that's the long and short of it. My kids don't fit. Hell, one's not even magical. Being misfits in your organization made sense when you were on the outskirts of the magical world. But now that you're a ruler, we're weighing you down. We'll make you a laughingstock if we haven't already. You didn't even mean to mark me. Eventually that'll get out and make us both look silly." I let out a shaky sigh. "This isn't working. I think it's time..." I had to stop speaking to force back the sobs. "It's time we let this go. This thing we have has run its course. I'll take the kids into hiding and you can get on with your life."

I hugged myself, hardly believing I'd actually said the words. Worse, that I intended to go through with them.

"I'm not sure how to handle this," he said after a quiet moment.

I shrugged. "It's not you, it's me. And probably for the first time ever, that is actually the truth. Just let me go—"

"No, I meant I'm not sure how to handle this—should I laugh? I can feel your pain, so you *actually* believe this is the right thing for me, but it's killing you...so is calling you an idiot out of line? Bitch-slapping some sense into you isn't my style... Should I get Bria to do it? Or maybe Daisy? Because I doubt Daisy agrees with any of this. That kid wouldn't go quietly, that's for sure."

"She'll see reason. And please don't joke. Don't make this harder than it already is."

Kieran sighed, but, thankfully, he didn't move closer. I didn't think I could hold firm if he did.

"Alexis, I know the last few months have gotten to you. They would've gotten to anyone. Literally anyone. Demigods and people of influence have training for all this—"

"For magic, yeah, but not for dressing yourself."

"Even for dressing myself. I've had tailors steering me since I was a child. My mother was a harsh critic, because she had to be. Now you know why. I've been taught how to dress and act my whole life. How could you possibly think you'd get it right out of the gate?"

"But—"

"No. Your pity party has gone on long enough. My turn. I didn't mean to mark you the first time, that's true. It was my natural reaction to you. And I will absolutely let that be known when the right time comes."

"What? Why? I'll look like a—"

"Because it'll prove I had no ulterior motive. It'll prove that your magic wasn't the reason for my mark. Those that aren't in the know might sneer and snicker, and you'll probably return to the tabloids—"

"*Return?* I've never left."

"—but those that *do* understand, the Demigods, for example, will feel the impact. They will know that my desire to protect you is not superficial. That I marked you because I couldn't help myself. If they ever try to tear us apart because of that mark, this will ensure they have no grounds to do so."

I remembered that Demigods had traditionally applied their mark to people they wanted to put dibs on. They'd used it as a brand, denoting certain people as *theirs*, whether that person was a king, a mate, or a slave. The practice of claiming in that capacity was now illegal.

Kieran had already worked out what he'd do if people accused him of illegally marking me in order to make me less desirable to the other Demigods. He was prepared to protect me in ways I didn't even know he needed to.

More tears slipped out and I bit my lip.

"No, I didn't mean to do it that first time, but I've meant to mark you every single time since. I bet you can't even count the number of times I've sizzled my magic across your skin. I even proposed to you, remember? Yes, the timing was more romantic in my head than in reality, but I still meant every word. And when I try again, hoping to catch you in the right mood, I'll mean it then, too."

I shook my head, my warming heart at war with my

logic, love dizzying my mind. I couldn't open my mouth, not sure what I'd say.

"That meeting today went exactly how I'd hoped. I purposely kept you in the dark. I instructed Bria and the guys not to coach you. And you shone like a star. You threw shade you didn't even know you were throwing." I could hear the pride and humor in his voice. "It was perfect. I escorted you out because your part of the symphony was complete. If I'd explained all this, it would've ruined what I'd been going for. And that's my fault. What you're feeling right now is my fault. I apologize for that. As for your not helping me lead..." He chuckled softly. "You might not see the bigger picture yet, but you're doing more than helping me lead. You're shaping my image. You're giving me goodwill with the people."

I startled, no clue what he was talking about.

"If you remember," he said, "I never said you needed to work at the government office. You don't have to work at all—most Demigods' wives or husbands don't. Girlfriends either, before you bring that up. As long as you're happy, it makes no difference to me. But you picked your own office in the bowels of the building and built various charities with moderate budgets that are making me look like a ruler for the people while still being fiscally responsible. You're kicking ass in a meaningful way and you don't even realize it." His footsteps whispered across the rug. His arms came around my middle and he pulled me tightly against his chest. "Right after everything went down with my father, do you remember what I told you?"

Unable to help myself, I snuggled into him, my mind still whirling. My resolve eroding. I was supposed to be doing the right thing and setting him free. Cutting the anchor. The whole situation was going tits up.

"I told you I'd sort things out, and then we'd move on. That we'd go shopping in France, visit my castle in Ireland—I gave you the idea that we'd be free. And then I took a leadership job and chained you here. That's why I've left you largely to your own devices. I let you get your feet wet, then go running. Literally. I framed that tabloid picture of you with the red shoes, by the way. It's on my desk. I was in stitches."

I pushed to get out of his arms, but he held me put.

"The way you're feeling now is my fault." He nuzzled into my neck. "All of it. You have an incredibly rare and potent magic. Everyone is curious about you. They're all dying to see you in action. Dine at your table. Lock you up on their staffs. I *wanted* you to blast the first Demigod to come through here. I wanted you to make a statement, then I wanted you to waltz out, as you do, seemingly without a care in the world. So what are you bringing to this relationship? Your love, your wit, your ability to put me in my place, and your unwavering, open-minded support. What are you bringing to my rulership? Resources for the people and a terrifying magic that makes me look damn cool. They're calling me an upstart, a child, but they aren't doing it to my face. Why?"

"Because Demigods lack a sense of humor?"

"Because you've got my back, and no one wants to mess with you. I'm not just an upstart Demigod—I'm an upstart with an ace in the hole. I have a woman that cannot be bought, cannot be dazzled with charm or lured away with extravagant gifts. A woman I can trust with my empire and my heart. I'm not starting at the bottom. Not with you beside me. Nancy placed you higher on the status scale than a level five. Than her whole prized staff of level fives, actually. She was trying to fight for her placement over me, but it took very little convincing to make her step down." He paused for a moment. "Notice I didn't say kneel down? My fly was closed, that's why."

I huffed out a laugh through the tears, most of them heartfelt and happy. Some inspired by the trigger that had caused this epic spiral.

The fear from earlier welled up. Might as well get it all on the table.

Chapter 8

ALEXIS

"I CALLED THE last Spirit Walker today," I admitted. Kieran stiffened behind me. "Before you get mad, we tried to call you. You were…busy."

"You should've been able to get through. Jack and Boman should've thought to call the other guys. Bria should've thought to call Zorn. The whole thing was a clusterfuck. I let you down. In fact, maybe we *should* break up. I'm not good enough to be your man if my people can't play a simple game of telephone. Yeah, let's break up." He squeezed me as he paused for a beat. "Too soon?"

I leaned my head back against his shoulder. "I *am* trying to break up with you."

"No you're not. You're trying to work through a few tough issues and doing some terrible problem solving. And just so you know, I was bored in there with Nancy today. The woman is clueless and her secrets are largely useless. I got a couple of nuggets and a few leads, but I couldn't work around to who sent her, and it doesn't seem like anyone trusts her. I could've used your call. So what happened?"

"I succeeded in summoning the Soul Stealer. I had to go really far in to get to him."

He slowly blew out a breath, and I could tell and feel that he was trying for calm.

"We have the same magic, but he dominated me. I couldn't get away from my own magic. I didn't know how to fight back. I just forced him back to where I got him. Or tried. He dragged me in with him. I struggled away, but then…I got lost. It was hazy and confusing. I felt like a sailboat in the middle of the sea with no direction and no wind. I was stuck. Unmoored. But then I grabbed what felt like an anchor—I think it was our soul connection—and used that to pull myself back out." I rubbed the back of my hand across my eyes, angrily wiping away the wetness. I pushed out of his arms. "I don't know what I'm doing, Kieran. I don't know how to get better. But there's more to this magic, I know it. More than just ripping out souls and creating obedient zombies. More than war. It can be used for a more noble cause. I need to believe that."

I rounded on him, wanting to punch him for no reason. Maybe just punch anything. "But how the hell am I going to find out? If my dad knows about me, he probably wants to kill me. The others want to use me as a weapon. Your new girlfriend doesn't have the answer with her kind of magic, and I have nowhere else to turn but a more experienced murderer that can flip me end over end in the spirit realm."

By the end I was panting, and Kieran was staring at me.

Silence hung between us as I watched the ocean churn in its endless loops beyond the cliffs.

"Did you like the necklace?" he asked. "I had it designed for you."

My eyebrows crawled up my forehead and I blinked at him for a moment. "Did you hear any of what I said? I'm shit at my magic, I nearly killed myself today, and I don't have one fucking clue what to do about it!"

A smile brightened his eyes and he closed the distance between us.

"You've got fire and determination. You can overcome the impossible. We'll figure it out, I promise you. We'll call the Spirit Walker again, and this time, I'll be on hand to lend you some might. He might be a strong spirit, but I am a Demigod. He won't dominate you a second time."

I dropped my head to his chest. "It's like a fairytale, the way you always save me, but honestly, when do I get to be the strong guy?"

"You turned the tide in my war against my father, fought him off when he was about to kill me, and saved the day. I'd say I've done my fair share of being the mansel in distress. You gotta let me swing my dick around once in a while or I might just get a complex."

I laughed and snaked my arms around his middle. When I tilted my face up to him, he bent down to kiss me.

"I absolutely loved the necklace," I murmured against his lips. "I have some ideas on how to thank you, but I'm actually trying to break up with you first, so…"

"Break up with me next time you freak out. I'm famished. Let's eat dinner. Nancy was sucking on strawberries all afternoon and it really put me off eating. Do you want to eat here…or with the others?"

"Is Jack cooking?"

"Roasted chicken and all the fixin's."

"We're definitely going over there."

He sighed, kissed me in a way that curled my toes, and put an arm around my shoulder, ushering me out. "Good. I'm tired. I didn't feel like making something."

"I like that you assume you'd be cooking, because I definitely wasn't going to."

"Isn't the rule that if it's my house, I cook, and if it is your house, you cook?"

He paused in the kitchen and pulled away so he could lower the blinds. Good thought. After last night, I needed to do that in my house.

"No," I said. "The rule is, if it's your house, you cook, and if it is my house, one of your guys cooks."

He laughed and rejoined me, leading me toward the door. "Or Bria."

"She's banned from the stove. She's burned too many dinners. And lunches. And once the breakfast."

"On purpose. She's actually an excellent cook."

I laughed. That sounded about right. She was better than me at getting out of things. "Are you going to fill the guys in on that?"

"Oh, they know. That's why they had her cook a few times instead of just the once. But when it turned out she'd rather accept my displeasure *and* eat burned food than cook for that many hungry guys, well…"

"She's a smart girl."

"Very. Listen, I was thinking…" He paused when we stepped outside into the crisp night, like he was waiting for something.

"What is it?" I asked into the hush.

He shook his head and started forward again. "Thought I heard something. I was thinking…I never stay at my house anymore."

"I know. Look, I'm sorry about that. It's just that Zorn's training is turning Daisy into a terror. Just the other night I caught her trying to set a tripwire at the top of the stairs for Mordecai. She's gotten out of hand. As soon as she gets a clue, I swear we can stay at your house again."

"No, it's not that." He stopped again on the sidewalk, his eyes roaming my empty grass. "Where's Frank?"

"After the fifth time I sent him rolling through a bunch of houses and streets, he got the hint that I need a break from him."

"Why? What did he do?"

"Tried to convince me that it was okay for you to cheat but not okay for me to retaliate."

Kieran froze and looked down at me for a long moment.

"The last Soul Stealer was on the handsome side. Frank thought I was bringing him back to…you know," I said.

Kieran's brow pinched. "Can you do that with a spirit?"

"I'd never thought about it, and now I'm afraid to ask."

A minute soul bleeped on my radar, but it wasn't a human. An animal, it had to be. Their souls weren't as complex, though they did pulse nearly the same. The creature was ambling in the trees beyond my house.

Kieran walked me to my door but didn't reach for the handle. "It's just that we spend every evening and night together. It seems silly to have two houses. It might be better, for a few reasons, if you and the kids and I all had just one place. Maybe closer to town. Nearer the guys and Bria."

I'd just tried to break up with the guy, and he was asking me to move in with him? We were both cracked. Still, I could barely contain my excitement. He was certainly getting the short end of the stick, but he didn't seem to mind. Given my feelings for him, I didn't want to push too hard. It was a complete role reversal from when we'd first gotten together. At first, he'd tried to push me away, convinced he was too much like his father to make a relationship work. Now, I'd taken on that role.

Yeah, we were definitely both cracked and maybe a little stupid.

"As silly as you marking me?" I smiled.

I expected him to bend and kiss me, but he looked out over the street, on guard. His emotions didn't tell me that he was spooked about anything, though. Probably just watchful after last night.

"Sillier," he said, a grin tugging at his lips. He shrugged. "Something to think about."

"I mean…" I dragged my teeth across my lip, still trying desperately to play it cool, but nearly bursting with love. I shrugged one shoulder. "If you don't need two houses to fit all your egos, then you're right— sharing a place wouldn't be much different than what we're doing now. I'd be in for that, as long as I get to keep mine so I can sell it when I break up with you next time."

"It's cute that you think I'd somehow *not* follow you around like a creep. I mean, how did we meet?"

"You followed me around like a stalker creep."

"Right. So…"

I laughed and rolled my eyes. "For the record, I do still feel like I'm weighing you down. It isn't sitting right with me."

He rubbed his hands along my upper arms. "You've been thrown into the deep end of this magical world. I appreciate that you want to do what's best for me. I'm hoping someday soon that you'll realize *you* are what's best for me. If you ever decide you need to leave San Francisco, we'll go together. I will not lose you over a job—let's get that clear."

I widened my eyes, not having expected that. The scenario hadn't even crossed my mind.

He smiled. "I win. So, about moving in together…"

Blood rushed to my cheeks and other, more delicate parts. "What about Daisy? We can't go very deep into the magical world with her."

"She's got that magical fake ID, she's the ward of a dreaded Soul Stealer, personally protected by the resident Demigod of San Francisco, and a little night-mare that no one would, in their right mind, cross. She'll be just fine."

"Resident Demigod?"

His smile slipped a little. "I rule, but in order to be

recognized by the magical political forces, I need to be officially put on the books. That happens at the next summit. It is rarely contested, but…"

There was so much I didn't know. I'd need to really hit the books if I was going to help him. Because I was tired of being dead weight. Starting tomorrow, I would pull up my britches and get to work. Right after breakfast. Or maybe after brunch.

The little bleep of a soul meandered closer, and I looked that way to see what might slip out of the trees and brush. Kieran's body tightened. "What is it?"

"Just a…" I squinted in the darkness before layering the world with spirit so I could see better. "Behold, it is a pale horse, and he who sits on it has the name Death, and Hades is following with him."

"What?" Kieran grabbed my arm.

The little creature's tail flicked as it slinked closer. It let out a loud *meow.*

"It's a cat," I said, laughing.

Wariness swirled within him. He didn't release his hold. "A shifter, or just a plain cat?"

"A plain one," I said, frowning up at him. "Shifters maintain their human souls after they shift. Are you okay? You seem really jumpy. I'll know it if one of the spirit monsters from last night rolls through. Probably."

He shook his head and pushed open the door. "It's nothing. Let's get something to eat, and then you can thank me for that necklace in creative ways."

Chapter 9

ALEXIS

KIERAN WASN'T THE only one feeling a little jumpy. I read it on Boman and Henry's faces. I noticed it in the absent way Donovan randomly used his magic to lift and lower things, as though testing to make sure he could. Thane would barely stay seated, preferring to stand near doors or hover near windows, and Jack burned dinner. The only one who was utterly calm and cool was Zorn, and that was probably the scariest of all.

They'd all be staying close tonight. I didn't know what they thought they could do against a Demigod wandering the streets in spirit form, but I knew I'd feel more comfortable getting some shuteye with them on hand.

I finished touching up my light dusting of makeup and fussing with my hair in the bathroom. I wore the absolutely gorgeous necklace Kieran had gotten me, feeling the weight of it as it hung between my bare breasts. I loved the symbolism of our entwined magics. Our entwined souls.

He waited at the window, his hands in his pockets, looking out at the blackness that blanketed the horizon. I took a moment to marvel at his broad, muscled back, cinching down into trim hips. His raven hair was long on top and short on the sides, a little messy from the way he'd been running his hands through it all evening.

Of course Nancy wanted him. All women wanted him. He was as handsome as he was debonair. As charming as he was big-hearted. He was a knight in shining armor who was confident enough in his masculinity to love a strong woman who could desecrate a battlefield. He was my dream come true, and here he stood, in a house he had selflessly bought for me.

He was too good for words. Much too good.

"Hey," I said softly.

He looked back, turning as he did so. When his eyes hit mine, he froze. They dropped, sinking down to the necklace adorning my nude body. Then lower, taking in the rest of me. Hunger raged in those stormy blue eyes. Desire. The effect boiled my blood.

"You are so fucking beautiful, Alexis," he whispered, facing me. His large bulge stood out in his pants. "There are no words."

He'd just said plenty of words. But with that look in his eyes, he hadn't needed to say anything at all.

"Sorry for what I said earlier," I said, slinking toward him. I trailed my fingers over the necklace, letting them descend to my suddenly taut nipple. "It was my own issue, not my lack of trust in you."

He shook his head, his gaze following my hand.

"I love you, Kieran." I trailed my fingers lower until they were at my pubic line. "I do want to move in with you. No, I do not feel chained here. I knew you'd take the position. That's fine with me. I'm happy just to be with you, wherever you are." I massaged my clit a little, and all the air puffed out of him.

He yanked me to him so fast that I sucked in a startled gasp. Before I knew it, my nipple was in his hot mouth and his hand was running up my inner thigh. His fingers replaced mine on my clit, working me to a fast start.

I knew the best thanks I could give him wouldn't be hours of pleasuring him, though that would definitely be round two. It would be to appeal to his raw, wild, primal side. To coax him into losing control doing what he was designed to do—guarding that which he deemed his.

"Mark me," I whispered. "Claim me."

He moved to the other nipple while laying his palm on the necklace. His hand moved so his fingers now covered my heart.

"I love you," he said, and picked me up, hurrying me to the bed.

I fell back on the soft sheets. He rose and grabbed

the back of his shirt, pulling it over his head. He ripped at the buttons on his trousers. I lifted my knees, spreading my thighs on the bed.

His breath turned harried. His emotions burned with need and spiraling desire. With that primal need to take his woman.

Feeling it, I worked myself until his large cock sprang free. I licked my lips in eager anticipation.

He crawled onto the bed after me, pausing to run his hot tongue up my center. He sucked in my nub, and I groaned in pleasure, running my fingers through his hair as his Selkie magic glided across my body. The sensations teased me in the best of ways. They drove into me as surely as he was about to—fiercely intimate and inhumanly delicious.

"Oh yes, Kieran," I said, swinging my hips up into him.

He threaded two fingers into me, pounding his fingers in rhythm with his sucking. With the other hand he reached up and tweaked a nipple, driving my pleasure deeper. Turning me wild with it.

"Yes. Yes. Oh God, yes." I arched on the bed, soaking it in. Rising higher. Words turned to moans. Heat burned through my body. My world reduced down to the exquisite sensations caused by his ministrations.

"*Yes!*" I blasted apart, sucked under the tide and happily lost. I shuddered, my eyes closing, as he moved up. His chest slid against mine. The necklace jingled between us.

"I love you," he said, and kissed up my neck to my collarbone. His lips then fitted against mine, our tongues soon twirling together. There would be no time to rest. No time to get my bearings before this next onslaught of divine lovemaking.

His large cock slid into me, filling me up. I groaned, my eyes fluttering with how good that felt. How right. His Selkie magic whispered across my skin, driving all thought from me.

He took my hands and threaded his fingers between mine. His kiss turned insistent. Dominating.

He pushed our hands up to above our heads and held them there, trapping me beneath him. Covering me with his size and strength. Doing as I'd asked, and claiming me.

The pace increased. He drove into me faster now. I tugged my hands, wanting to run them down his muscular back, but he held on, in control. My inner beast mewed for more power from him. For the might I knew he was capable of. I wanted a show of it as my man consumed me in a way only he could.

"Harder," I begged, gyrating up to meet him. Desperate for him.

He made a sound halfway between a groan and a growl. He swirled his tongue with mine, his lips forceful. His kiss nearly bruising. He continued to hold my hands as he rammed into me rhythmically. The bed thumped against the wall and I moaned into his mouth.

The world vanished. I felt spirit flood the room around us. The Line pounded into being and magic filled me to bursting.

"Yes," Kieran said, pushing himself up a little on his hands so he could work harder. He thrust into me with wild abandon, having completely lost control. I arched into each thrust, angling to get him deeper. Needing him with every ounce of my person.

His magic seared across my skin. The waves pounded the cliffs, as loud as if the ocean were right outside the window. My magic throbbed in time to his hungry thrusts.

I arched. "Almost...there," I managed, the drumming of pleasure beating on me. His magic feeling so damn good. Almost as good as his body inside mine. Almost unbearable. "Almost..."

A punch of pleasure hit me. My vision went splotchy black as an intense orgasm consumed me. Dragged me under and spun me around.

"Oh!" I yelled out, clutching him with my legs.

He shook, moaning as he emptied himself into me. Pounding into me once more, twice.

Another wave rolled over me. I clenched my teeth and shook, vibrating with pleasure. Barely able to breathe.

"Oh yes," I said, coming down from that high. Shuddering a third time, feeling light as a feather and electrified. "Hmm."

Kieran kissed me before collapsing. His weight, pressing me into the mattress, felt better than good.

"That never gets old," he murmured into the skin on my neck.

My hands freed, I wrapped my arms around his shoulders. "Take a break, because then it's my turn to be on top."

He kissed my neck. "If it weren't for the possibility of an intruder showing up to spoil our party, I would say you'll have a hard time getting on top when you're tied to the bed, but given the circumstances…"

I smiled in the dim light. My power still throbbed and my sex drive was ready to join the party. With him, I was always ready to go again. "Rain check."

"I'll hold you to that."

I wiggled to get him to move off me, then reached for the side table. I pulled out a black blindfold and dangled it from one finger. "But you can choose who wears this."

His eyes flashed desire again. "I will. I want to be surprised when you move from teasing to taking my cock deep into your throat."

"And then you'll rip it off so you can watch me suck

you off?"

A grin pulled at his lips. "You read my mind. And take that necklace off. I don't want to get cum on it."

Giddy, quickly moving to close the blinds, I found myself longing for the day we could be carefree and do all this for real, without worry we'd be interrupted.

I hardened my resolve. I'd call that Spirit Walker again, and this time, I'd make him my bitch.

Chapter 10

ALEXIS

THE NEXT MORNING, I arrived in the kitchen refreshed and determined. Today was the first day of my new life. My new *adult* life. I would get a real job, a real office, and a real place in the magical world. I'd been in hiding for far too long.

Bria sat at the island with a breakfast sandwich and a plate of fruit. Daisy and Mordecai were at the kitchen table, eating similar meals. Boman stood near the doorway between the kitchen and dining room wearing the black cargo pants he usually donned for breaking and entering or combat.

I frowned as I glanced at Kieran's assistant, Red, standing near the window, her fiery hair glowing in a stream of sunlight. Leaning against the counter near the stove was a woman I'd never seen before. She stuck out like a sore thumb. Her makeup was perfect, her hair blown and styled *just so*, and her feminine clothes accented her slight curves just right.

"Where's Kieran?" I asked, looking at Red.

"Oh." The unidentified woman straightened up with a pleased smile. "Alexis, hell—"

"He's at the office with the rest of the Six and the paper pusher," Red cut in.

"So then…why are you here?"

"He got word from Demigod Nancy's office," Red said. "She will be supplying someone to train you. A level-five Defalcator. Kieran has shifted me to protective duty. He doesn't completely trust Nancy's motives."

"A Defalcator? I've never heard of it," I said, grabbing the one remaining breakfast sandwich from the platter. I'd taken a little longer getting ready this morning. I really wanted to look the part today. I'd wow people, damn it. No more worst-dressed lists for me.

"Of the Hermes line," Daisy said as though reading from a flash card. "A Defalcator can move objects into the spirit realm for retrieval at another time. These items are typically smaller, but the best of their kind can move something up to the size of a medium-sized dog. They must be inanimate items, however. A Defalcator is no kidnapper. He must touch the items he wishes to transport. Keep his fingers off your possessions. He'll be a master thief and pickpocket."

I poured myself some coffee, realizing that Zorn was training me up a little magical almanac. That would be helpful.

"What can someone like that teach me about my

magic?" I asked in confusion.

"Damned waste of time," Bria murmured.

I had to agree with her. I might be able to glean a few lessons from context, but I wouldn't be breaking down any walls.

"Refusing the tutor might damage Demigod Kieran's fragile relationship with Demigod Nancy, and—"

"His fragile relationship, yeah." Bria snorted. "Nothing is going to damage that relationship unless he actually sleeps with her and then ghosts her. A woman scorned and all that. Otherwise, she'll just keep trying. And if someone else picked out this tutor for her, when or if Kieran refuses the offer, the secret string puller will just come up with something else."

Red turned from the window, her eyes smoldering with annoyance. Speaking of fragile relationships, I didn't have high hopes for theirs.

"It's fine." I held up my hands, talking around my food so this didn't escalate. "It's fine. I'll see what the tutor has to say, and..." I hadn't registered the soul until it was right under my nose. A little white cat rubbed against Boman's leg and mewed softly. He bent down and scooped it up, cradling it in his big arms. "Who let the cat in here?"

Boman scratched its head and then under its chin. It purred softly. "This little fella was hanging around last night. Sounded hungry, so Jack gave him a little tuna. He ate it up and looked for more—didn't you, little guy, huh? Poor thing was probably brought out here and left for dead."

"It can't be feral. Those things never have both their eyes," Daisy murmured.

"That's not true," Mordecai responded.

Daisy's eyes turned haunted. She'd spent her early childhood in and out of foster homes, each of them equally bad. She'd seen her fair share of horrors. "One of the homes was by a creek. More than a few kittens wandered up, missing—"

"All right, Death's raven, we get the picture." Bria shuddered.

"This little guy has both his eyes, doesn't he?" Boman nuzzled his head against the cat's. The purring was so loud that it reached me across the kitchen.

"I don't want to sound like a dick or anything, because starving is no fun," I said, trying to be delicate, "but what is it doing in here?"

Red huffed out a laugh, turning back to the window.

"Ah, isn't it just the cutest thing." The unidentified woman crossed the room in dainty little strides, like a little pixie or something. She stopped by Boman's side to pet the cat. I didn't miss her goosebumps—probably a reaction to the handsome, well-built man next to her. A man directly connected to the Demigod of San

Francisco. The way she kept batting her eyelashes drove the suspicion home.

"Also, who are you?" I asked her.

"Jack brought the cat in this morning, because he, like all the guys, are big ol' softies without a clue." Bria shook her head, not giving the unidentified woman time to answer me. "You can't bring a cat into a house with a shifter. And if you do, it's only a matter of time before one starts marking. That's not a good scene."

Mordecai turned around to look at Bria, his expression sour. "I have more control than to go around peeing on walls, thanks."

"You wait. I see a very embarrassing sleepwalking situation in your future," Bria said, rinsing her dishes.

"Excellent." Daisy clapped. "That's a good reason to set up motion-detecting cameras."

"That's an invasion of privacy!" Mordecai was back to hollering. She'd really developed a talent for getting under his skin, lately.

"It's the common areas. It's not like I would set them up in your room." She made a face and stuck out her tongue. "Gross. I do *not* want to know what you do in there."

"Good time for a subject change." Bria slipped her dishes into the dishwasher. "It's your house, Lexi. If you want to drop the thing at the pound, it would find a home really quickly. It's got that soft, snowy coat—

someone is bound to pick it up." She tucked the fruit bowl into the fridge. "And that woman is your new stylist."

"Oh. Yes." The woman, who looked to be in her early twenties, flashed me a set of straight, blindingly white teeth. "Hi." She practically pranced up to the other side of the island. "I'm Aubri, with an I. Like Bria mentioned, I'll be helping you with styling. Demigod Kieran called my office this morning asking for a representative. We're usually booked up solid, but…" She rolled her baby blues. "When I heard *you* were looking for someone? Of *course* I jumped at the chance."

"I told Kieran he needed to outsource because you were dragging your feet," Bria said, switching off the coffee pot. Apparently I was done with it. "He had only held off so long because he didn't want you to think he was calling you a mess."

"She is a mess. Always has been," Daisy said.

"That's part of her charm!"

Daisy exaggeratedly leaned away from Mordecai. "Oh my God, Mordie, I am sitting right here. Why are you yelling?"

He looked abashed. "Sorry. Autopilot."

"All the big dogs use someone." Aubri nodded at me with big, serious eyes. "All of them. Life in the spotlight can be harsh. It's best to go in armed."

I sighed. "I'm not going to lie and say this isn't a

huge relief, but I feel…unfeminine. Like, I should know how to dress myself and do makeup. Isn't that a girl thing?"

Aubri stuck out a hip. "There is dressing yourself, which you really excel at." She nodded adamantly. Daisy turned in her chair and draped an arm over the back, a goofy smile on her face. "And there is *dressing* yourself, you know?"

I didn't.

"So I'm just going to nudge you in a focused direction, that's all." Aubri squinted as she looked me over. "It'll be so easy, just you watch."

"It wasn't all that easy when I was doing it myself," I murmured.

Aubri leaned against the counter. "You look really great, by the way. You have a natural beauty my clients would *kill* for. I love your spunk."

Daisy's lopsided smile grew.

"A few little touches, a quick clothing change, and you'll be singing." Aubri beamed at me.

"A few…touches?" I looked down at my outfit. "But this was how it looked on the mannequin."

Aubri nodded with a supportive smile. "Totally. And it really smashed the runways last season. But I think we can get something a little more"—she pulled her lips to the side and squinted one eye in apparent thought—"your style."

I slid off the chair at the island like a lost lamb. "My style?"

Boman set the cat down and grabbed my dirty dishes. "I got this, Lexi. Go get beautified." He unleashed his wide, glittering smile. Aubri froze for a moment, looking at him like she was staring up into the sun.

It occurred to me that I was the butt of the joke in an ongoing sketch.

I spent the next hour listening to Aubri sing my praises while she compiled a lengthy list of clothing that would suit me better. All my makeup was scrubbed off, but only to give her a "blank canvas" for the entire store of new products she'd brought. Finally, I was given the green light to leave the house.

"But what about my hair?" I asked, looking in the mirror at the same old face but with way too much makeup. I looked like Bobo's wife, about to head into the circus. "And I'm not feeling all this makeup. It makes me tired. Like, physically. It physically makes my eyes tired."

"It makes you tired?" Aubri looked down on me, trying to make sense of my nonsense.

"Never mind. But what about my hair?"

"Oh no." She waved it away, packing up a little bag that she then strung over her shoulder. "We're going with a shabby *chic* style for you. Your hair, a little wild, really sets off the whole look."

"Shabby?" I asked, following her down the stairs to the front door. A new handbag awaited me. I didn't recognize the symbol on the side, let alone the name stamped on it, but you'd think it was made of gold from the way Aubri gingerly handed it to me.

She laughed as everyone else filed in the doorway, including the cat, who clearly had been taken hostage and was desperate to escape. "I just mean...we're doing a play on a half-tamed wild thing. You have this raw...like"—she looked like she was grabbing and manipulating something in the air—"violent exuber-ance about you, but then you're so pretty and graceful. It's a really fun mashup. It'll be the next big thing, just you wait. After this season, we're going to see a lot of people trying to duplicate this look. But there is only one you."

Bria checked her watch. "See?" She headed out the door first, followed by Red. "Didn't I tell you that one time? You got that look down pat."

"The makeup is way overkill," Daisy said. "You look like a crack whore who tried too hard, one rock away from waking up in the gutter."

I opened my mouth to chastise her, but honestly, I was still working through what she'd even said.

"Good notes." Aubri nodded at my other side, also analyzing my face. "You know her best. Comfort is a real concern. I can already see this tightening her up.

Yes, I'll think about that."

"I think you look pretty," Mordecai said, following us out.

"Why is everyone going with me?" I asked as the sunshine and Frank greeted me.

Frank let out a long, low whistle. "Look what the cat dragged in. I knew you had it in you. Your mother, in her heyday, would be hard-pressed to outdo you. I wish she could see you now—she'd be so proud you finally cleaned yourself up. Now this is the way to keep the boy from straying, Alexis. You've got the right idea."

"Frank, I will throw you over the Line, don't think I won't," I said.

He put up his hands. "You look very nice. Like a lady. That's all I'm saying. Oh, and there was some riffraff around here not that long ago." He pointed off to the right as I slowed.

The others fanned around, Aubri somewhere between slightly confused and incredibly wary. She knew what I was, but not many people knew how it worked. I hoped she wasn't afraid of spirits.

Frank turned and pointed in the opposite direction. "It was very strange. I thought I saw someone over there, walking along the side of your—*Scat*, you vile thing." He kicked at the cat, whose tail flicked as it sauntered by. It clearly was not susceptible to spirits. "That thing came from the other side of the wall." He meant the dual-society zone. "You better be careful with those things around. They'll lie on a baby's face and suffocate it."

"I don't have a baby, Frank," I said dryly.

"Well, someday you will. Demigods don't shoot blanks. They've got real strong stuff, I hear. Like shooting it out of a cannon."

I sighed. "About the riffraff?"

"Yeah, I thought I saw someone walking on the side of the house last night. The house was dark and everyone was asleep except for that prowling girl you got. You're really going wrong with her." The move from my old house—which I really needed to fix up and get rented out—to this one had made Frank much surlier. I kept hoping he'd simmer down, but he'd just doubled down on the worst parts of his personality. "But when I went to check it out, he was gone."

"You're sure it was a he?" I asked as Bria drifted closer.

He thought for a moment. "No, as a matter of fact. It was all shadows. I couldn't make out any distinct features."

Cold dribbled down my spine. I'd checked my repellent magic this morning. It was still there, so nothing had gotten in—they would've had to tear it down for that. Nothing from the spirit world, anyway. But I didn't have repellent magic on the grounds. Nothing had gotten in, but that didn't mean something hadn't been scoping me out from a distance.

"How big was the shape? Enormous?"

His brow pinched. "No, it was just…" He put his hand up, gauging height, then lowered it about level to his own head. "Normal height. Then, when I was coming back this way, I thought I saw him again, on the other side." His eyebrows lowered. "Whoever it was just wasn't right. They were standing there, staring at me. Still in the shadows, mind you, keeping hidden, but I knew they were checking me out. So I yelled, ran after them. I'm no coward. That scared 'em off."

"So…now…" I crossed my arms, remembering the other night. "You ran toward the…man or woman last night, but the night before, you ran *from* the creature that showed up."

His eyes widened. He'd apparently meant to keep that little episode a secret. A moment later he puffed up, trying to recover his pride. "Well, yeah. It was a creature, as you say. Some sort of demon, I'd wager. It was sending out a real strong vibe for me to get lost. I didn't want to set it off and leave you to deal with it."

"Riiight."

"What'd he say?" Bria asked.

"We got another one." I walked around Frank, my mind whirling. "Doesn't sound like the same intruder. This one didn't mess with my magic, and while it acknowledged Frank, it didn't run him off. Any idea how we can tell them apart?"

"Not a clue. I need to start making some calls. Someone will know what spirit forms the various Demigods take."

I nodded then halted, not seeing my car parked in the driveway. Confused, I searched the curb, wondering if Kieran or someone had needed to move it for some reason. Boman's black BMW was there, with the ding in the door, and Bria's old, faded Mazda with a key scratch down the side. A red Beemer, which hopefully wasn't Red's, because that would be too much, and a pink Corvette, which hopefully wasn't anybody's and was a practical joke.

I put my hands on my hips. "Where's my car?"

With a little grin, Boman tapped his phone, and my garage door shuddered to life. A bumper came into view, but it wasn't the black one I was expecting. It was a deep, shiny blue.

I walked closer, Boman on my heels.

High on the rounded back end, in the middle, was *Maserati.*

The breath left my lungs. "What is this?"

Daisy squealed and danced around. "Right? Oh my God, when Jack showed me this morning, I nearly peed. Lexi, *I nearly peed myself.*"

"But…" I entered the nearly empty garage—it was

the first garage I'd ever had, so I didn't have much to put in it—checking out the sleek design, the huge wheels, and the tinted glass. "The BMW wasn't even a year old. What do I need with this?"

"I told you she wouldn't be excited," Mordecai said. Both of the kids had hustled up on the other side of the car. "You owe me five bucks."

"How the hell is she not excited? Lexi, how are you not excited?" Daisy spread out her hands aggressively. "Lexi, this is a Maserati. A Mas-er-ah-ti. James Bond drove this car."

"No, that was an Aston Martin," Mordecai murmured.

"Whatever, fine. James Bond wishes he drove this car. It's gorgeous. On what planet do we live on that we get this car? *On what planet?*" She had an ear-to-ear grin on her face.

"Daisy, this money situation has gone to your head," I said. "Which reminds me, you need to pull way back on spending. It's gotten out of hand. Kieran said to get what you needed, not put him out of house and home."

Both of the kids' expressions closed down. They fought like cats and dogs when it didn't matter, but when it came to the important things, they were tighter than any blood relations could be.

They had a secret. I'd been so wrapped up in my

own problems that I clearly hadn't made enough time to check in with the kids.

"Boman, close down the door real quick," I said in the mom voice I couldn't help.

The motion-sensor garage light clicked on as the door touched down.

"What aren't you telling me?" I demanded.

Nervousness crossed Mordecai's face. He was always the quickest to crack, not wanting to upset me. Daisy didn't so much as twitch.

"Spill it," I barked.

"She'll see reason," Mordecai whispered to Daisy. "It's for all of us."

I lifted my eyebrows. "You better not be selling something illegal."

"She can't make us give it back. She doesn't know where it is," Mordecai continued.

"Give. What. Back?"

Daisy huffed. "Fine," she said with a condescending smile that was all teenager. "I haven't kept all those clothes and accessories."

I waited for more. When none came, I said, "*And*?"

"And I returned them, obviously."

"Oh." I squinted at her. "Why would you be slow to admit that? What are you leaving out?"

"She buys them on the credit card and returns them for cash," Mordecai said. "Not to mention what she's taken from the house and pawned."

Daisy's expression turned defiant. I just waited. She
knew I was going to chastise her for stealing, so there
was no point in wasting my breath.

"I will not get in a situation where he owns us,
Lexi," Daisy finally said. "You guys are in love or
whatever now, but what I heard about that twat Nancy
just cemented why this is necessary—"

"Big no on that swear word. Big no."

"He's going to end up super powerful, we all know
that," Daisy said. "And girls are going to be throwing
themselves at him. One misstep and you're done, we all
know that. And that's if he doesn't go crazy like his dad.
We need an exit plan, but guess what? You're in his
house. Sure, your name is on it now, but if you tried to
sell it? That nut-sack would just close you down. If you
need to leave, you'll need to leave quickly. You'll need to
get out from under him. We all will. You don't really
have a job anymore, and that hundred grand you got
isn't enough to buy new identities. If this goes sour,
we're worse off now than we were. I'm just looking out
for us. Making sure we have a nice nest egg and a few
unseemly friends who can help us if it all blows up. I got
this, Lexi."

My heart was full, but my head could not believe my
ears. I didn't even know how to respond.

"Kieran was Valens's heir," Mordecai, the more reasonable of the two, said. "His dad hadn't changed that before Kieran killed him. So Kieran got all Valens's holdings, plus the millions he already had. He's a billionaire, Lexi. He's sitting on an empire. He won't even miss a million or two."

"It's like Robin Hood," Daisy said.

My mouth dropped open. "A *million*? When have you had time to buy all these clothes?"

Daisy rolled her eyes. "He means long term. I'm going at a reasonable pace, Lexi, don't worry. I'm very careful to show off everything in front of Kieran at least once. I gush a little and everything. I only buy as much as an air-headed, spoiled teenager would. And I never return too much at one store. I spread it around. Disguises, too. Or I have other people do it for me."

"What other people?"

"Street people. Or college kids who have showered. Whatever the situation calls for."

"Street people? College—Where are you meeting these people?"

She looked at me like I was dense. "San Francisco State, city college—the other day, I got a guy from the art school to take back a TV. Two grand into my pocket, a hundred spot for him. Everyone was smiling."

I leaned against the car, then jumped back, afraid I'd scratch it somehow. My mouth opened and closed like I was a fish out of water. I just could not believe all this had been happening without my knowledge. When we were poor and in that tiny house, with nothing but each other, I knew absolutely everything that went on. Everything. But now, when life was so much easier financially and I had a plenitude of time to look after them, everything was going sideways.

"Stop it." I put out my finger, knowing I'd get flack. "Just stop. That is stealing, it's immoral, and it's not right."

"Whatever happened to taking the handouts?" Daisy pushed back.

"Take the handouts." I gestured at the car. "I'll be taking this. It's way too much—*way* too much—but it's expected of me, he is at fault for that, and I need to look the part. But it wouldn't be okay to sell it and pocket the money. That's wrong. If you aren't going to use what he gives you, fine. But don't steal."

"Okay, but it's not really stealing, is it?" Daisy pressed. "He sees the purchases. He's not batting an eye. What's the difference between cash and clothes? He's giving me the same amount; they are just in a different form."

"He's giving you clothes as a basic necessity of life," I said.

She laughed theatrically. "The clothes we've all been buying over the last few months are *not* the necessities of life. The clothes we used to wear? Yes. Our new clothes are outrageously expensive because of stupid labels. Do I love wearing those stupid labels? Yes, I do. But not as much as his kind of people do. So I am living up to his standard, yet I'm also taking what I don't need *at present* as cash. I will need it down the road, so I'm putting it away. It all comes out the same."

A knock sounded at the garage door. I stared at Daisy, fuming. "Mordecai, what do you think about all this?" I asked, needing some sense here.

Daisy smirked. "Yeah, Mordecai, what do you think? Better yet, tell her how often you help me."

"She does have a point, Lexi," Mordecai said. "He isn't worried about what we're spending, so why would he care what we're doing with it?"

The knock sounded again.

"Because you're lying, don't you see that?" I walked over and slapped the garage door opener. "Don't say you are buying clothes when you aren't. Don't..." I threw up my hands. "No more, do you hear me? No more. You are both grounded. You will train, and you will stay in this house. That is it. Do I make myself clear?"

"Yes," they muttered, Daisy with more sauce than was good for her.

The cat zipped in under the door and disappeared amongst the boxes on the shelves.

"I'm not looking after that thing," I said, rounding

to the door of the shiny masterpiece I was almost afraid to drive. A part of me wondered how much I would get if I *did* sell it. "I can't even look after the wards I do have."

"We gotta go," Bria said. "We need to meet up with that trainer and then get organized for tonight. Kieran said we're a go for calling that Spirit Walker again. We know what he's about this time. We won't be surprised by what he can do."

I nodded, pulling open the car door. Boman jogged in and handed off the keys, his grin showing his delight. "I'll follow behind," he said. "I'll close the garage door, too. We should leave it open a crack so the cat can get out."

I pointed at the kids. "What's your plan?"

"Jack is on the—"

I put a finger up to silence Boman as Bria got into the passenger seat of my new car. "I want the kids to answer."

"Jack is going to train us pretty soon," Daisy said, plenty of attitude in her voice. "Kieran wants Zorn close at hand."

I hesitated a moment, wondering why Jack wasn't sticking around if he was doing a morning training with the kids. That wasn't normal. Just like it wasn't normal for all the guys but one to go to work with Kieran. He'd only pulled them in yesterday for the Demigod meeting, and last I heard, she'd headed out of town.

I pushed the ignition button and the engine roared to life, giving me a little thrill. But I couldn't shake my growing sense of unease. Kieran was always cool under pressure. I hadn't felt any anxiety from him. But his actions spoke of him being under attack.

My gut twisting, I opened my mouth to ask about it, and instead blurted out, "The kids are stealing from Kieran."

"He knows." Bria pulled out her phone and looked at the screen. "We're going to be late, so take it slow. Enjoy this fine new automobile that came at a very steep price. Toot, toot."

I pressed my lips together. "Toot, toot" was her way of saying I'd boarded the train of bad decisions the first time I hooked up with Kieran, and the steep price was all the crap I had to do to fit into his life. He was worth it, but I was hard-pressed to convince her of that. Or, last night, myself.

"Wait…" There was a lot to unpack in this conversation suddenly. "Don't you mean I should see what this baby can do so I make it in time? And also, what do you mean, *he knows*?"

"If we're going to be late, we need to be fashionably late so this tutor knows who pulls rank. You do, by the way, in case that wasn't clear. Nancy gave you clout. You need to take that shit to the bank. So slow down.

We'll make this baby work another time.

"As for your wards, Kieran is not an idiot, and he wasn't born yesterday. That said, it was Mordecai who blew their cover. He's a genuine, honest kid that will make a really fair, reasonable alpha one day. Thank God, because he'd be a shit thief. That kid is not sneaky."

"I wonder why Kieran didn't say anything," I said, taking the turn a little too fast. The car stuck to the street like glue.

"I don't know for sure, but my guess is he was tickled by Daisy getting one over on him. Zorn, who has known since the beginning, because he *is* a sneaky fucker, didn't mention it because he was studying what she was doing. He said she was clunky at first, so he tailored a few training sessions to address her shortcomings. Then she was off to the races. I've never seen a man prouder of his pupil's ability to steal from his boss."

"A member of Kieran's Six is teaching Kieran's girlfriend's ward to steal from Kieran. What kind of screwed-up scenario is this?"

"I mean, not really. This is helping Daisy's training, and the money is making those kids feel more secure. Kieran wouldn't begrudge them that. He isn't Valens. But Daisy really shouldn't have trusted Mordecai to help her. Or maybe it's her supervision over Mordecai that is lacking. Zorn is trying to figure out how to adjust that."

I just shook my head. I'd always been pretty vague when it came to morals, thinking of them more as a set of guidelines, but this was beyond me.

"So I shouldn't shut this operation down?" I asked helplessly.

"I don't know. Ask Zorn about it. He might have you deliver another test for her."

I shook my head again, stopping at a light. A little fear wormed through me. "What else don't I know? Why are the guys acting strange?"

Bria slowly blew out a breath. "I don't know. Zorn took someone down yesterday, I'd bet my life on it."

"Took someone, meaning…"

"Took them out. Killed them. Damned if I know who. Couldn't have been someone with Nancy, or she wouldn't be sending us a tutor of sorts."

"But why wouldn't they mention that?"

"My guess is Kieran doesn't want to shift your focus from what he deems important—learning your craft so you can protect yourself." She snorted. "Men are so stupid. They don't listen. They don't realize women are designed to handle multiple things at a time. It's in our genetic makeup." She shook her head, her lips pressing together in annoyance.

"In fairness, I did almost kill myself yesterday."

"Different scenario." She waved that away. "So now we have no choice but to operate blind. No problem. I can work with that. Here's what we'll do—you meet that tutor. *Do not touch him.* If he reaches out to shake your hand, you give him a flat look and clasp your hands behind your back. Got it?"

"It's a bit rude—"

"Got it?"

"Yes."

Bria nodded. "I'll put a few spirits in a couple of rats—"

"That math is wonky…"

"—and have them check things out. I'll ask a few questions, too. You talk to Mia on your way in, see if she's seen anything amiss. But don't mention any of this to Kieran. If he hasn't told you, that means he doesn't want you knowing."

"Right, but what if we learn something? Then what?" I asked.

"Then we confront the guys. If Kieran has become a target, it's to make you more vulnerable. And mark my words: anyone going after him so early in the game is playing with spirit. No one admits it, but a lot of people have a blind spot when it comes to battling spirit. They simply don't know how. But you do. You might be shit at it sometimes, but you always seem to find a way to pull through. If someone is going after Kieran, you are the only defense he has."

Chapter 11

MAGNUS

"WE'VE JUST GOT word, sir."

Magnus slowed his stride as he made his way through the ground floor of his mansion. His servants pushed away to the sides, holding trays of food and waiting for his go-ahead on the menu choice for that evening. A couple of old friends would be calling in on him, privileged to get Nancy's firsthand account of the child Demigod and his potent weapon. Magnus wanted to make sure they knew an allegiance with him would grant them sought-after rewards.

First he'd need to prep Nancy. Whenever she spoke of the child, she sounded star-struck to the point of distraction. She needed a good lay, a new lust to obsess over. He was well equipped to thoroughly distract her, and for this, he'd make the effort.

"Go ahead," he told Gracie, something like his right-hand woman.

She stopped in front of him in a soft pink dress, her hair in cute little curls, her expression pleasant. To look at her, one would never guess she had such a foul temper, incited at a moment's notice and with very little rhyme or reason. She was responsible for the highest body count in the mansion, and fifty percent of them were Magnus's staff. One could never tell when her smile would turn vicious and she'd brandish a knife. It kept the staff performing at optimal standards, not to mention on their toes. Those who died...well, magical Darwinism at its finest.

"I've confirmed that the Body Jumper was definitely Aaron's, and has been killed," she said.

Magnus lifted his eyebrows and turned his face a little, a silent directive to his head cook. The staff moved away to the kitchens. Magnus led the way out to the garden. It was monitored and protected from eaves-droppers, living and dead alike.

"Are you sure he's been taken out?" Magnus said once they had some privacy.

"Killed yes, but the spirit has not been treated, apparently. It still wanders the living world. Aaron questioned the man himself. A powerful dark Djinn got to him. One of Kieran's Six."

Magnus bent to smell a particularly foul flower, something to clear his head. "The girl was not involved, then? Or else she is not aware she needs to dispose of the spirit so it cannot be used again?"

"She was gone from the building at that point, so

no, she was not involved. I don't know if she knows how to dispose of ordinary spirits. She handled Valens well enough, but as far as I've heard, she can only push people across the Line. She doesn't trap them there. They are free to be called again."

"It's a wonder she is any use to the child Demigod at all with so little knowledge about her magic."

"Yes, sir. I was thinking this exactly. We'll rectify that soon. Amos is in position."

Magnus clasped his hands behind his back and looked at a weeping tree. He'd known Aaron would insert himself into the situation, but he hadn't known what angle he would take. Aaron was lazy at the best of times, but when he was moved to action, he was usually cunning and unpredictable. Or at least he had been in times of old, when there was more strife between Demigods. This time, it seemed Aaron was taking the blunt, obvious, and entirely too predictable approach. Known assassins? Going for the child after work in a public place? There was no finesse. It made things easier for Magnus.

Magnus pursed his lips in thought. He couldn't very well announce he had a claim on the girl. Times had changed. Daughters were no longer bought and sold, traded to establish and form alliances. The other Demigods of Hades might step aside out of respect had she been a normal magical person, but she was a Spirit

Walker, and he had publicly wiped out his children and heirs. The other Demigods would not want to see her in his hands.

So. Where did that leave him?

He relayed all of this to Gracie, his best sounding board.

"I don't think our strategy needs to change overmuch," she said, standing a little behind him. "Aaron wants the child gone so he can have access to the girl, same as us. But he doesn't have anyone in his arsenal that can grab her once the child is out of the way. We do. As a Possessor, Amos is better than anyone Aaron could send for this job."

Magnus had to concede the truth in that. A good Possessor was nearly as rare as a Spirit Walker, and although they were not equally feared, they should be. They could do exactly what their name said—assume control of another person, like the fairytales of demon possession.

There were limitations, of course. When a Possessor took over the body, the host stopped recording goings-on. They would wake with a black spot in their time table. One too large to be shrugged off as forgetfulness or daydreaming. If enough people experienced the same thing, they'd eventually trace the cause to the source. So a Possessor had to carefully plan out whom to possess and for how long.

Another problem in this situation was where to leave the body. A Possessor didn't so much walk in the spirit world as zoom from one point to another. If it had an item belonging to its target, which was where Nancy's chosen tutor would come in, Amos could leave his body in a safe location and inhabit the target's body. When it came time to evacuate, Amos would zip back into his own skin. This was great for assassin jobs, since he could quickly leave the scene of the crime, but it wasn't as easy when it came to kidnapping. He'd have to leave the girl with a trusted friend in order to assume his own skin, return to the girl, take out the friend, and then transport the girl to the next location. Magnus would probably need to orchestrate a bigger team for that. He'd work on that while Amos was taking care of the child Demigod.

"I don't think your end result should be to kill the girl," Gracie said.

"Oh?" He turned to her, wondering about her reasoning. He had some clear ideas on how he would go forward once he met the girl face to face, but he hadn't discussed his plans with anyone. Not yet.

"Not at all," Gracie replied. "Times are different than they once were. There is a peace treaty with humans, making today's risk more about financial rather than physical survival. Children have plenty of options for leadership. You could set her up anywhere.

She will have no wish to take your territory if she is established and happy."

"And yet Valens's heir ripped him off his throne and assumed control of his territory."

A little line creased the skin between Gracie's brows. "Valens tortured the kid's mother. From what I've heard, Kieran didn't set out to take the territory. His goal was vengeance. He fell into his role. This situation is wholly different. You can present yourself as blameless to the girl. You didn't know about her. How is that your fault? At least, as far as she is concerned, you didn't know about her. Her mother kept her word and did everything exactly as the two of you agreed. The girl was hidden, kept away from the magical world at all costs, and hence, she lived. The mother could've had no way of knowing what the girl was."

Magnus held his tongue. Iris wasn't anywhere near a dumb woman. She very well might've known the truth, but the girl had apparently inherited a bit of her magic too. A stroke of luck. Very few magics could evade the magical screenings. Given the girl was still largely clueless about her power, it was clear that if Iris had known, she hadn't told anyone, not even the girl. Not at all a dumb woman. She'd sacrificed greatly to see her child safe. Too bad all good things had to come to an end.

"You certainly have a point, but I doubt the girl will

be all sunshine and roses after I kill her beloved."

Gracie smiled, this time a chilling sight. "Since when have you been bashful about assassinating a leader and blaming it on someone else? Demigod Aaron has been complacent for too long; this weak effort on the child's life proves it. Maybe he needs a worthy adversary, like a trained-up Spirit Walker under the protection of one of the most powerful Demigods in the world…"

Chapter 12

ALEXIS

I WALKED INTO the government building with Bria at my side, both of us stewing about the way we'd been sidelined and thinking about how we were going to work our way back into the main battle. Kieran's desire to protect me was sweet, but when it came to family, sweet didn't cut it. Red and Aubri, who'd ridden with Boman, trailed behind us on the sidewalk. I felt a tug on my jacket, Aubri adjusting it so I looked the part. I tried not to feel annoyed.

"I'll meet you in your office," Bria said, about to peel away. She stopped short and put her hand on my arm to stop me. "Not your current office. The larger, lighter, nicer office you better pick out while you're up there. I'm tired of that musty cat smell. I don't even want to know how many cats that lady had living in her office, but if it still smells like that after two years of industrial cleaners, it must've been a good few."

"Why didn't you mention something before?" I asked.

"You seemed content thinking you could blend into the background and quietly sponge off your rich boyfriend. What was I going to do, piss on your parade?"

I lifted my eyebrows as she walked away. The answer was yes, since that was her MO, but I didn't want to shout it across the expansive lobby.

As I got to the stairs, I felt the strangest sensation, as though a spirit were physically touching me. But I didn't see one. The only person nearby was a living man heading down the wide stairs opposite me. He stared sightlessly in front of him, his mind clearly elsewhere.

I paused and glanced around, seeing a guy at the front desk who drew my eye. From my vantage point, I could only see the back of his head and his ear, but that was plenty. It was his posture that gave him away. His confident lean, one ankle crossed over the other, bespoke power and a nonchalant ego. His clothes were of a good cut and quality, and they fit him perfectly. They were expensive, something I now knew from experience. His styled hair and expensive watch perfected the image.

"Do you know him?" I asked Red, trying to get a feel for his soul. I was too far away. I could probably slash at it, or bang on his soul box, but the power would be minimal. Grabbing his middle would be beyond me at this distance. Not like I needed to do any of those things. For all I knew, he was a high-level official. I only knew a handful of faces in this place. That was it. I needed to get better at creating a list of "friendlies."

"No. I've already made a mental note to identify him. Salesmen and admirers hang around the front desk. He is neither. Nor is he very good at disguising his interest in you. And here I thought the Demigod's mistress would be a boring detail. I should've known better."

I felt my face sour at the title. "You discourage friendships, then?" I asked as I started climbing again, continuing on past the first landing. I wasn't going to the musty cat room this time. "Not well liked?"

"Correct," she said.

"Ah, that can't be true," Aubri said. "I'm sure a lot of people like you."

"I hope you don't become one of them."

I couldn't help a grin as I reached Mia in her usual alcove, picking at a large button on her ratty blue sweater, her large eyes solemn.

"Hey," I said, stopping.

"A spirit has been wandering around," she said. "One I don't know. She looked like a spy."

I repeated what she said for Red's benefit.

"How can you tell?" I asked.

"The living try not to act suspicious. The dead don't think anyone can see them, so they peer in closets, in desks, watch people…"

I repeated that as well.

"Appearance?" Red asked.

"Middle-aged white woman with short hair. She looks pretty athletic, but she kinda stoops when she's creeping around," Mia said. "Reminds me of the Hamburglar in that way."

"Who?" I asked, getting out of the way of someone coming up the stairs.

"An old McDonald's character," Red replied. "Stole burgers, that sort of thing. I like weird retro stuff. That qualifies."

"Strange detail, but okay. Is she still here?"

Mia shrugged and glanced around. "She disappeared on this spot. She'd just finished looking around Demigod Kieran's assistants' desks, but didn't go in his office."

Red stiffened when I relayed that bit.

"She's not a shadow?" I asked. "You could make out her appearance and everything?"

Mia nodded slowly. "But I've seen those shadow types around here lately. They dart around me. They burst into view and dart away a second before I can get a good look at them. I think they're taunting me. Telling me it is time to retire from the living world."

A chill ran down my back. The same thing had happened to me leading up to our battle with Valens. I'd seen strange, shadowy creatures from the corner of my eye. I hadn't had a chance to really think about it at that time—it had always happened at some crucial moment—but Mia was describing my experience exactly. It was like the creatures didn't mind if we knew they were watching us, but were great at not getting caught.

"Keep an eye out, if you don't mind. In the meantime, I need more people watching things," I said, finishing the climb of stairs and heading toward Kieran's office. Someone was getting intel through the spirit world. With enough energy, a spirit could open drawers. Maybe lift files. No energy and they could still monitor conversations and comings and goings. Kieran could see most spirits, thanks to our soul connection, but he still couldn't see the Demigods. One of them could park in his office and he'd never be the wiser. He needed a spirit bodyguard like I needed a living one.

"John," I said, standing in front of the receptionist's desk. The desk was familiar, but the person behind it was not.

"Sorry, what's that?" the middle-aged woman asked me, her round face turned up with a somewhat strained smile. I noticed she didn't acknowledge Red's presence.

"That's Rena. She's the new help," Red said, probably reading my confused expression. "Hopefully she'll know to patch through an important call during a non-important meeting."

"I know my job just fine, thank you." Rena pursed her lips. Apparently, she wasn't one of Red's few or nonexistent friends. That had to be an awkward working arrangement. If the job hadn't been working for Kieran, for a Demigod, I would've wondered why she'd taken it.

"I should contact John." I cocked a hip, thinking of all the spirits that had helped me take down Valens. Many of them had said they owed me one for freeing them. Maybe they still wanted to help. "Oh"—I snapped—"and what's-his-face. The experienced guy I summoned with the locket. Chad! Maybe he got a taste of the action and wants another go, this time without a gross body to maneuver."

"You want"—Rena's hand hovered over the phone—"me to call...John?"

"Jesus Christ, if you were any worse at your job, they'd take away your participation ribbon." Red steered me past the desk and toward Kieran's closed door.

"A little harsh, huh? It's her first day."

"I'm helping her. If she hates me, she won't want to talk to me, and then she won't have to pretend we're friends. She can focus solely on her job."

"Uh-huh."

"Wait, wait." Aubri hurried to my side as Red turned the handle. Aubri peered at my face, ducking this way and that. She stepped back with an "mhm!" and a smile. "Still perfect."

Red thrust open the door, glanced back to make sure I was on her heels, and led me inside. She paused for a moment, as if gauging the situation, then peeled off to the side.

Kieran looked up from the couch. He sat across from an unremarkable, aging man who nonetheless had a sharp stare and a lithe body. I got the feeling the man wanted everyone to know they were in plain sight. None of the Six were in the office.

"Alexis, please, come in." If Kieran was mad that I was late, he didn't show it.

It didn't make me feel any less awkward. I barely kept myself from apologizing and throwing Bria under the bus.

He smoothly stood and put out his hand, welcoming me closer. "This is Nester, the Defalcator that Demigod Nancy sent to help you explore some more facets of your magic. Nester, this is the infamous Alexis Price, not quite so scary as everyone would think."

Nester rose and lifted his hand in a salute. I suspected I knew why he didn't go for a handshake. My magic wasn't the only one that came with a reputation. No one liked being robbed.

His smile didn't reach those calculating eyes. "Hello, Miss Price. Nancy spoke highly of you. I'm excited to be working with you."

He lied well, at any rate.

"Hi." I copied his hand gesture. "Thanks for helping me out. A few nudges in the right direction and hopefully I'll be off to the races."

"Hmm, yes." He put his palms together, his fingers spread out. "I feel it is my duty to be upfront regarding the help you might receive from one with my magic. The only similarity between our magics is the commonality of spirit. I have, essentially, one function as it pertains to spirit—to hide things. Things, not humans. Not souls. But I can, of course, walk you through how I store the items, and maybe you can garner some understanding about the nature of spirit that way. But I must be clear: I *cannot* show you how to wander through the spirit realm. It is a dangerous practice and I simply do not have the skill set. I'd as easily kill you as help you if I even tried."

Kieran nodded as though he knew all that. I twisted my lips to the side. My "teacher" would be even less help than I'd originally thought.

I'd definitely need to wrangle that Spirit Walker, and I would not feel bashful about having Kieran help me.

Chapter 13

ALEXIS

"**O**KAY, NO. OUT." I sternly pointed at the door. Jack froze, the white cat, a dwarf in his big tan arms, hugged to his chest. "What?"

I pointed out of the kitchen, having just grabbed some water on my way to the backyard. It was dusk and much of the crew was waiting for me to summon the past Spirit Walker. They all worried something would go horribly wrong. It probably had something to do with the way he'd yanked me into spirit limbo last time...

Word had spread that the Spirit Thief, as I'd started calling my would-be teacher, was mostly useless. After waiting around the office for half the day, Kieran had just excused him, letting him know that he'd be contacted when needed. I didn't blame him. Regardless of Kieran's wish to get further into Nancy's good graces, the guy was a waste of time.

"Get that animal out of the kitchen," I demanded. "You have no idea where it came from. It can't be in here."

A wounded look crossed Jack's face. "He's hungry. I'm not going to keep him. I'm just giving him a little food and love until we find his owner. I had the staff put up a few signs."

"It had no collar and was on the outskirts of the dual-society zone. Frank said it came through the hole in the wall in the backyard. That animal was left behind. And if it wasn't, the owner will be looking at the pound—if there is one over there—not a gated community."

"Well…" Jack ran a big hand over the perfectly content animal. "I can always leave a sign at the non-magical shelters. The last magical one has been closed. A Bray Road Beast escaped from its handler and ate its way through the mundane animals. Now we ship all our strays to the non-magical zone. If they aren't found and killed for sport on the streets. Which will probably happen to this little guy if we don't at least help him."

I sighed. Why was the magical zone so messed up in so many ways?

"Fine, whatever. Give all the shelters its picture."

"*His* picture. He's a boy. He still has his balls and everything."

I leveled Jack with a look. "*He* better not spray, or *you* will find a new place to hang out."

Jack lifted his free hand. "He's a good boy. He won't

spray."

"But in the meantime, *out*! He could have fleas or ticks or who knows. I want it—him—out of the kitchen and away from couches, chairs, beds—"

"I know, I know. I was just heading outside." Jack hurried up in front of me. "You'll see, Lexi. Cats and kids—they just bring everything together."

"Someone is bound to agree with me about this," I muttered, heading through the back door to find everyone sitting in a semicircle around an enormous circle of two-by-fours, the ends just touching, in the grass. On top of them burned all manner and size of candles, interspersed with stinky incense and the occasional bell.

Bria knelt on the grass beside a large, flat piece of wood holding the rest of her Necromancer tools. She'd decided part of the problem with our last attempt had been a lack of firepower. She clearly intended to fix that issue this time.

Kieran sat in the middle of his Six, though a little rug sat empty in front of him, between his chair and the nearest two-by-four.

"Really? I get the rug?" I asked, drawing everyone's attention. "I don't even get a chair?"

"Oh." Jack hesitated at the end of the semicircle of chairs around the wooden circle. "I thought you'd want to be mobile?"

The cat, perfectly content up until now, hissed. It bit Jack's arm, raked suddenly clawed paws across his skin, twisted, jumped, and darted away into the trees, all in a flurry of movement.

I lifted my eyebrows and pointed at it. "It's possessed. The witchcraft portion of this summoning scared it. See? It probably ate its last owners. It probably turns into some sort of...hell cat in the nighttime or something. It doesn't need to be in the house when we're all sleeping. Or anytime, actually. Cat dander can't be good for the sinuses."

Thane twisted in his seat to look at me more closely. "Cats do that, Lexi. Jack was probably squeezing it too tightly. They don't put up with bullshit. Have you never owned one?"

I crossed Thane off my list of no-cat-in-the-house allies.

"Any animal that turns on you is not to be trusted," I muttered, waving Jack away. "It's fine. The women will take the ground, at the men's feet. It's where we belong."

Daisy huffed, at the opposite end of the semicircle from Jack. "No ground for me, thank you very much. These are new jeans."

I pursed my lips but didn't comment on her moneymaking scheme. "*Ladies.* You don't qualify."

"Quit yapping and let's get going," Bria said, looking at the sky. I didn't know why.

Red and Aubri clearly got nights off, since they weren't on scene. Lucky for them.

I took a deep breath. "Fine. Okay." I'd just bent at the knees when a blur of white froze my heart. The cat zipped past me, randomly pivoted near one of the candles, batted at Zorn's legs, dashed between the chairs, and ran back out of sight. I clutched my chest. "What in the holy fu—"

"Don't worry about that. He's just playful," Boman said with a smile that would normally melt anyone's resolve. I wiped that smile off his face with a heartfelt scowl.

"That thing needs a leash," I said, trying to calm myself. Trying to re-center. Or even center for the first time.

Donovan chuckled. "You don't put leashes on…" His words died when he got the next scowl.

"Ready?" Bria asked, her focus intense.

I swallowed and nodded. Showtime.

Kieran's movement had me glancing over my shoulder. He held out the pocket watch, which he then placed in my waiting palm.

"I'm right here," he said softly, his sweet breath dusting the side of my face. "You have a lot of power sitting right behind you. Nothing, not even a Demigod's army, will get through us. Do whatever you need to do.

We've got your back."

Jack and Thane both grunted their agreement. I could see the others nodding out of the corner of my eye.

"Okay," I said, breathing out a little more stress. Reaching for the power of the Line.

Spirit crawled across the ground and filled the circle, not stopped by a few boards and some stinky candles. The Line pulsed, comforting, its nightmarish colors not instilling me with any fear. The watch felt like it was pulsing in my hand. Like the guy on the other end of it was waiting for me to reach out and reel him in. Like he was challenging me. He'd gotten the better of me last time. He expected to do it again.

I gritted my teeth and hardened my resolve, sinking into a trance, the act second nature now. My consciousness followed the signal from the watch.

Time dropped away. My stomach rolled, and I felt like I was rolling with it, the laws of gravity ripped out from under me. This had never happened with any other spirit, and I knew the rogue Spirit Walker was somehow to blame. I was being manhandled.

Boy did I hate handsy fuckers.

I held on to my confidence and rolled with the feeling. Focused on the task at hand with the determination born of keeping two kids alive in the crack of the world. I was a survivor. When the going got tough, I pushed through with a little creative courage.

Free-falling now, I nonetheless sensed I was moving steadily across a flat plane. The logic made no sense, but I forced myself to focus on the end game. Soon enough, I bumped into the same wall, or door, I'd encountered last time. Again, I wondered if it were a cage, if somehow the guy was imprisoned in this realm. That would explain why he hadn't found his way back last time in order to mess with me. Or maybe just wander the world and cause havoc. A spirit that strong certainly could.

The wall nudged, opening slightly as the presence slammed against the other side. Crashed into it, shaking the very foundation of the spiritual plane. Strange colors, like a blood blister spreading under the skin, pulsed around me. Tendrils of it licked at my limbs and slid down my back.

My resolve shook. Fear worked through me. I stayed the course, but my mind was fixed on the one unshakable link connecting me to the real world.

It leads back to your Demigod. To your soul mate.

The voice seemed to curl around my ears, but the words hadn't been spoken.

He is a strong root for you. He will stop you from losing your way.

I opened my mouth…until I realized I didn't have a mouth. Communication was different here. I remembered that from before. There was no air. There were no words. I should know this by now. I'd been in this plane before, many times. Maybe not this deep, but it shouldn't matter.

Why did I keep forgetting things?

You need guidance. Practice. I will help.

Spirit ripped and tore at me. Rolled my spectral body end over end.

Panic tightened my chest, but I clutched what I knew was the soul link and held on tight, rolling with the feeling. Refusing to be knocked around this plane like a rag doll. This thing was the same power level as me—less, actually, after death. I should be able to withstand him.

I had to learn how to withstand him.

If I met a Demigod in this plane, the effect would be a whole lot worse.

Laughter rang through my ears. Roared all around me.

Still I held on, refusing to be budged.

Chapter 14

KIERAN

THE STRANGE FEELING he'd felt yesterday tugged on his middle. Kieran leaned forward, bracing his elbows on his knees, and stared at Alexis's back as she sat cross-legged in front of him, her head bowed. Bria peered intensely at her from across the badly orchestrated wooden circle. The precautions Bria had insisted on taking, including her insistence that all of them needed to be present, told him she was scared of this spirit. Something he'd rarely seen.

"What are we thinking?" Kieran asked, rising from his chair and then lowering beside Alexis.

Bria shook her head. "I don't know. She wasn't in the trance this long last time. I have the bells that should speed her way back to the surface, but it's all book knowledge. I don't want to use them unless it's dire."

"She's okay," Daisy said, nudging her chair to the side of the circle so she could scrutinize Lexi's face. "She's okay right now. She's got that little stubborn crease between her brows."

Mordecai stood and knelt next to Daisy's chair, his focus on Alexis. "Yes, she's right. Lexi always makes that look when we point out she's missing something. She's frustrated she doesn't know something, I'd bet."

Bria nodded, an unlit candle in one hand and a bell in the other. "I'd listen to the kids. They know her best."

A hard tug made Kieran grit his teeth. Those occasional tugs on their soul connection helped him feel closer to Lexi. Her presence, her emotions—they were all gone. Even seeing her living and breathing next to him wasn't quelling his anxiety. Her body might be safe, but her soul was not.

He took her hand, cool to the touch, and focused on that tug. On grabbing the other end. Maybe if he...pulled it taut? He didn't even know if that was possible.

Hell, he didn't even know how to grab it.

Alexis suddenly jolted backward. She sucked in a deep breath, blinked her eyes open, and then scrambled further back. Kieran's empty chair tumbled away as he stood. The guys all jumped up, clearing their chairs away too. Magic built around them, rolling and boiling, waiting for the enemy to emerge.

If only this were a normal battle. But no, they were dealing with the magic of Hades, the pit dweller, king of the underworld—a blind spot for most of the other gods and their descendants. Hades had been dealt a bad hand, but he'd turned it around into something hard to combat.

A man stepped out of the air and into the center of the glowing circle. Wearing a smirk and tousled, wheat-colored hair, he looked around him in amusement.

Bria was staring at him as well. Then she was moving, grabbing up various candles and moving them around the circle.

"This all for me?" The spirit put out his hands, his smile wider now. He zeroed in on Kieran. "Look at *you*. You have the power of a Demigod, but you're only a quarter god. That's quite rare." He hooked a thumb in his pocket. "I think you got touched by the divine, that's what I think."

Alexis stood slowly, her hands out, braced for action.

The spirit turned in a circle, looking at each of the Six in turn, none of whom could see him. Didn't matter. All of them awaited Kieran's orders.

"Loyalty. I like it." The spirit nodded, coming to the kids. "And children, in a potentially dangerous situation. Odd parenting choice."

"I never claimed to be mother of the year," Lexi said, then her teeth clicked shut. She hadn't meant to say that.

The spirit chuckled, as though he could tell.

"And then our resident Necromancer, with all her

bells and whistles. Or…candles and boards, in this case. You've gone old school, my dear."

Alexis repeated what was said.

"I had to brush up on my reading skills, but yeah, I got the gist," Bria said as she finished shifting a candle and picked up a bell. "It oughta hold you. I have everything placed exactly as it should be, moved at the right time. I'm sure of it. It'll hold."

The spirit bent to study the boards, turning as he did so, until he was all the way around. He pointed at one. "Weak link, right there. It is an inch too far to the right."

After Alexis relayed what was said, Bria paused in what she was doing, studying the offending candle. She ignored it and turned to another. "He certainly doesn't have any problem with lying."

The spirit laughed merrily. He turned to Alexis. "And another quarter god, this one without the divine touch. Our god clearly doesn't like you as much as his god did him. But look, you've tried to amend that all by yourself. That shows initiative. I don't think any other Spirit Walker in history has had a Demigod as a soul mate."

"Is he still talking?" Bria asked, checking her watch and then moving around the circle to switch out a candle.

"Mouthy, that one. I like her. She's definitely one of

Hades's." The spirit winked at Alexis. "So." He sat down with crossed legs. "Why have you called me? I don't feel your influence, which means you aren't trying to control me. You have faith in your friend."

"Kind of. Look, I'm just…" Alexis lifted her chin and walked closer, stopping just in front of Kieran. She was assuming control of the situation. "I'm not trying to control you because I'd like you to help me of your own volition. I don't like the idea of forcing people to do my bidding."

"But I am not a person. I am a spirit."

"The only difference between you and me is the outer crust. I have a body. You do not. But a soul is a soul. I'd prefer not to force anyone to do something they don't want to do."

"Very poetic of you. Yet you dragged me here and trapped me in a poor man's circle."

"Number one, I didn't drag you anywhere. You chased me…"

"Yeah, that was good sport. I couldn't refuse."

"Two, you tried to root around in my middle last time. This is a necessary precaution."

The spirit spread his hands. "Touché. So. Why am I here, then, in this poor man's circle?"

"You're really worried about the engineering of the circle," Alexis muttered, sitting cross-legged in front of Kieran. Bria muttered about the wastefulness of blowing money on a fancier setup. "I called you here because I'm in need of training, and I don't know anyone else who can do it."

"Don't you? You must've come from someone. Who is your father or mother?"

"My mother was not a Demigod, and she died. She asked not to be called back, and I will respect her wishes. My biological father kills his kids."

"Ah." The spirit nodded. "Not ideal, no. Magnus would crush you. Well I'm sure the other Demigods of Hades would give their left foot to have you at their disposal. There is no one better to train you than them."

"They'd give their left foot to use me. To turn me into something I don't want to be."

The spirit's eyes flicked to Kieran. "But hasn't he used you in the same way?"

Kieran shifted slightly from side to side, guilt pressing into him, but Lexi didn't even hesitate.

"No. He tried to push me away. I became the weapon I most feared in order to protect the people I love. I'd do it again if I had to, although I hope I never have to."

"Hmm." The spirit looked over the flickering candlelight into the growing darkness. "I've killed a great many people."

"I know."

"Good people, too. I've trapped and used spirits at

will. I've toppled leaders and murdered minions. Babies? Sure, why not. Killing good people for money? Yes, please. I do love gold. Some would say I don't have a heart. Others that I do, but it is as black as the hole whence I came. Many agree that I am the absolute worst. Just the worst. The worst what? Everything. It's a catchall. And yet you want to be trained by me?"

"I'm kind of between a rock and a hard place right now. You're all I've got."

He laughed again. "Way to make a guy feel wanted." He nodded and looked around at the grass, the trees, and the house. "A palace would've been nice. This is a little…domestic for my tastes."

"Weren't you kept in a dungeon?"

The spirit stood in a fluid motion. "You should never listen to gossip." He dusted himself off and shot a pointed look at the boards in front of him. "Yeah, sure, I'll train you. But you gotta let me out of this place." He met her eyes again. "Without trying to control me. I'll only do this as a free man. I was forced into slavery in life. I will not be forced into it in death."

A shock of anxiety rolled through Kieran from Alexis, matching his own. She hesitated, thinking about it. Then she moved forward to let him out.

Chapter 15

ALEXIS

"**W**AIT," BRIA SAID after I'd filled her in. She moved another candle. How she could keep the positioning straight was beyond me, because she hadn't written anything down. "Wait. Let's think about this."

I took a step back. No emotion crossed the spirit's face. He was too calm by half. Smooth as they came. More charismatic and handsome than a spirit had any right to be—at least one I'd need to spend a bunch of time with.

"What happened that last time he had free rein?" Bria asked as hot wax ran over her fingers. She grimaced but didn't move to put the candle down.

"We didn't have a chance to chat last time," I answered, adrenaline running through me. I was making things up at this point. I didn't trust him to save my life. But I needed him. I hadn't been lying about being between a rock and a hard place. It was either him, a spirit I could control in a pinch, or a Demigod who could control *me*. Eventually, the choice would be taken from me. "He was disorientated."

"I was testing her," the spirit answered. "This time, too. Your soul mate has boosted your power, Alexis. He's positioned you smack dab in the middle of a level five and a Demigod. I want to play with it. Maybe with you, if he'll share."

"Ew." I didn't relay that last bit to the rest of the group, although Kieran, of course, heard it. His muscles went taut.

"But you have been raised with morals," the spirit went on, his smile faltering. "You have been raised to know the difference between right and wrong. It is one of the first things stolen from a Spirit Walker. And while you are courageous in the face of your fear, determined when you are out of your league, and steadfast when your loved ones are in danger, you are still mortal. You are still human. You can still be broken and then reprogrammed. A Demigod will know how. It is only because of the Demigod beside you that it has not happened yet. You got lucky, lady. Real lucky. But luck is not eternal. You need to start designing your own fate."

"Yeah." I gestured at him, suddenly impatient. "That's why you're here."

His smile spread again. "So it is."

"What's he saying?" Bria asked, still moving around

the circle. Another dribble of hot wax ran over her fingers.

"What we already know," I answered. "Except he's surprisingly horny for a spirit."

"Slap him in a woman's body and let some nasty-ass taboo hunter take a turn with him," Bria replied. "That'll calm him right down. They don't like when they're the ones who are put upon."

"No one likes being put upon," I muttered, shivering in disgust.

Amazingly, the spirit's smile just kept spreading.

He turned as Bria walked around to another spot on the board circle.

"I take it back," he said. "I'll take her. She's more my speed."

I rolled my eyes. "Okay, is everyone ready?"

Bria straightened up, her expression surprisingly serious and intent. "You need to be absolutely sure about this, Alexis. This is on you. You are the only one here that can control him. The only one that can send him back. He's above my pay grade. I can help, and I've got a few tricks I can use, but you are the muscle, and neither of us have experience. Think this through. We can find another way if we must—"

"No, you can't," the spirit said over her. "The buck stops with me. Well, me or the kid-killing Demigod with love issues. If any of the other Demigods land you, the kid killer will just steal you away again. He's the strongest of them all."

Bria's mouth stopped at the same time as the spirit's. I almost asked her what she'd said, but I already knew. She was saying she couldn't get me out of this one. The pupil had finally surpassed the teacher, and unfortunately, the pupil still had no real clue.

"Take the spirit by the balls," Daisy said, making a fist. "You can do it, Lexi."

Mordecai nodded. Light flickered across his strong features. "This is the only way. If anyone can do it, it's you, Lexi."

Warmth and fear unfurled in my chest. Those kids usually forced me out of terrible ideas. That they were behind me, rooting for me, meant they believed in this. In *me*. Believed that the only way I could properly defend myself was by rising to the challenge of potentially controlling a strong spirit more experienced in my magic than I was. If I could see this challenge through to the end, I could face the next one.

I nodded, and Bria nodded with me.

"Just go ahead and blow out the…red candle. Yes, the red candle," she said. "Blow out the red candle on that board in front of you. If something goes wrong, force him back into the circle, keep him there until I can relight the candle, and Fanny's your aunt."

"Fanny." The spirit grinned. "That's what the Europeans call a lady's poontang." He waggled his eyebrows. "Gives fanny pack a different meaning, doesn't it? I'd like to pack her fanny."

"Gross," I said softly, bending quickly to blow out the candle. I didn't want to give him any ideas while I was down there.

The spirit watched the smoke rise for a moment before stepping over the board. On the other side, he rolled his shoulders and then his neck. When his gaze came back to rest on me, he said, "Now what?"

I stared back at him. I had no idea.

"Why don't you start with checking the repellent magic on the house?" Kieran said softly. "We'll stay close, just in case."

"But if we do that, I can't wander in at inopportune times to stare at you." The spirit winked.

"Good point, Kieran." I wanted to clarify which idea had been the good one. I started walking toward the house.

"Lesson one, and a little payment toward mutual trust." The humor dripped off the spirit's face. "When you call someone from behind the veil, especially someone that was in there deep, or someone that was there for a long time, they will be attached to the item used to call them. In this case, my pocket watch. That is now my home base. Not you, not this place—unless I eventually grow more attached to you than the watch.

Now, I can still roam, but it will drain me quickly when I'm away from the watch for any period of time."

I nodded, since I already knew that about spirits wandering. I stopped at the back of the house.

"Show me the watch," he said, standing beside me.

I hesitated, and he waited patiently. He probably had the power to move the watch. Take it from my hand and place it elsewhere. But he wouldn't be able to hold it for long. He might be powerful, but he was still a spirit, governed by the same rules as other spirits. The watch would be safe.

However, it was essential for me to keep the pocket watch away from that living magical klepto I'd met earlier.

I held out the watch in a slightly shaking hand I was not proud of. The spirit met my eyes before his gaze dipped to the watch. Suddenly, spirit blanketed my hand in a way I'd never seen before. Sparkling and almost living, it roamed my palm like tiny mites.

"Wait, wait. Is he showing you something?" Bria darted toward us holding a stick of burning incense in her fingers. She pulled a candle still emitting smoke out of her open backpack. She was clearly not worried about her own safety. "Here, here. You need to see it with your eyes first. That's how you learn."

"Oh, really?" The spirit cocked his head. "That's an unfortunate handicap. We need to rectify that somehow. I don't have all the time in the world."

"But don't you?" I asked sarcastically as smoke rose around us.

"No. You'll bore me eventually. And then I will try to get one over on you, and you'll send me into the bog again."

"Good tip." I studied the spirit floating around him, now turning colors in the smoke. Oranges and blues—what I'd already determined as the power of the Line and spirit, respectively. But he called upon different colors, too—purples and reds, pinks and greens that reminded me of the little ribbons attached to the souls of the living. I could grab them up and yank on them when they were still in a body. But as he coiled and turned them over the pocket watch, I realized he was making a sort of box. A cage. He draped it over the item, spinning it like a spider.

"It keeps falling away," I said, watching in awe. Feeling the pulls and yanks in the fabric of the spirit around me, telling me someone was messing with it.

"That's because I am without a body and also because I can't cage my own spirit."

"I'd be caging your spirit?" Tingles of apprehension moved over me, reminding me of Kieran's mom's skin, kept in a cage so Valens could ensure her spirit was caught in the world of the living. Of the way spirit magic could be woven with air magic to keep spirits imprisoned in a building—the opposite of what I did with my repellent spells. The magic was complex, beautiful, but I had sworn I would never do that to a spirit. I would never be as vile and disgusting as Valens.

The spirit, sensing something was wrong, stopped his hands and chuckled. "What if you need to protect those you love?"

I squinted at him, knowing manipulation when I heard it.

"You need to learn it, but that doesn't mean you need to use it," Kieran said softly.

I gritted my teeth and nodded my head. His mom had been hurt by a spell like this. If he wanted me to learn how to do it, I couldn't really say no. Besides, I did basically know how to do this. I'd already taught myself what this spirit would probably call the poor man's version. Learning to do it correctly made sense.

Or so I convinced myself as I tried to replicate what he was doing.

A half-hour later, I was doing the spell like I'd been trained all my life. All it had taken was a guiding hand, *so* much easier than trying to figure it out myself without knowing the rules.

"Right. Good work. Now, through the watch, I am tied to you. Maybe you can slap me in a body and I can be tied to you in—No, that's not right. Never mind." The spirit's face soured. At least he had standards.

"What if I lose the pocket watch?" I asked.

"Yes. Good point. You could use the watch to compel me more easily. If someone else should get the watch, I will still be tied to it, but the new holder will not be able to compel me unless they break your magical hold and apply their own. Given the power you applied, only a Demigod or Hades himself could make that happen."

"But I thought you said you wanted to be free?" I asked, sensing a trick.

He shrugged. "You're easy to trust. What can I say?"

"He knows that he is vulnerable with that watch out in the world," Kieran said, studying the spirit. "You are easy to trust, that's true, but he's only doing it because you're likely the *only* one he can trust in the Hades line. If that watch fell into almost any other hands, he'd end up right where he was in life."

"But there are a few things people can use to summon and bind him, aren't there?" I replied.

The spirit was analyzing Kieran the same way he was being analyzed. A smile slowly spread across his face. "You are older than your years, junior. Well? Answer the lady."

"Demigod Zander has his possessions, and Zander is of Zeus's line. He doesn't want anyone to be able to access your spirit. Bria could give the Hermes Demigod's guy a run for his money in thievery."

"Cheat to win," Bria murmured, now monitoring the incense.

"But now an item is free. If anyone finds out, there will be a race to acquire it," Kieran finished.

"A new, untested Demigod and an untrained Spirit Walker—I normally wouldn't play those odds," the spirit said.

"Yeah, you would," Kieran replied. He didn't need to smirk with all that confidence and ego he was whipping around—it was implied. "It would make you a rich man."

I would still need to keep the watch away from the magical klepto. Even if he didn't immediately take it to his boss, he could still prevent me from getting training. Given I didn't trust the side he was on, I had every reason to suspect he would attempt to nab it.

I blew out a breath. I also needed to learn the politics and manipulation side of things if I ever wanted to sit at the adult table.

Baby steps. Magic first. Politics later.

"Now." The spirit stepped back and looked up at the house. "We need to apply the same sort of magic to this house, just in reverse. Instead of tying a spirit in, we want to push them away. Luckily, the house is tiny. It's good practice for a beginner. That's the thing about Poseidon. He and all his heirs are cheap, cheap. Cheap and lazy." He turned to me. "He didn't build his own palace; he made the ocean gobble up someone else's hard work. That's what happened to Atlantis. Mr. Cheapy-Cheap thought he'd save a penny or two and just sink something rather than build it himself. It's not like anyone would want it back once it had been dunked. Everything would have been ruined. Kelp in stuff, crustaceans—tragic. And here we are, only a quarter Demigod and still as cheap as they come."

I opened my mouth to defend Kieran then closed it. I really didn't need to get involved. Especially since someone razzing Kieran for being cheap, which obviously wasn't true, was pretty funny.

"Okay," the guy said, and spirit didn't just crawl across the ground and rise around us—with his help, it floated through the sky, connected to all our souls, and swirled up like mist. He didn't need air to plaster a spell to the house. With his training, I might not need it either.

If he was trustworthy.

Chapter 16

ALEXIS

A COUPLE OF hours later, after a hot shower and a back massage from Kieran, I trudged downstairs and half fell into a seat at the kitchen table. Working my magic around the watch had required more technique than power, but casting a protective net over the whole house had drained me.

First of all, it was incredibly hard to call enough power to see the spirit floating all around the house. The other Spirit Walker had made it look easy. He hadn't even strained. I'd looked like I was sitting on the toilet in need of Ex-Lax. Or so I imagined, given the way Daisy and Mordecai kept laughing at me. Thank God Kieran loved me.

When I asked the Spirit Walker why it was so hard for me, I got a disapproving look. Apparently I hadn't been pushing myself. I could have come up with a list of explanations. That I'd only been at this for half a year. That I couldn't have known I needed to push myself in the first place. But there wasn't any point. As far as the spirit was concerned, it was my fault.

And then there was the challenge of *feeling* spirit, something that was even harder for me. Finally, I had to twist and nudge and bend and braid spirit around every inch of the house (which was easier, the Spirit Walker claimed, since it was so "modest"). Sweat was running down my face at this point. I might have piddled myself a little.

The protections wouldn't be enough to stop a Demigod, but they would severely slow them, and by that time, Kieran and I could combat them. All other spirits or magical workers wouldn't stand a chance.

Or so the smug spirit had claimed. I got the feeling he'd been testing me all along. If my undies weren't that little bit damp (super embarrassing), I might've felt a little pride in my accomplishment. I was new, fine. A novice. But I was no dummy. I could be taught.

Just maybe not without a few minor accidents.

One thing I did pick up on: with spirit hovering around me, I could tell when another spirit worker was using their magic in the area, something the Spirit Walker helped me to see.

That realization earned me a nod of approval from the spirit. I nearly clapped in glee, and would've if I hadn't been worried I'd look like doofus with wet drawers.

"What's for dinner?" I asked as Boman put a glass of

water in front of me.

He hesitated. "Or did you need a beer?"

I let my head thunk down on the table. "Water is fine."

Jack and Donovan turned around from the grill and stove respectfully, delicious-smelling smoke rising behind them. "Steak," they said in unison. "Potatoes."

"What's this, the Tweedledee and Tweedledum show?" Bria asked as she walked in, burns on her hands and a backpack slung over her shoulder.

A little mew preceded the cat sauntering in behind her, its tail curling at the end like it owned the place. Zorn followed them in. Both Zorn and Bria had showered and changed, but only one of them looked fresh and revitalized. Zorn got benefits from the blood bond. Bria was just a trooper.

"You can make a salad," Jack said to Bria. "You can't fuck up a salad."

"Are you sure?" Bria shot back.

"I got it. The girls did all the heavy lifting today. They deserve a rest." Boman smiled and winked at me before pulling a little glass tube filled with green gel from a pant pocket. He set it on the table next to my arms. "Aubri would like you to smear this under your eyes when you are feeling tired, fatigued, or puffy." From another pocket on his Mary Poppins cargo pants, he pulled out a lemon zester. "Oops. That shouldn't be in there." He placed it on the island. Next, out came a little plastic tube of aspirin. "Here we go. This'll help."

"I'll make her a martini," Bria said. "That'll help more."

"No alcohol," I said. "It'll put me to sleep, and we've had watchers. I need to be alert."

"No problem. A Jaeger bomb will keep you up," she replied. "That failing, narcotics, though those'll probably hurt more than help."

"Where would you even get narcotics?" Jack asked, flipping a steak. Loud sizzling filled the kitchen.

"Boman's pants, obviously. He's got everything else," she said.

"All out, I'm afraid," Boman said, heading to the fridge.

"Just set up the salad stuff here." Bria patted the counter, leaning back to catch Boman's eye. "I'll help cut. I need something to do."

Zorn slipped into the chair next to me. Apparently he wasn't planning on helping. What a coincidence; neither was I.

"What name did that spirit give you, by the way, Lexi?" Bria asked, centering her cutting board.

"Why, does he have more than one?" Donovan asked as Thane stiffly walked into the room. I could barely see the kids heading up the stairs behind him. They'd gotten in some training of their own while I was wrestling with spirit.

"What happened to you?" Boman asked, pausing in rinsing lettuce.

Thane braced against the island and winced. "The wolf lunged, distracting me from the gremlin, who used the opportunity to kick me in the nuts from behind." Half the room busted up laughing. Jack danced over and punched him in the arm. "It's not funny. I think a surprise kick to the nuts hurts more."

"As opposed to asking for a kick in the nuts?" Jack asked with a grin.

"If you're Donovan, yeah," Thane said, adjusting his junk.

"Dude, I was checking to see if that cup worked," Donovan said, moving something around on a pan. "I'd forgotten I'd taken it off because it had gotten itchy."

Bria blinked at him incredulously. "Thank God you're pretty, because wow, you sure are dumb."

The guys laughed again, even Thane, who immediately followed it with a groan.

Kieran strolled in a moment later, his hair wild, his eyes bright, and the smell of the ocean rolling off him. My heart leapt at the sight of him, warming me from the inside.

"You good?" he asked me softly, stopping next to me to knead my shoulders. "As good as you can be in this itty-bitty house?"

I laughed. "Yeah, just exhausted," I replied. "Not to worry—Boman has supplied me with green goo so that I won't look too puffy or tired. Lord knows I wouldn't want to offend the menfolk by not looking my best."

"Aubri said so, sir. I wasn't commenting on Lexi's looks," Boman said.

Silence trickled through the kitchen. The guys all sent incredulous glances at Boman.

"I said I *wasn't* commenting," Boman said, his voice rising. "That I *wasn't*. I wouldn't comment on a girl's looks—you know that, Lexi. I mean, not to say I wouldn't compliment you if you were all dolled up and looked really pretty because—"

"Oh, so she's ugly right now, but you're being a gentleman and not acknowledging it?" Jack asked with a lopsided smile.

The color drained from Boman's face. "No! That's not what I meant. She's always pretty. She's one of the prettiest girls I know. I've always thought that." Kieran turned to him slowly. Boman put up his hands and took a step back. "Sir, let me explain. What I'm saying is, pretty girls don't like to be told they're pretty because it makes them feel objectified—"

"Which you just did...even though she currently looks ugly," Thane said seriously, cupping his balls.

Donovan's back was shaking with his failed attempt to hide his laughter. "Oh yeah, a real gentleman, sure. I noticed she barely sat down before you ran over there with serum to fix her up."

"I did not—"

Zorn leaned closer, catching my attention as the guys picked on Boman. Even though he didn't look it, Boman was the youngest of the Six, which meant the guys often chose him as the fall guy. When they really got going, they made fun of him ruthlessly. Actually, Zorn was technically the youngest, although everyone knew better than to mess with someone whose reciprocal humor was so violent.

All the guys aged really slowly because of their blood bond with Kieran. I wasn't sure if they were immortal, though. I wasn't sure if Kieran was, since he was only a quarter Demigod. Frankly, I was afraid to ask. I didn't know what that would mean for us.

"I heard you found out about what your wards have been up to," Zorn said softly. I could feel Kieran's attention shift.

"Yeah, look, I didn't know," I said. "It's not right, what she's doing."

"It's exactly right," Zorn replied. "Exactly. She's had a hard life, and she's in a situation where she has no control over her fate. A survivor doesn't just accept her circumstances—a survivor finds a way to gain some control. We think she's collected a nice little nest egg so far."

"Over fifty thousand, I think," Kieran said, taking the empty chair on my other side. My mouth dropped open. "That's an estimate. I think she's sold or returned roughly seventy-five percent of her purchases."

"Kieran! How could you let her spend so much? Are you out of your mind?"

"Shh." Zorn looked up at the corners of the kitchen. "I think I got all her listening devices, but I'm not positive. She's gotten good."

"Two reasons," Kieran said, his gaze delving down into mine. "I want her to be comfortable here, and this nest egg she has created herself will help her do that. The second is because Zorn is studying her and tweaking his training accordingly. That we have no idea where she is putting the money means she is a better pupil than I think any of us anticipated, especially for a non-magical."

"It's *because* she's non-magical, I'd wager," I said. "She is spending her time learning, analyzing, and applying. The only thing she has to fall back on is herself. She has no magical crutch. No advantage. You're forcing her to adapt, and she's using her brain-power to do it."

Zorn and Kieran both nodded.

"I would ask you," Zorn said, "to just forget about this. Don't mention it again. If you have to, tell her to do the right thing. I want to see how far this goes."

I shrugged, happy to be left out of it. "Fine by me."

The cat leapt onto the table and sauntered across it, as though it was perfectly normal for an outdoor animal to traipse across a surface where food was consumed.

"Get down," I said, pointing at the ground. "Shoo. *Go!*"

It stretched, completely ignoring my fervent movements. It kicked out its back legs, one at a time, then took a seat next to my glass of water.

"Seriously, do they not listen?" I asked in bewilderment. "Its butthole is on the table."

The cat batted my glass of water.

"No—"

Water splashed as the glass tipped. I reached out to grab it, but was too late. Liquid sloshed across the surface of the table and spilled into my lap.

"You little shit!" I jumped up, bending over to look at my soaked jeans. "What in the absolute hell?"

Zorn rose and scooped the cat off the table.

"Don't tell me you like cats, too," I asked incredulously as Zorn retreated to the other room where two cat bowls had mysteriously appeared, one for water and the other for food. "They don't listen. They just do whatever they please."

"They're like women," Jack said. "They stare at you flatly, reading you, judging you. If you are worthy, they will allow you to pet them, but only on their terms and only when they're in the mood. Treat them well, though, and they'll give you all the love you can handle, sometimes with a little painful nibble to keep things interesting."

"Well, that one is a moody jerk who doesn't listen." Realizing what I'd said, and in what context, I held up a finger. "Don't you dare say that's like a woman."

"Hear that, Boman?" Thane said. "*Don't* say that a moody jerk who doesn't listen is like Lexi. Keep it to yourself and only passive-aggressively give her Midol to combat the issue."

"Keep it up and I'll treat your nuts like a soccer ball for the second time," Boman replied.

"I'd like to see you try."

"Shifting back to things that are actually important, did that spirit ever tell you the name it wanted to go by?" Bria asked.

The mood in the kitchen changed on a dime. I shook my head. "I make it a habit not to ask for spirits' names, so I didn't even think of it, and he didn't offer. But we know his name, don't we? Or don't you?"

"I know all three. His birth name, the name he gave himself in school when he grew confident in his magic, and finally the name he was given after he was broken and re-formed with a killer's mind. I'm interested in which name he goes by now."

"You can still feel him?" Kieran asked me.

I nodded, because yes, I could. His presence existed at the edges of my awareness—the pulsing sensation that I held someone's soul on a rope. When I pulled that awareness front and center, I felt the string connecting us. I knew I could use that string to easily compel him, as he'd said. I could even force him, regardless of his power. I'd bound him to me. And he'd shown me how.

"Yet he can't come inside?" Bria asked.

I shook my head. "He's bound, but he's still at arm's length." A payment in trust indeed. From now on, I would need to run all of my interactions with this spirit through Kieran, because if this spirit was manipulating me, I doubted I'd know. I simply didn't have the experience to always think someone was lying. It was draining. Kieran could shoulder that burden.

"But Demigods can come inside," I said. "The boosted protections won't change that. They can still rip down my magic and come on in."

Kieran leaned forward, bracing his arms on the table. Thane and Boman both leaned against the island, their eyes intense.

"A Demigod in shadow form, right?" Kieran clarified, probably for his guys.

"Yes. In the form from the other night. Whoever it was didn't have any problem with the old...spell, or whatever you call it, and while it wasn't well done, it was still powerful. A Demigod, even in spirit form, trumps me."

"He didn't show you how to set alarms to alert you if someone tampers with your magic in real time?" Bria asked.

"You can do that?" I reached for my glass, which Kieran had refilled, then hesitated, wondering if cat hair had gotten in it.

Bria shrugged. "Don't know about yours, but I can set little warnings to let me know if inhabited cadavers cross into my defined space. It should also work for a strong soul. The only problems are: one, this is a house and I might set the whole place on fire, and two, I don't know if a Demigod can circumvent it somehow. I would assume one of Hades's line could, although I have no proof."

"They'd see your warning system only if they knew to look for it," Jack said, plating the steaks.

"If they didn't, there's still the issue of possibly burning the house down. I have some of the tools, but don't have the sand pits to keep the fire contained." Bria reached for her backpack. "I can try, though. I can poor-man-set-up anything. I'm not proud. Poseidon ain't got nothin' on me."

"No, he does not," Zorn said from beside the door-way. I hadn't even heard him sneak back in.

"Oh yeah, you can talk," Bria retorted. "Why have a nice meal when you can save a dime and eat some frozen hot dogs."

The guys in the kitchen made "uh-oh" faces and turned away. Bria and Zorn had some strange friends-with-benefits situation that was turbulent at best. No one else wanted to get involved. We had enough problems.

"Okay. Well, worst-case scenario," I said, "we eat a good, big meal, all tuck in for the night in the two itty-bitty houses that our benefactor seems to like—right, Kieran?"—everyone chuckled or smirked—"and we battle if we need to. We've been through worse."

Chapter 17

ALEXIS

"**P**ROTECT YOURSELF."

The strange slide made of rainbows disappeared from my dreamscape. I floated toward consciousness, confused, but was waylaid by a playground made out of melting chocolate. I bent to lick the ground, not a rational thing to do, perhaps, but the chocolate was calling.

"Rise. Protect yourself."

It was a man's voice, at the edge of the playground. Something zoomed past me, rubbing against my legs. Little feet pitter-pattered.

I jolted and felt my physical body jolting with me. I was near wakefulness. This was usually when the shadow thing would swoop in and take me into the spirit land. When I was strangely conscious yet not awake.

A strange little chirp met my ears, then a small weight settled onto my left thigh.

I froze as candy apples fell into the pooling chocolate. It occurred to me how fucking weird my dreams were.

"Wake up! Something is here!" the voice repeated.

I looked around the nightmare candy land, the apples now glowing a toxic red, looking for the source of the warning.

The weight moved up my body, and something rough, like wet sandpaper, ran up my cheek. Again. The third time it scratched against my nose before the weight settled on my chest.

I jolted again and fluttered my eyes open, struggling to wake up.

Something small and furry stood on top of me, looking down at my face.

It was the damn cat.

It chirped, an unexpected sound. I froze. Cats didn't chirp, did they? Was I still dreaming?

My inactivity was apparently a green light, because the cat kneaded at the edge of my boob with its paws, taking turns pushing and releasing with each foot. A moment later, a claw dug into my skin. Pain shocked into me, and I slapped at the creature.

It was already moving.

It let out a small meow-purr as it bounded away, hitting the floor with an elegant plop, if such things existed, before darting into the shadows.

My heart thudded. I sucked in startled breaths, staring wide-eyed in the direction the creature had run.

"What is it?" Kieran asked sleepily.

"I'll tell you what it is. It's a dead cat, that's what it is." I flung back the covers and threw my legs over the edge of the mattress. The door stood cracked open. The cat was nowhere in sight, but I doubted I was lucky enough that it had left the room. "Out," I whispered, bending to look under the bed.

Without warning, something darted at me, swiping. I flinched, nearly losing an eye but refusing to lose the battle. I rushed forward, reaching out for the blasted thing, but it took off, its bright body streaking across the floor and through the black crack out of the room.

Opening that door was probably Daisy's idea of a joke. Or maybe a challenge to see if she could pick the lock and open the door without getting caught. Well, the joke was on her—or it would be tomorrow when I punished her within an inch of her freedom.

Speaking of Daisy, I did a quick check to make sure she wasn't wandering around the house, looking for more mischief to make. I found her soul in her bed where it should be. Mordecai's, too. Donovan was in the spare room, and the cat was nowhere to be found. It had probably taken off downstairs after realizing it was in mortal danger. Its soul had a smaller signature than a human's, more of a wisp, but for some reason it seemed even wispier tonight. The spirit floating through the air in droves had clearly messed with my reading ability.

Still annoyed, knowing I wouldn't get back to sleep right away, I wiped my face and stepped into some jammies. If I didn't get some water and regroup, I'd just toss and turn and bother Kieran. There was no point in both of us losing sleep and being grumpy in the morning.

The house was quiet as I walked down the hallway and descended the stairs. The curtains and blinds had been drawn so no one could see in, and I navigated mostly by memory. I walked across the chilled floor to the front door and pulled the shade a little, just making sure all was well. The darkened street lay deserted, the few streetlights covering the ground with circles of light.

I turned and walked down the short hallway to the kitchen. Halfway there, the cat darted out from the side and clawed at my ankles.

"What the—" I jumped and kicked and staggered in surprise, ramming my shoulder into the opposite wall. The vile thing took off toward the back of the house. "Your days are numbered, you little dickhead," I said through gritted teeth.

I stared after it for a moment, half inclined to stalk it around the house, catch it, and toss it outside. But the little bugger was fast, Daisy was asleep, and a locked door really should suffice. Tomorrow, though…

Continuing on, I nodded in determination. Tomorrow, that thing was goneskies. I didn't care if it made me public enemy number one in the house.

Someone had left the kitchen curtains open, letting in a little light. Frank stood out in the middle of the street, still as the ghost he was. He faced away from the ocean, as though watching for intruders. Which was odd, because usually he stood on the grass.

Does he see something?

"What is it going to take to get you to follow me?"

My heart ratcheted up to an alarming speed. I froze. Felt my eyes widen. Turned around slowly.

Nothing stood in the entryway.

My gulp was loud in the quiet kitchen. I hurried to the door and looked out, my rampaging heart now in my throat.

A dark, quiet house greeted me. Nothing was here.

But I had heard a voice!

"Is my sanity slipping?" I whispered into the hush.

"I've never in my life"—I whipped around—"seen someone so clueless"—I darted to the edge of the island—"in the face of danger as you"—and stared down at the cat.

Its mouth hadn't moved. But it was standing there, staring up at me as though it had just spoken. As though it was now waiting for me to take action.

"I'm still dreaming," I said with a slack mouth.

"The back of the house," the voice came again, and

damned if it didn't sound like it was coming from that cat. The logical explanation was that Bria had thought it a hilarious joke to put a spirit in there, but the cat was very much living, and no human soul was hunkering in its furry little body.

"I'm going crazy," I whispered, unable to tear my eyes away.

"No, you're going stupid. Hurry!"

"You're a cat. I'm dreaming, I must be."

It bristled, hissing, then pounced and wrapped itself around my ankle. Its sharp little teeth and claws bit into my flesh.

I let out a high-pitched squeal and shook my leg, trying to get it off. Trying to wake up.

It jumped back like it was on a pogo stick. "Focus! We don't have time for you to be this clueless. Hurry! She's at the back of the house, and soon they'll be all over. I don't have time to explain. Suffice to say, you still have my pocket watch, it's in your Demigod's silly little safe, which can easily be broken into, and we'll need to have a few words about why you have an office filled with cats when you clearly don't like the bloody things. But we'll worry about that later! Hurry. I'm not about to see my newest pupil end up…like almost all of the Spirit Walkers before you."

Disbelief bled through me. I could hear spirits in their cadavers, but…

"That cat is alive. You can't shove spirits into living things."

"I am not inhabiting this cat. I am possessing this cat. There is a very big difference."

"How much of that cat's personality are you controlling?" I asked as I followed it.

"Get a hold of yourself," it called back, loping in front of me.

I slowed, reality *finally* seeping in.

"How can you be in here when I coated this whole house with magic-repelling spirit?" I asked.

"By being in this cat. My perfect god, you are slow. It would be awe-inspiring if it weren't so sad. It's a real shame what they let women get away with just because they're pretty."

I opened my mouth for another question when a soul bleeped onto my radar. Warning crept through me, sending a shock of cold down my spine. The soul moved slowly, like it was creeping, sticking to just outside of the house.

I hurried forward, all my senses on high alert. Near the laundry room, I slowed down.

"Finally," the cat said, and leapt onto the dryer, closest to the window. "She's out here."

"How do you know?" I asked suspiciously, eyeing the drawn shades.

The cat's head swiveled around and it stared at me

condescendingly. The spirit had picked the perfect animal to be an asshole in, that was for sure. Two peas in a pod.

"You're a Spirit Walker, right," I said softly, batting it off the dryer. I still didn't trust him, especially since he hadn't bothered telling me he would be assuming this other form for the time being. "Can I possess animals?"

"When you come back as a spirit? Most likely. Shall I kill you and see if you can figure it out?"

The soul slinked just a little closer. Through the window, I could see a shapely form dressed in dark clothes—a woman's body. She paused by the door and reached into a utility belt. I didn't need the Spirit Walker to tell me she planned on breaking in.

I could take her down right now, easily. It was a living human, the soul was throbbing right there, and I had lots of experience. Hell, I could yank out the soul, stuff it back in, and make her tell me who'd sent her. But why in the hell would anyone break into this house?

"Yes. I can see the wheels are turning. Talk me through it," the cat said.

"Kieran is inexperienced for a Demigod," I whispered, "but he is still a Demigod, and he took down Valens. He's not to be underestimated. Then there's me. I'm also inexperienced. Everyone knows that. But I can still rip out souls. Nancy would've confirmed my magic by now. And if not, the way I helped Kieran take down Valens probably unnerved a lot of people."

The lock jiggled on the door. I paused, my heart hammering. Everything in me quailed as I thought like a single woman with two kids and no weapons, feeling vulnerable and helpless.

Only I wasn't that woman anymore. I didn't just see ghosts—I *was* a weapon. A weapon with a brain.

"Kieran often has at least one member of the Six around, and all the cars are here tonight. Only a fool would break into this house…"

I let the thought drift away as that feeling from earlier commanded my attention. Someone was manipulating spirit.

I stepped in front of the back door, bracing myself for whatever awaited me on the other side. It wasn't a Demigod—thanks to Kieran, I could sense power, and this woman was barely a level five. I doubted she had a power that I couldn't combat with my own.

The lock clicked.

I waited, holding my breath, ready to stab with my magic.

The handle didn't move. Instead, the soul drifted away, moving slowly and silently across the grass and into the trees in my backyard. She crouched there, clearly waiting.

I dropped my hands slowly and felt my brow furrow.

Waiting for what?

A throb of spirit pulsed around me, disturbing the stagnancy. A distant yelling drifted through the quiet house. It sounded like Frank.

I remembered him in the middle of the street, watching.

I remembered what types of things he ran from.

My heart sank and I felt the blood leach from my face.

"My, my. I've changed my mind, you do learn fast. You've got the broad strokes down of feeling the spirit in the air, you just need to learn the nuances, like where and who it is coming from."

"The *who* is a Demigod," I said with a suddenly dry mouth, turning slowly. "The *where* is in front of my house, and from the sound of it, my guardian spirit just took off running."

"Sure, if you want to make light of your training and pull a Sherlock Holmes, no problem."

Little ripples of spirit drifted around me now, and a weight pushed on my chest. Dread. The Demigod hadn't come alone this time. He'd brought friends.

I re-locked the door then pulled a rubber door stopper from a drawer and wedged it in the bottom. It did okay with strong breezes, so hopefully it would do something against a shoulder.

Just in case, I had to get the kids hidden or out of the house.

"Kieran!" I shouted, running for the stairs. Souls popped up on my radar like firecrackers, hurrying down the street toward the house. Another huge pulse of spirit pummeled me like currents in the ocean, and I ripped at the cords to draw the curtains from around the door. The huge shadow form from the other night stood before me, back to the house, waving a great hand at the street as if to wave someone on.

"Kieran!" I shouted again.

"There are intruders in our yard," Daisy said, pounding down the stairs. She wore tight black clothes bulging with various weapons strapped to her person. "They emerged from the trees down the way. They must've been hiding there."

"Astute kid," the cat said. "What's her magic? I can't feel it."

"Doesn't have any," I said, hurrying to the kitchen to look out the window.

I caught a glance at what—or rather whom—the shadow man had been waving at. Someone walked down the middle of the street with straight shoulders, head held high, and sword handles sticking up from his or her back. The light showering down from the streetlights slid over the person's body without high-lighting any features, almost like the light diffused into a black cloud. The moonlight, though, shone on waxy white skin and pale hair, the human embodiment of a ghost.

"What?" Daisy asked, breathing fast and standing behind me. She couldn't hear the cat talking. Before I could shrug it off, she said, "Oh shit."

A small army marched behind the man, and if they weren't stopped, they'd cut us off from the rest of our crew.

Fear made it hard to swallow. There were too many of them, especially since they were led by a Demigod of Hades in shadow form. There would be no soul for me to grab and yank.

Footsteps pounded down the stairs. Donovan appeared first, followed by Mordecai in wolf form.

"You and your brother need to hide, do you hear me?" I said, rounding on Daisy. I turned and clamped a hand on her shoulder. "You need to hide. We don't have enough people to protect you. You have the money you got from Kieran. If something should happen to us, you take that and get out of here, okay? Don't tell anyone who you are. Take it and go."

Mordecai whined softly, and I was reminded of the last time he and I had been ambushed. Only this time, the cavalry wouldn't run in and save us at the last minute. This time, we were grossly outnumbered and would stay that way.

Chapter 18

KIERAN

KIERAN STOOD AT the window in the guest room, staring down at the street below. He had already awoken by the time Alexis called his name, responding to the panic coursing through the soul link. He'd lain there for a moment, unable to believe what he sensed was true, unable to believe the Demigod from before would disrespect him a second time.

Last time, the Demigod of Hades had come to suss out Alexis and her power, but this time he was threatening Kieran's family. And he didn't have the balls to do it in person. Hiding behind his shadow form, he'd collected a little army and marched into Kieran's territory in the middle of the night.

Kieran sucked his teeth, letting the fire build in his center. He could understand why one of the other Demigods might want to attack him politically, before his views and positions were known. Or why Valens's allies might want revenge. Hell, he could even understand why greed might drive someone to take advantage of a young Demigod newly in charge of an influential and prosperous territory.

But there was a way things were done, even among thieves and cowards. This was not it.

This was a declaration of war.

The tides rolled and boiled. The air whipped around the street, responding to Kieran's inner turmoil. Fog rolled in, settling low. He'd cut off their sight, confident his people knew how to work in a state of near blindness. They'd trained for it.

Footsteps thundered up the stairs. Daisy ran past him, followed by Mordecai in wolf form. The boy put on the brakes, nearly making Lexi fall over him.

"What are you... Oh." Lexi, out of breath, hurried across the room with the cat at her feet. "There's one person out back, waiting in the trees. She unlocked the laundry room door and then retreated. She's obviously waiting for us to be drawn out the front. I can't fathom what she wants—could it be that pocket watch?"

"It's you," Kieran said, the fire boiling within him. His power swelled around the room. "They want you, Alexis. They want to weaponize you, like the last Spirit Walker."

"Sure, fine, but when did they think they would grab me? I'm obviously going to be out there with you."

Kieran laughed, the riddle too easy to solve. "Clearly the coward on that street thinks I will try to hide you away to protect you. He thinks I wouldn't dare risk you in a skirmish like this."

"A skirmish?" Alexis turned to face him, her eyes filled with fear. "Kieran, they must have three dozen magical people down there. And a Demigod that no one but me can see." She huffed. "Yes, I know you can see him, but what are you going to do, claw his ankles?"

"What?" Kieran's attention strayed from the intruders for a moment.

"Sorry, not you. I'll explain later."

He let it go. He didn't have the time. His guys and Bria were almost ready, and the enemy forces were almost in position.

"They have less than three dozen troops unqualified to handle me, my Six, and Bria, even with that excuse for a Demigod. Aaron sent one of his best after me, and defeating his assassin was child's play. If this is Aaron, he won't risk more prized staffers so soon. If it isn't Aaron, the Demigod will have heard about Aaron's guy, and will also shy away from the risk. I bet it is Aaron, though. Magnus would never be so stupid as to assume I'd pit you against my father only to hide you now. He'd never be so bold as to challenge me like this. Lydia is much too subtle. She's known for her cunning and nuance. No, Aaron's making a play for the prize. You. And after he realizes you aren't his daughter, he'll want you in his bed. He'll torture your sanity away, then shape you into a bed-sharing weapon." Kieran ground his teeth, pain and disgust stoking his rage.

"You are really hot when you're this frightening, but we can't stay in here, Kieran. We're wasting time. That Demigod is doing something with spirit and I have no idea what. Soon he'll unleash his power and I have two kids in here."

"We fought Valens, too," Daisy said. Mordecai gave a little yelp.

A pulse bloomed in Kieran's middle. That was Zorn. Bria was ready to go. Boman had yet to signal, though. He needed more time.

"I hated that you were there," Lexi told them, "and you were shielded by large groups of fresh soldiers. This is different. You *will* hide."

"Can you sense anyone beyond that woman out back?" Kieran asked, time ticking away. He felt power building. Aaron was ready to make his move.

"I couldn't earlier, but I'm too far away now to double-check."

Kieran glanced at the kids, who were ready to fight. They had courage in spades. "Follow me."

He stalked down the hall to the small closet between the guest bath and Lexi's room. Lifting a little latch near the bottom, he pushed the button beneath it. The wall of linens popped forward.

"What the…" Lexi's words died as another pulse

blossomed in Kieran's middle. Boman was in position. It was time.

Working fast now, he pulled open the hidden door, stepped in, and flicked the switches to power the room up.

"I didn't think you needed more space in the master bedroom," he said, glancing down the long, narrow room. "I also figured you'd appreciate it if I made some precautions in case things went poorly with my father. I didn't think I'd need to use them after the fact."

"Yeah, he *was* a good find," Lexi said, but Kieran hadn't heard Daisy say anything.

"Sir, we've got movement," Donovan called up.

"Why didn't you tell any of us about this?" Daisy asked. She thought she was old enough to join the battle.

"Because you're Zorn's star student. If you'd known about it, you would have figured out how to get in here, and then no one would be safe." Kieran stepped out of the way. Neither of the kids moved.

"Now!" Lexi barked. The kids grudgingly shuffled forward.

"Demigod Kieran," Donovan called, apprehension coming through the blood link.

Kieran shut the door behind Daisy, knowing they could figure out how to latch it from the inside. He shut the closet, too, and took a spare moment to grab Lexi's upper arms and look down at her angelic face.

"I love you with everything I have," he said, his emotions swelling like the tide. He wanted her to feel it as well as hear it. "We're better together. But so help the heavens, if anything happens to you, I will follow you into the spirit realm and drag you back out, kicking and screaming if I must."

A lopsided grin broke through the apprehension on her face. The kids were taken care of. Her worries were over.

His middle throbbed with the power of her magic running through their soul link. "Stay safe. You are my soul mate. That is forever."

Her grin grew. "You say skirmish, I say practice. No one messes with my kids and gets the nice Lexi."

✕　✕　✕

DAISY

DAISY LOOKED BETWEEN all the monitors, each showing a different portion of the house, inside and outside. They could see most everything from here. Most. She'd already identified four blind spots. Zorn would probably quiz her on them when this was over.

"Why haven't I noticed these cameras?" she asked quietly, observing the large gathering outside. She remembered how blindsided Lexi had been when the Demigod's shadow form had shown up near the house the other night. How hard it had been to get rid of it.

She shook her head.

"This isn't a skirmish, Mordecai. Kieran always sounds super confident even when he's in over his head. Our people are going to get slaughtered."

Mordecai emitted a soft growl.

"Ew. Obviously I didn't mean for real, come on. But this is bad. They need all the help they can get."

He moved around and bumped up against Daisy's thigh. He was probably trying to talk to her with his weird shifter movements.

"I told you, I don't speak canine. If you want to communicate, you have to change. Not like we need a wolf in here, anyway. This place is tiny and no one is getting in."

A moment later, Daisy was edging away from Mordecai's nudity. Thank God there was a blanket right on the other side of the door.

Given the battle hadn't even kicked off yet, she quickly unlatched the door, pulled it open, and snatched a towel from the shelf.

"Wrap up, dickhead," she said, hiding a smirk. Mordie hated when she swore at him for no reason.

"Shut the door," he said urgently.

She turned to do exactly that when the closet door swung open. The hall light flared behind a massive shape, cutting off her field of vision. Surprise punched her, and she slapped down on the handle.

"That's Jack," Mordecai said.

She paused in yanking the door shut, knowing Mordie was using his shifter smelling.

Sure enough, Jack filled the doorway with his large frame and massive arms. Through the glare she could just see him blinking at her, as though he didn't really know her.

"What's the matter?" she asked him, a small warning tickling up her spine.

"Come with me," he said, his words wooden, his inflection off. He didn't sound like the Jack she knew.

"Kieran put us in here…" Mordecai started, but Daisy put up her hand to stop him. Something wasn't right.

"What are your orders?" Daisy said, dropping her hand back to the door handle. She didn't know what was going on, but something felt *off*. If there was one thing Zorn constantly beat into her it was that she had excellent instincts. She should trust them at all times.

Jack reached out a hand like a Neanderthal. Like a big guy with a lot of muscle instead of a graceful shifter, waterborne or no.

Like someone would guess that was how Jack moved.

The warning screamed through her body: *Now.*

She slammed the door shut before fumbling with

the latch. The handle turned. Daisy attempted to hold it shut, but she was no match for Jack's muscle. It moved against her palm, then swung open with her still attached to it.

She staggered, but she was already reaching for her knife. Jack's strong fingers curled around her wrist as she wrapped her palm around the knife hilt. He jerked her wrist away. The *crack* sounded bad. The pain nearly made her black out, raging up her arm and through every nerve in her body. He'd broken her wrist.

She bumped into the wall, trying to compartmentalize the pain, to get out from under it. Jack palmed her head and smashed it into the wall. Splotches of black clouded her vision and made her dizzy. Pain dominated her thoughts, blaring through her.

Mordecai screamed, not usual for him, and Daisy barely registered a huge fist reaching its zenith and crashing back down. A sickening crunch and Mordecai silently fell.

"No," Daisy screamed, drowning in pain but struggling to the surface. "No! Mordecai!"

Jack stepped back, a bloody mallet in his hand. Something glopped off it and onto the floor.

Brains.

The word swam lazily through her mind. Terror rooted her to the spot. Anguish consumed her, and it wasn't from her wrist or her head.

"Mordecai," she screamed again, digging for her knife with her working left hand. But she wasn't as diligent with her nondominant hand. She didn't even get close to grabbing it.

Jack moved, and suddenly the back of his hand cracked across her ear and cheek, knocking her into the wall again.

Her thoughts dimmed and suddenly she was in the air, a band of steel around her middle, her body dangling from either side of his enormous arm. Tears she hadn't realized she was crying dripped from her face as she howled silently through the pain, the horror.

Mordecai was her brother. Her lifeline. Each time she had a nightmare, he'd gently shake her awake and then sit up and talk with her until she felt safe to return to the darkness of her mind. Of her past. Before the Demigod, it had been just the three of them, Lexi, Mordie, and Daisy, struggling together. Mordie had been her partner in survival. Her only friend. Her only confidant. He was everything light and pure in the world. Everything good and wholesome. She'd promised him they'd train together until he was good enough to meet his pack. She'd promised she would stand by him one day when he assumed the role he'd been born to fill—the alpha.

Her actions had killed a member of her family. She'd opened the door and invited in a snake.

She didn't deserve to live instead of her brother. Not instead of him.

"Please," she whispered as Jack jogged her down the stairs. "Please God no," she begged as he turned the corner to the back of the house.

A shadow down the hall froze. Daisy hadn't even realized she was looking forward rather than backward. Even through the fog of pain and life-altering horror, a part of her mind recognized the knife throw, where it would hit. She shifted just a little so when Jack recoiled and staggered, her head wouldn't be bashed against the wall for a second time.

Another knife, dead center. One more into his throat.

Jack gurgled up blood. His arm came loose and Daisy dropped to the floor like a rag doll. She landed on her broken wrist, and the explosion of agony shattered her. She screamed and rolled, holding her injured arm to her chest.

Move, girl! You're free! Get moving!

Tears and blood clouding her vision, she struggled to sit.

Jack convulsed next to her, a cry of shock and renewed pain escaping him before he clutched at his neck, as though he'd only just realized he'd been wounded. The woman, who had been moving in for the kill and hadn't seemed to care about Daisy, jerked to a stop. She straightened up woodenly, then stilled.

Daisy shakily pushed onto her knees and emptied her stomach, then pushed to standing, refusing to give up, needing to kill this bitch and get back to Mordecai.

The woman rolled her shoulders before she burst into action, slicing her knife across Jack's throat before punching Daisy in the forehead. Daisy's head snapped back and she was falling. Before lights out, the woman bent over to scoop her up as Jack's movements slowed.

Chapter 19

ALEXIS

I COULD'VE SWORN that was Jack's form hustling past me in the swirling mass of fog and darkness as I made it to my front yard, but his soul was...off. It felt like his, but also like someone else's. It didn't make sense.

Then again, I couldn't think straight, not in this thick, soupy mass of white-tinged darkness, the moon and streetlights illuminating the fog in places. The stuff rolled and boiled around me, suffocating, messing with my mind.

"Was that Jack?" I asked Bria, her shape enlarging as it got closer, her soul identifying her. My words didn't seem to travel as far as they should. They seemed muted. "Where's he going?"

"This shit is a mind-fuck, am I right?" she said, stopping beside me. She was close enough that I could just make out dirt and sweat or moisture smeared across her face. "Yeah, that was Jack. He's supposed to be meeting up with the guys and Kieran, due west of here, in the middle of the street. But I don't know. He was acting strange earlier. I think he's worried about the kids. Listen, we got work to do."

She grabbed me by the arm and yanked me with her, heading toward Kieran's house across the street. Something brushed past my leg and I jumped. I could just barely see the cat streak by.

Shadows writhed around us, and what I could only describe as a sucker punch smashed against my chest. Bria grunted at the same time, but didn't slow, pulling me along behind her.

"That is really annoying," she muttered, jogging now.

"Where are we going?" I asked as the ground underneath us trembled.

"We've dug up the cadavers I had stored in Kieran's backyard. This potential situation is why I went with shallow graves and loose dirt. We need to get them active. Get your bearings. That Hades nut sack is about to shake this party up."

A tremor rolled through the asphalt, followed by a small earthquake, shifting my balance. Kieran could rumble the ground with power, maybe give it a little wiggle, but this felt more like the other Demigod's work.

The ground dropped away, giving me a moment of fright, before launching back up and knocking the soles of my feet. My knees buckled and I hit the deck, only to be shaken like a snow globe in the hands of a child. Spirit condensed around me, making me feel sluggish, followed by a blast of unspeakable terror. Fear like I'd never felt before blasted through my mind and locked up my body.

"Fight it," Bria shouted in my ear. "That's the Demigod's magic. Fight the feeling. It isn't real. If metal is thrown at you, though, run. That *is* real."

She hoisted me up and dragged me along, clearly unwilling to let the manufactured terror we both felt tear her away from her duty.

"Get moving." The cat darted in and batted at my ankles. I kicked at it. "Get going!" he said. "The troops are advancing, your Demigod is stalling for heavens only know why, and the dickhead Hades Demigod is headed for your house. This is all about to unravel."

I repeated what the cat had said—and quickly explained who had said it.

Bria looked down in bewilderment, then stared at me for a long beat, her expression clearing to one of neutrality. She thought I was crazy.

"Fine, if it is just a voice in my head, it's been right so far," I yelled, stubbing my toe against something with a little give. I stepped around it, only for my other toe to hit something with no give. I fell over a curb and onto an unnaturally soggy body. "What the—"

"Hurry, we need to get souls into these bodies and get them moving," she said, grabbing items out of a box she must've brought out before she'd run to find me. She handed a few of the things to me, relics attached to spirits we could call from beyond the Line. "Kieran should be keeping them busy to give us a second."

Worry dripped through my middle—Kieran's. A burst of emotion followed it, trailed by shock, sadness, confusion. I didn't know what it meant.

"Something is happening," I yelled as the ground heaved again. The need to tear at my hair in fear and scream nearly overcame me. The spirit around me felt like a shroud. The fog was too thick, cutting out my favorite sense. The sense I used as a crutch.

The sound of yelling cut through the pounding of my heart in my ears. Battle cries. Someone had given the enemy troops the go-ahead to attack.

"Go, go, go!" Bria shook me. "Focus on one spirit at a time. Focus on your job. Block out the rest." The flame of a candle barely illuminated the fog before it went out. "Shit. My magic doesn't like all this moisture."

My heart rattled my ribcage wildly, responding to the magical fear even as I tried to force my mind to ignore it. Sweat joined the moisture of the fog on my skin.

"One at a time," I said, someone's scream renting

the night. "One at a time."

I closed my eyes, the constant press of spirit on me starting to piss me off.

Frustrated, unnaturally terrified, fucking angry, I *pushed* out around me, shoving the Line, the spirit, and everything else, trying to get a little breathing room, to clear a spot for myself.

"Yes!" The cat darted in, stood on its hind legs, and tried to paw at the chain of a gold necklace swinging down from my cupped hands.

"What the hell is your problem?" I ripped the necklace away.

"I can control the thought processes of the cat, but I cannot control its instincts. In this case, I need to attack that waving, dangling, sparkly chain of madness."

I felt the soul connected to the necklace pulse, so much closer in the spirit plane than the Spirit Walker had been, as a boom of power slammed into me. The sound of waves crashing against the cliff face not far from us, unnaturally, magically loud, drowned out the battle cries and yells.

I pushed out again, this time with the magic I'd received from Kieran through the soul connection.

"Yes!" the cat yelled again, jumping at the dangling chain, doing a half backflip and landing on his feet. "*That* is why you choose a Demigod of a different lineage for a soul mate. I was on the fence, but now I'm a believer."

The soul of a sleepy woman in her sixties appeared before me. I didn't have time to explain. I thrust her into a body, clamped her soul into place, and moved on to the next as Bria started loading up weaker spirits next to me.

The souls were all easy to find, and I picked up a quick rhythm—relic, soul, body, relic, soul, body.

"You're a machine!" the cat yelled with delight, sitting down for a moment to lick his paw. The exuberance didn't match the lazy fur cleaning, but then, his excitement didn't match the situation at all. He was clearly reacting to his murderous past. "I didn't think there was any way in the great god of Hades that you'd get all this done in time, but here you are. Fantastic. Great work ethic."

"That cat is getting on my last nerve," I muttered.

A wave of power rolled over us, barely kept at bay by the spirit I was constantly shoving out to keep us unscathed. The ground jumped again, throwing me at a jerking body filled with an unhappy soul. Kieran had just gotten started, but I could plainly feel his impatience through both of our links—he was clearly waiting for us to get going. The enemy troops were probably almost upon us now, picking their way through the murky night, slowed by the fog—slowed but not stopped.

"You filthy, soul-stealing…" One of the spirits started before I gave it a kick with spirit.

"Yes, okay, I see what you did there," the cat said. "Look at you improvising in a violent sort of way. I like it. You'll get along just fine with Ares types."

"Enough from the peanut gallery," I grumbled, not needing one more distraction. Power throbbed within the newly filled bodies, higher and higher, until everyone had obtained the max level they were capable of in spirit form.

"We're ready," I told Bria, clutching souls by their strings, not compelling but controlling. I'd apologize to the spirits later.

"Tell Kieran through the blood link," Bria said, her animated bodies jerking and twitching like zombies in the movies as they gathered in a neat little cluster.

One of mine took off running, one poorly attached leg wobbling dramatically. Another started off in the other direction.

"Get a hold of them," Bria hollered.

I tried to communicate to Kieran as I battled the fear still poisoning my blood, the push of the various magics messing with my head, the thick fog and darkness hindering my vision, and my zombies' attempt to scatter. I had no idea what message Kieran would receive.

"Direct them at the enemy troops and make them

use their magic," Bria instructed me, yanking me into action again. She seemed to have the directional sense of GPS. "This way. Just make them use their magic. You know how!"

I called up her teachings from my memory. All the practice sessions. I tried to focus on that as I forced my crew into a jerking horde.

Shapes moved through the glowing darkness, passing under a glowing streetlight. Spirit punched my middle, the same magic as before. A black strobe blotted out the glowing streetlight, restoring the darkness. It didn't matter a whole helluva lot here. It was impossible to see anyway.

I imparted my will onto my troops, forcing them to lurch after Bria's well-organized group. Their souls, like little ribbons gathered in my hand, strained to break free. I relayed this to Bria.

"All spirits try to break free. Yours were all level fives in life that didn't die too long ago," she said. "Real nasty people. There are only a handful of people on this great green earth who could control them all. Welcome to the elite. Now hurry up and get them doing their magic."

A black stick swung through the murky white, and I realized too late it was a sword. It sliced through the arm of one of Bria's zombies. The creature jerked, outraged, and I heard its spirit yelling obscenities from within the rotting corpse. The disembodied limb fell to the ground and a ball of fire exploded from its remaining arm. More shapes pushed through a slice of one of the still-glowing streetlights. Three of them in a row. More followed in the murk.

I cursed myself for forgetting that I didn't need my eyes to see. I opened myself up, feeling the souls. Dozens of enemy troops bleeped onto my radar. Kieran and the guys were a ways behind me, standing together on my house's side of the street. They were taking on the Hades Demigod, I knew, keeping him or her busy until I could join them. Or maybe keeping him busy so he wouldn't know I was right here, fully exposed, ripe for the taking.

The Line appeared beside me, but before I could draw power from it, someone slapped me in the face.

"No Soul Stealer magic yet," Bria hissed. Someone screamed ahead of us. Then another. Her zombies were doing magic. "That Demigod would be down on you in a minute."

I gritted my teeth, not arguing. She was right. Instead, I bore down, forcing my zombies to do as Bria had said. Use their magic. Help us fight.

Lightning rained from the sky.

"Oh shi…" I couldn't even finish my thought because the next bit of magic took my breath away.

Zigs and zags of electrical current ran through the

fog like a living thing. Kieran had clearly used precipitation from the ocean—the salt with the moisture a great electrical conductor—in preparation for this spirit-zombie's magic. Somehow, he'd been ready for an oncoming battle. He'd made preparations.

"He was worthy of the divine hand," the cat said quietly beside me.

A glow preceded a flailing man running. The fireball zombie had sent out another one, and it cut through the air around the man, sending out forks of fire as it touched down on his skin. He screamed, the top of his body already consumed in fire and now convulsing, his legs somehow kept running, shaking but determined. Right at me.

I back-pedaled to buy time, sucking in a startled breath, but the body wouldn't go down. Without thinking, I yanked the man's spirit out, injected it with my desires, and shoved it back in, locking it into place. All in the space of seconds.

Fire spat at me from two feet away. The guy jerked to a halting stop. He'd gone from dying to dead to zombified with head-spinning speed, and clearly had no idea what the hell was going on. Without hesitation, I gave him a little nudge. I didn't even feel bad about the situation, the bastard.

He turned around, smoother than any zombie because of the familiarity of his body. He faced the shapes moving through the darkness. Faced the screams, zombie and enemy both. Faced the carnage.

And then he started running right back the way he'd come.

A glowing ball of flame slammed into the enemy troops, knocking into them. More lightning rained down, too. Souls bleeped out as our enemies took down the spirit-controlled bodies and vice versa.

"And now we see what you can really do," the cat said as Bria said, "You've done it now. Might as well just go whole hog."

A shock of spirit pulsed through the air, freezing my blood with fear. Bria screamed and ducked, clutching her head. More screams rose from the enemy.

And then Kieran was running my way, the others behind him.

The fog lifted in an instant, pulled up high overhead. Suddenly the moon was free to rain down on the battle. The street lamps could brighten small pockets of action.

A quarter of the enemy force lay on the street. Half of the zombies. The battle raged on.

The soulless Demigod of Hades stood back where Kieran had been, its full focus on me. Its shadowy form had grown to a height of twenty feet, its muscles popping out like a Berserker's.

"It literally thought I was in the house," I said quietly, my heart ricocheting around my ribs from the magically induced fear. Spirit wrapped around my insides so tightly that I didn't know if I could move.

"Without fear, there can be no courage," Bria said. She straightened in strained, jerky movements. "Fear does not rule me. Fear will not control me. Fear is but a speed bump on my journey to victory."

The Demigod took a step toward me, and power boomed out from it. But not the power strength of Kieran or Valens. Leaving the body behind lessened the spirit. It was as true for a living Demigod as it was for the dead.

He was still more powerful than me.

"Fight back," Kieran yelled, nearly to me. "Fight back, Alexis."

The fear in his voice shocked me. The fear in the blood and soul connection. I was a part of this equation. I was a part of this plan. I needed to show up and own my position.

Another wave of heady spirit pounded into me, trying to force me to submit.

I gritted my teeth and called forth buckets full of power from the Line. I'd taken my brief training earlier to heart. When it came down to survival, I remembered what I learned.

The world around me filled with ultraviolet rays of spirit, layered on the ground, crawling up the streetlights and hovering around all of our bodies. A veritable fountain of it rained down on us from the Demigod, who was dousing us from his position across the street.

Chewing my lip, I let part of my mind run through that problem while I grabbed up the nearest bunch of enemy souls. Just as I was about to reduce them to the ground, Kieran pushed out his hand, five feet away. A blast of air ripped past me.

Wide-eyed, I glanced back. Bodies tumbled across the ground, and the souls I held popped out like champagne corks.

"Well, that was easy," I murmured.

Kieran reached me and spared one moment to inspect my face. He nodded, as though assuring himself of something, then said, "Take out the rest of the enemy. Show them what you can do. When that's done, let's make a statement to that coward hiding in shadow."

Anger and pain rang through our connection, making me hesitate, but impatience and fierce determination colored his words. I'd ask him about the emotion later. First, I needed to clear the field.

Bria jogged to catch up with me, moving stiffly, responding to the terror but not letting it run her down. The cat loped on my other side.

"This is ridiculous," I grumbled, feeling the power pulse through me. A splashing sound attracted my attention, and I looked back to see a monstrous water tornado splash through the trees. A whirlpool on land. That was terrifying. Thank heavens Kieran was on my side.

I drew more power. As much as I could.

"If I'm going to own this horrible Soul Stealer mantle," I said, "*I* should be Death upon the pale horse, not the cat lady in her jammies."

"Whoever owned that office in the government building before you was probably more terrifying than any lunatic riding a horse," Bria said, fighting the magic. "Don't underestimate crazy cat ladies in their jammies."

We neared the spread-out crowd of enemy, those whose souls I hadn't ripped out. They were down the block. Many of them struggled to rise on broken limbs, injured by that burst of air from Kieran.

"Never own the mantle of Death," the cat said from beside me. "You were not designed to be Death. Nor does your magic have just one purpose. You are the yin and the yang of the living world—you can save a life as easily as you can destroy it. Your Demigod is not Death, either, though he kills just as readily as you. Besides, you are not killing these people; you are simply setting their spirits free."

"Tom-ay-to, tom-ah-to," I said, raising my hands to make it easier to envision grabbing all their soul ribbons.

"Though if your Demigod *was* Death, he'd probably

use a giant goldfish for a trusty steed. He's too cheap to buy something as cool as a pale horse," the cat murmured.

Wind from the Line rustled my hair, only it suddenly struck me that it wasn't wind at all. It wasn't relegated to the spirit world, only affecting me because I was working with spirit—it was the hovering spirit all around me. When I drew all the power to use in this manner, I was unknowingly messing with the spirit and creating that movement.

And if I was creating it, I could control it...

Chapter 20

KIERAN

A POUNDING ACHE filled Kieran's middle, threatening to derail him. One set of emotions was missing from his Six. One complex weave of feelings had fallen away, leaving a void.

He gritted his teeth, the rage roaring through him. The need for vengeance dizzying his thoughts. But even if there was a way to kill this Demigod here, tonight, doing it would be the wrong play. It would bring down too much heat on Kieran. It would open up Alexis to more danger. No, he needed to focus on the long game. He needed to cool his rage with logic.

The backs of his eyes stung, but he clenched his jaw and sent another wave of power at nothing more than a feeling in the air, stopping the Demigod from advancing. All he needed was Alexis to make an impression with her magic, and they could send this sad excuse for a Demigod packing.

He turned back to her. Wind didn't blow her hair to the side this time; it circled her like a windstorm. Her cotton jammies lifted at her sockless ankles and worried an undone lace on her runners, drawing the attention of the cat at her side, who promptly pounced at it. She slapped at her face, and the wind suddenly changed, blowing at her face and whipping her hair behind her. It also caught Bria, sending her back-pedaling, using her forearm to block the magic.

"She's figured out another facet of her magic," Zorn said, his voice strained.

"She needs practice," Donovan said, his words hollow.

She did indeed, but even though the display was amateurish, the effect was not. The enemy screamed and clutched at their middles. One by one they fell, bonelessly sliding to the ground. And one by one the bodies rose again, twitching as they did so. The effect worried a person's primal side, hinting at forces not known to the living. Hinting at death walking among them.

"She's just getting started," Kieran yelled as he turned back around.

The ground bucked and Kieran nearly lost his balance. But the power was weaker now than it had been at the onset of the attack. Even then, it had been weaker than Kieran on his worst day. The magic of invisibility clearly had its cost.

"I have found a trainer for her," Kieran yelled

through the street, in the direction of the invisible pulse of magic, "and you are a dead man!"

Newly dead and reanimated cadavers lurched up and readied themselves for battle, their hands up, magic spinning. Alexis jogged forward, the wind blowing her hair elegantly to the side, her eyes on fire, her newly stolen army at her back. She and Bria could've handled them all on their own. Kieran merely needed to chase the Demigod coward from the battlefield.

Kieran jogged to stay by Alexis's side, but he looked back at Thane, his heart aching. "Take someone and go. See if he can be revived." They all sensed one of them had fallen.

Thane glanced at Henry and they were off, sprinting toward the house and Jack. Hoping against hope he was still clinging to life.

Filled with sorrow and rage, Kieran pulled the water tornado from behind the creature and strained to focus and contain it. It was the Demigod's shadow form he wished to destroy, not the neighborhood. Alexis's magic rolled in, slashing and tearing, cutting through the creature. When he was beside her, he followed her gaze and moved the water, covering the area she was focused on. Covering the invisible coward.

"Higher," she said, slowing, letting her newly created zombies continue the charge. "If you want to drown it, go higher. It's almost twenty feet tall."

"Can you drown a spirit?" Boman asked, scoping things out.

"No, but the mind will forget that," she said, working her hands. Her magic. "His mind is attached to that shadow, and his mind is programmed to protect his living body. Unless he has trained in pushing through the feeling of being drowned, his mind will revolt." She looked at Kieran, seeming suddenly unsure. "Do you guys train in withstanding each other's magic?"

"No." Kieran moved the water up, sweat popping out on his brow. Anguish bled through his middle, but he gritted his teeth against the onslaught. He didn't want to know what had caused that emotion in Thane and Henry. "That would take away our advantage against one another."

Pain throbbed now, and urgency took over.

"Go, you sonuvabitch," Kieran said through clenched teeth.

"What's going on?" Bria asked Zorn quietly.

"Good." Alexis nodded, her eyes intense, a smile spreading across her face. "Yes. Yes! He's thrashing. He's trying to step out—here." Alexis's brow scrunched and she raised her hands higher. Her army circled the water tornado, magic firing from their hands. "A little to the left, Kieran."

Kieran complied, impatient, wanting this done. Why was the Demigod hanging around, anyway? His army was destroyed. His body was elsewhere. Alexis was protected. What was he hoping to achieve?

"There you go," Alexis said, and did a fist pump. "I know he's gone—I was just about to say that." She turned to Kieran. "He's gone. You're good. We're good."

Kieran barely stopped himself from asking whom she'd just been talking to. Nobody who was physically present had spoken. But it didn't matter right then. He didn't want to waste any time. He turned the water into fog and pushed it out to sea. It would disrupt some weather elements, but it couldn't be helped. He'd fix it later.

"Make sure everyone is incapacitated," he yelled over his shoulder.

"Got it," Bria said.

"Alexis, you help." Maybe it was selfish, or cowardly, but he didn't know what to expect, and if the worst had indeed happened, he didn't want her to see him cry.

He made his way through the door and immediately saw a prone body lying in the hall, surrounded by a lake of blood. Neither Henry nor Thane were there.

Heart in his throat, Kieran fell to his knees and pushed his fingers against a spot of clear skin in a half-ruined neck. But the skin was cold. No pulse pushed back.

Agony rose in his chest. Hand shaking, he pulled it

away from Jack's neck. He let his hand hover over Jack's middle.

Where the hell was Henry? Where was Thane? Why weren't they here with Jack? Why weren't they keeping watch over him, trying to resuscitate him?

Kieran put his hands over Jack's heart, but before he started, a flicker of movement caught his eye.

He sucked in a breath, jerking to standing, reaching for his power...only to feel his hands drop limply to his sides. Heat pricked the backs of his eyes, and all the fight went out of him.

Jack stood without a body to house him, blinking at nothing. He clearly didn't know where he was. He probably didn't understand he was dead.

He needed someone to shepherd him across the Line. Someone who understood the transition. He needed help. Help Kieran didn't know how to provide.

For the first time, he understood the full spectrum of Alexis's power. Why spirits tried to latch on to her. Why they made their homes close to her. She was the rock they clung to like a barnacle, their shelter in the turbulent world of the living when they didn't want to, or couldn't, find their way to the beyond. She had always had one foot in the physical world and one in the spirit realm. She was the protector of the dead. The Spirit Walker.

And Jack needed her.

As Kieran watched his friend, confused and help-less, it felt like the world opened up and swallowed him whole. The pain was so great that he didn't want to feel anymore. He couldn't help the tears pooling in his eyes.

Then another blast of emotion rocked him from Thane. He was upstairs in the panic room. The kids!

A cold sweat broke out across Kieran's face and his heart stopped in his chest. Another blast of emotion from Boman, way out toward the back of the house but now working his way in.

"Kieran," Thane yelled. "Get Alexis."

Chest tight, heart pounding, Kieran hurried to the front door and yelled her name. She was already running at him, her face ashen and eyes wide.

"What is it?" she asked, the corners of her lips pulled down. She stopped just inside the door, her focus on Kieran acute. "Why do you feel like that? What's happened?"

"Sir." Boman ran through the door behind her. He'd clearly run all the way around the house so he wouldn't have to cut across Jack's form to get to the front. "They've taken one or both of the kids. They went over the wall—they must not have known about the illusion covering the break in the bricks. There's a lot of blood, and it looked like it was from drag marks. One or both is wounded but not dead."

Alexis's face drained of color. "Daisy. Daisy is

gone—" Her voice cracked. Her head snapped up right before she sprinted up the stairs. She must've felt Mordecai. And if she felt him, maybe he hadn't gone the way of Jack.

Chapter 21

ALEXIS

I COULDN'T BREATHE. I couldn't think. A hole was eating through my heart and terrible, white-hot agony ripped down my middle. Daisy was gone. Taken. Wounded and probably terrified.

I choked back a sob.

But Mordecai wasn't. I could feel his soul throbbing erratically. I'd never felt that before. I didn't know what it meant.

I slid to a stop outside of the open closet door and stared down at droplets of congealed blood. My eyes burned with unshed tears. Taking a deep breath, I braced myself for what I would find inside.

Thane sat on the floor in a puddle of blood, leaning over a lifeless form, his hands shaking as they hovered in the air. Next to my foot lay a sort of mallet coated in red.

I could barely feel my feet as I took another step into the room. Helplessness overcame me. Sobs bubbled up through me.

Thane looked up, and beyond him all I saw was red where a face should be.

"Lexi, I…" Tears dripped down his face. "I…" Thane shook his head, looking back down.

I stood frozen for a moment, too numb to move closer to my kid or kneel beside him. Boman hurried in after me, bending over Mordie's legs like Thane was bending over his face. Still, I didn't move.

The numbness spread. To feel would be to crawl in a hole and die with Mordecai. It would be to give up, and Daisy was still out there. She still needed me. I couldn't shut down. So if I needed to stop feeling, so be it.

A strong hand covered my shoulder. "I don't see his spirit."

I blinked stupidly.

"Do you feel his soul?" Kieran continued urgently.

Fog clung to my thoughts. I tried to find reason in what Kieran was saying.

"There's no pulse," Thane said, a tear dripping off his jaw.

But there *was* a soul, still erratically throbbing. A soul hunkered down in a limp body, clinging on to dear life.

Choking back another sob, I dug my nails into my palms. The pain cut through the haze of my thoughts. I sifted through my memories and pulled up what I needed.

*You are the yin and the yang of the living world—
you can save a life as easily as you can destroy it.*

I pushed Boman to the side and then recoiled when I saw the crushed side of my kid's unnaturally pale face. My stomach swam, but I held on to my gorge. If there was a chance I could do something, it was a fleeting one. If there was time, it was almost up.

"Souls can live as long as the body can house them," I murmured to myself, trying to work through all I knew.

With my magic I seeped into Mordecai's chest. All but one of the prongs holding his spirit into its casing had broken. The final one was basically threadbare, holding on by the grace of God.

"All healers do is magically fix bodies," I said softly. "They fix the bodies, and it is up to the ailing person if they can cling on until their spirit settles again. But Mordecai is his own healer; he just needs to be furry. When in shifter form, they heal at lightning speeds."

You can save a life as easily as you can destroy it.

"I just need to keep his spirit docked until his body can recover." I knelt at his side. "He's strong. He's been battling all his life. He has experience holding on until I can save him. He's waiting for me to save him."

"But there's no pulse," Thane whispered.

I stopped from lashing out. "Then give him a pulse,

you useless sack of monkey balls!" Kinda.

Kieran stepped over and pushed Thane out of the way, determination lining his face. He clasped his fingers and went to work, performing CPR.

With my magic, I held Mordie's soul in place while I fixed the prongs, knowing the real challenge would be keeping his soul in place through the shift. The soul casing changed with the rest of the shifter's body, and for one weightless moment the soul was just hanging out, willy-nilly, with no docking. If it went fast enough, all was well. But Mordecai's casing was badly damaged, and I wasn't even sure if I could get him to shift, let alone quickly…

Desperation clawed at me, reminding me of the improbability of all this working. The first person I'd killed with my power had been a shifter—I'd ripped his soul out, and although I'd put it back, he'd died upon shifting. The prongs hadn't held up.

But I had to try.

"Is there a way to force him to change?" I asked, one of the prongs crumbling in my magical grasp. *"Is there a way to force a change?"*

"Yes." Boman searched through his pockets with amazingly steady hands. He was clearly good in a bind. "Yes! Because of Jack, I always carry one when we go to battle." He pulled out a little vial as well as a Q-tip. The Q-tip went back in his pocket. He searched another side. Then two more pockets. "I don't have a syringe. How can I not have a syringe?"

I thought back to moving into this house. "We have one. It should be in Mordecai's bathroom."

"Give it." Kieran reached forward and snatched the vial. He leaned the tip against the ground and used his other hand to smash off the top. Half spilled out, and Boman and I both sucked in a breath. Kieran poured some from the jagged top into the horrible wound at the side of Mordecai's head. "I don't think dose matters at this point. Alexis, get ready."

But I was already working on him, gingerly repairing each prong as it broke over and over again, the body trying to eject the soul. Kieran kept pumping the heart, not giving up.

Tears ran freely down my face. Boman and Thane waited with us, ready to take over for Kieran if need be, I had no doubt.

"Come on, buddy," Thane said softly. "You can withstand pain better than anyone I have ever met in my life. If you can do that, you can withstand death, too. Come on. Fight it. *Heal.*"

"Steroids." Boman hopped up. "Steroids! That'll give him a boost. I have some back at my house. All he needs is a boost and the shifter will kick in."

"Adrenaline is what he needs," Kieran said, holding out his hand. "Give me your knife. My blood can act as adrenaline."

"He can't be an alpha one day if he is bound to you," Thane said.

"He won't be bound to me. This is a gift, freely given, to save a life I have put in jeopardy. Give me your knife."

I stared, mute, knowing this was unheard of. Kieran had freely given his blood to each member of his Six, amping up their power and abilities, but they were bound to him. He'd given it to me, too, but he'd also marked me. We shared a soul link. He had been thinking about forever. But Mordecai wasn't his kid. He wasn't his responsibility. And if Mordecai lived—*when* he came around, I corrected myself—he'd one day go off and lead his own life. Lead his own people. Hell, if Kieran went crazy, Mordecai might even use the gifts he'd received from a Demigod against said Demigod. That was how a Demigod would think, anyway. That was how my biological father would have thought. Or Kieran's father.

But I would not dare voice any of that. Kieran's blood might be the only thing that could save my ward.

Kieran pricked his finger with the knife as his power ramped up around us. Waves sounded like they were crashing right outside the closet. The tides pulled in the distance. He lowered his finger to Mordecai's lips.

I focused on the prongs, another crumbling. The

Line throbbed in the room, trying to suck Mordie's soul toward it.

Heart in my throat, sweat and tears running tracks along my cheeks, I struggled to keep his soul in his body, to get him to hang on, as Kieran's magic reached a fever pitch. It throbbed around us, as though we were in the middle of a squall way out at sea.

Mordecai's soul continued to pulse, each one sending a wave through the spirit around me. It strengthened.

And then the shifter emerged.

The density of his soul casing changed, followed by the shape of Mordecai's body.

Somehow, I kept his soul from ripping loose.

Kieran kept pumping his heart, trying to change position with the morphing form. When Mordecai's face turned into a bloody wolf head, Kieran closed Mordecai's snout with his hands and breathed into his nose. Still he kept up the CPR, not slowing.

Thane and Boman leaned forward, their eyes on Mordecai, looking hopeful.

Sobs convulsed my body and I closed my eyes, working on those prongs. Slowly, ever so slowly, they stopped ripping away. They stopped breaking and needing to be reattached. Mordecai's body stitched itself back together.

Eventually, when minutes felt like they'd stretched

into years, Kieran straightened up, his back clearly stiff. Thane let out a ragged breath.

"He'll live," Boman said, and I bent over as sobs of relief racked my body. I welcomed Kieran's arms around me, holding me tightly. I welcomed Thane's hand on my back, and Boman's on my head, all of them wanting to share in my relief.

"That kid is his own miracle," I said, wiping my eyes.

"No," Kieran said. "You are his miracle. You are *our* miracle." He fell silent for a while, resting his hand on Mordecai's fuzzy ribcage, clearly making sure his heart kept beating. When Mordecai's soul burned brightly once again, and his side rose and fell naturally, Kieran said, "There's something I need to ask of you, Alexis. Jack needs your help."

Chapter 22

ALEXIS

J ACK STOOD IN a little alcove in the hall, looking around as though he didn't understand what he was looking at. The colors of reality had changed on him, I knew, shifting to the odd ultraviolet light of the spirit realm. The feeling of reality had changed on him too. And his body, full of holes and short on blood, lay on the bed upstairs where the guys had moved it. I wasn't sure if he knew he was dead.

My heart broke all over again. I'd helped Mordecai fight his way back to life, but I couldn't help Jack. Not by the time I'd finished with Mordecai.

"You couldn't have done anything for him even if you'd gotten to him first," the cat said from beside me, his tone respectfully somber.

"Can you read minds, too?" I asked as the others drifted away, giving me space. They trusted me to help their brother in arms. Only Kieran had stayed, both because he could see Jack and, knowing him, because he felt responsible for Jack's death. He watched with glassy eyes, sorrow written plainly on his face and dripping through our links.

"Don't need to. You show all your feelings on your face. You're probably the world's worst poker player."

"I wouldn't know. I've never had the money to play."

"Well, trust me, you'd lose."

I eyed the Line, feeling it sending out a welcoming vibe, trying to coax Jack to cross over, to get his bearings in the beyond. So far, he was resisting, but his gaze was on it. I didn't think he'd noticed us yet.

I shook my head. "I don't know what to do here," I whispered. It felt good to have someone else I could talk to about this kind of thing, even if it was a possessed cat. "I could easily give him a nudge to send him over, but I'm not sure he wants to go. If he stays around here, though, it's going to take him a while to figure everything out, and Kieran probably won't take it well. It can be heartbreaking to watch if you're familiar with the person."

"You know, there hasn't been a female Spirit Walker in..." The cat rubbed against my leg. I shook him off. A real animal was one thing, but this spirit-animal hybrid weirded me out. "Rude," he said. He licked his leg. "A long time. Genetics got it right with you. Your empathy sets you apart. It'll be the thing that makes you fly true, I have no doubt. Assuming you don't end up in the wrong hands. And with your Demigod at your side, you won't. That guy... He's a budding powerhouse. I think genetics got it right with him, too. The Fates are at work here. Buckle up. This'll be a good show."

"None of that matters in this situation."

"I know. I shouldn't have to tell you how to do your job."

"I mean...you're the one that's supposed to be training me to do my job," I whined.

I hesitated for a moment, then slowly walked over to stand beside Jack, facing the same direction he was. I stood silently, seeing if he would notice me. When he didn't, I said softly, "Hey, Jack."

To my surprise, he didn't startle. "Hey, Lexi."

I leaned forward to look at his face, wondering how the hell he could look so confused and sound so rational. "You've had better days, huh?"

"I'm dead, right? I bled out before I could heal?"

Tears came to my eyes and I blinked them away. "Yeah, buddy. Did you see your body?"

"See it? I stood up out of it. I didn't realize I'd left it behind until I tried to grab the back door handle. I couldn't. I stood there for..." He paused. Time was already slippery for him. That part of the living world seemed to fall away almost immediately for a spirit. "I stood there, confused, while she got away."

My heart sped up. "*She* got away? Who did? Was

Daisy still alive?"

Jack held up a hand and turned it over, checking the back.

"You'll get used to it," I said, my hands shaking with the need to ask him about Daisy. But you couldn't force the newly dead to hurry. The mind usually erased many of the details of a traumatic death, which he'd definitely had. Confusion muddied what was left. I didn't want to make anything worse. I wanted to preserve what had survived. It was our only hope for Daisy. "Soon all this won't feel so…different."

"She'd been roughed up. Her face… Lexi, I think I did that. I think I did that to Daisy. Blood was…on my hands. I hurt in a lot of places—I only vaguely remember now—but I had blood on my knuckles. On the backs of my hands. And her face was… She was right next to me when I came to. Like I'd dropped her weak little body before I took a knee." His voice quavered. "She tried to get up. She was broken, but she tried to get up…" He blinked a bunch, trying to recall memories that had been erased by trauma like ink on a whiteboard.

Kieran stepped up, faster than thought, now right in front of Jack's face. "Tell me what you know."

Jack blinked at Kieran, but the confusion cleared instantly. The focus of the living crept into his gaze. He was latching on to Kieran as a known quantity. The

Line dimmed around us. "Sir, I can't be sure exactly what happened. I have a big black hole in my memory. I remember waking up in your house, getting ready, and running to the door to answer your summons. Then..." His jaw set. "I...woke up, sir. It felt like it, anyway. Next thing I knew, I was...in pain, I think. Not terrible. I could get over it. I remember thinking I could heal through it. But then I saw..." He couldn't keep that quiver of emotion from his voice. The trials of the living clung to his spirit. "Her arm was messed up. Her face. She was in so much pain. And I think—I don't remember doing it, or even how I got to that spot—but I think I did it, sir. And I froze. I froze solid, watching her struggle to sit up. I was scared to help. I was scared to hurt her... I got myself killed and Daisy taken. I—"

A shock of spirit slashed through Jack, and he startled, his eyes going wide. Kieran was using my magic to shock some sense into him, to keep him from unraveling.

"What's done is done," Kieran said, leaving no room for emotion. "You can still help us. If you stay in this world, you can help us find her, starting by giving us details about this woman."

Jack's nose crinkled. "Do I have to put on one of those rotten corpses?" His expression cleared, as though he'd just realized his insubordination. "Sorry, sir. A lot's happened in the space of..." He shook his head. "How long has it been since…"

"Ages and no time at all," I said, fatigue making my mind fuzzy. "Come on, let's go write down all the details you remember."

✕　✕　✕

KIERAN

KIERAN STARED DOWN at Jack's still form while Lexi took Jack's statement downstairs. His brother in arms lay with his hands at his sides, his face pale and his neck ruined. He might've come back from his first wounds, but no way would he have survived getting his throat slit without a magical healer to quickly stitch him back up.

Kieran blew out a breath and directed his gaze out the window.

No, not *Jack's* still form. Jack's body. The body that Jack had stepped out of.

Lexi had looked at it before they'd brought it up. She'd said all the prongs had crumbled away. The cat holding the deceased Spirit Walker had apparently told her Jack's body was too far gone to hold a spirit now.

The situation was a mind-fuck. Kieran wrestled with the knowledge that Jack was physically dead—and yet he'd just spoken with him.

How the hell could you cope losing some-one…without actually losing them?

A tear worked down Kieran's cheek, and he let it. He was glad he hadn't possessed this ability before his mother had moved across the veil. He didn't know how he could've handled that. How Lexi handled any of this. Even now, exhausted, terrified for Daisy, probably eager to sit by Mordecai's side, she was working through Jack's account of events with a level head and a sympathetic ear. She was putting her own issues aside to help a removed spirit cope with the transition. Yes, she was getting valuable information, but it had to be hard for her. And she made it seem easy.

Kieran put his hand on Jack's cold fingers, trying not to flinch away from the chilled skin. Pain and emotion welled up as the door opened. He stood, schooling his expression. A man didn't cry. His father had drilled that into him as long as he could remember. A man held back emotion.

Lexi stood in front of him, her lids heavy. Dawn peeked in the window, highlighting her still lovely face, the warm sympathy in her eyes.

The lid over his emotions wobbled. He reached for anger to well up and overshadow it, but then pushed it down again. He wouldn't reach for anger with her. Not with her. Not given his family history and what his father had done to his mother. That way lay damnation.

"Hey," she said, and soft comfort flowed through the soul link, warm and welcoming.

He clenched his teeth, not trusting his voice.

She nodded, as though to say she understood.

"It's late." Her eyes flicked to the window. "Or early, I guess. Mordecai is still in wolf form, but his pulse is strong. Boman and Thane are taking turns watching him. You know that Henry went to the office for a while—I heard him tell you while I was getting paper." Her brow knotted. She was putting all her ducks in a row. Probably trying to organize the chaos. "Zorn and Bria have exhausted..." Tears filled her eyes and her fists clenched. Terror and sorrow pumped through the soul link.

He put his arms around her. She shook against him, giving in to her tears. He held back his own, knowing she needed strength.

"Daisy is gone. We aren't going to find her tonight," she went on through sobbing hiccups. "I have to sleep. Tomorrow I can..."

"*Shhh.*" Kieran rocked her. "We've grounded all private jets in the entire Bay Area, something only possible because she isn't magical. She's still on the books as a missing child. We've issued an amber alert for her and closed the magical borders. We've also alerted non-magical police officials and have video facial-recognition searches going for Daisy. Henry is working on identifying the woman, and soon we'll have her info, too. They won't get far. As soon as we can…process all this, we'll get down to business and find them."

She shook her head, her tears soaking through his shirt. "How can you sound so confident when I know you are breaking up inside?"

The lid wobbled. He needed to go for a swim and clear his head.

"Training." He pulled away enough to softly tip her chin up, getting her to look up at him. Tears beaded in her long eyelashes. "They tried to kill Mordecai, but they *took* her. If they were going to kill her, they would've done it by now. They probably want to trade her for you. Have faith, baby. She's already walked through hell and come out smoking. She's not helpless. They are bound to underestimate the feral being they have in their midst, and when they do, she'll react as she's trained to do. As Zorn trained her to do. She'll give us time."

"I'll trade for her in a heartbeat."

He didn't argue with her. It wouldn't come to that. He'd make sure of it. He'd failed Jack, but he'd be damned if he would fail Daisy.

He traced Alexis's perfect lips before trailing his fingertips down her soft, tear-streaked cheek…and found that he didn't want to go for a swim in the deep sea. He didn't want to lose himself in the ocean—he wanted to lose himself in *her*.

He scooped her up into his arms, cradling her against his chest. He didn't speak. Didn't explain. He walked her into her room and hooked his heel on the door before swinging it closed with a bang.

She kissed him first, just as eager to take a break from life, just as desperate to use him to do it.

He set her down on the floor, ripping into her clothing. Pulling off her shirt. Her pants. He paused so she could rip his shirt off, too. He unbuckled and shoved down his pants.

She crawled onto the bed, her watery eyes on him. Scared. Hollow. There was a hole in her heart where Daisy fit. Kieran knew how it felt. But his situation held no hope. Jack would be dead forever.

The lid wobbled again. Emotion threatened to break free.

Settling into her welcoming embrace, he lined himself up and thrust without preamble, physically sinking into her. Emotionally sinking in as well. He let the world drift away, the pleasure of her muffling the pain. He let their mutual love shut out some of the heartache.

"I love you," he said softly, next to her ear. He pulled out so he could push into her again, groaning with her. Hugging her tight. "I love you so much."

"I love you too, Kieran." She clutched his shoulders and swung her hips up to meet his, crashing against him.

He buried his face into her neck, smelling the sweet perfume of her skin. Their pleasure worked higher. Their desperation to be together mounted. He filled her, over and over.

"Yes, Kieran," she said, digging her fingertips into his back. "*Yes!*"

Their magic swirled around them, fusing together, burning across their skin. Pleasure rolled through them, turned them end over end. He lost himself in it. In her. He hit the peak…but then kept going, kept pushing, wanting to forget, giving himself to her totally.

A tidal wave of sensation crashed down onto them. She cried out his name as he shook with the orgasm, so intense that he felt dizzy. Their panting filled the suddenly quiet room, but he still wasn't ready to release her.

"It's okay. I won't tell," she said, and even though she didn't give any details, he knew exactly what she was talking about. She could feel the emotion in him. She could read him in a way no one else had ever been able to.

So, despite his upbringing, despite his father's lectures about what was and was not proper, he trusted her—and finally, for the first time with another human being…*let go.*

Chapter 23

DAISY

PAIN RATTLED DAISY'S nerves, pounding through her body from her broken wrist. It dulled the throb in her face from smacking into that wall. That had been a helluva strong push.

A different pain filled her. One of betrayal. She'd thought of Jack like family, the uncle she'd never had. She'd loved that fucking guy like he was blood. Only to have him do *this*? Betray their pack, as Mordecai would say?

She sucked in a breath as white-hot agony pulsed through her, and not from her arm. Her arm would heal. The loss of Mordecai would not. He'd been more than blood. You didn't go through a life like they had and come out without an attachment forged from iron.

Jack and that woman would die for what they'd done. They'd die slow, too. Real slow. With much suffering. They'd killed the wrong one of the Daisy-Mordecai pair. For all Mordecai was levelheaded and soft-hearted, Daisy was a monster in a doll's skin. She was a villain with a cherub face.

She was hell in razor-spiked heels.

But first, she needed to get the hell out of here.

Zorn's voice floated out of her memory: *Step one, assess your surroundings.*

In other words, where was *here*?

A leather office chair hugged her butt, and ropes, loosely and probably clumsily tied, held her hands around the back. Light showered down from a bare bulb suspended from the middle of the ceiling. It didn't penetrate the black shadows lining the edges of the window, covered with a cream-yellow shade. Linoleum with brown in the cracks lined the floor, not dirty per se, but old. Nothing hung on the walls. A small round handle adorned the cheap wood door.

It was still night, and she'd been stowed in some sort of storage room in an office building. Nothing fancy, and not in a nice part of town, but serviceable. Whoever owned or rented it had been doing so for years. Maybe decades. Otherwise the flooring would've been changed out, and little details like the knob would have been updated. It was easier to sell a building when things looked good.

A sort of...dampness filled the air. Not moldy, but...damp. The mustiness carried traces of salt. This place was near-ish the ocean, but not so close that the waves could be heard.

She was being held. It couldn't be for ransom. The people Lexi and Kieran were messing with had plenty of money. It was probably to bring Lexi to heel, or maybe to control Kieran through Lexi. Hell, maybe they were after some sort of trade. Daisy wasn't fluent enough in the games of Demigods to know exactly where she fit in. She'd need to work on that. She needed to know enough to make educated guesses, not blindly grasp at straws.

She twisted her chest. The hard hilt of a small blade pushed against her skin between the pads in her bra. Thank God for guys' obsession with mammary glands. Big boobs helped hide weapons, and the stores were all too happy to sell overpriced bullshit to create that effect. The knife at her waist was gone, of course, having been the cause of Jack breaking her wrist.

She moved her right ankle. The hard nylon holster was gone, and obviously the blade with it. Interesting. The woman had done a light frisk, but hadn't checked Daisy's cleavage. That bespoke a man more than a woman. When there was no purse to be had, the bra was a great place to store something. Ladies knew about this hiding place, especially violent ladies. Bria was adamant about that.

She crinkled her brow as a muffled voice rolled through the door. The words didn't take shape. There would be no eavesdropping in here. That gave her a big blind spot. She also didn't know what kind of magic she was dealing with, not to mention how far the treachery in Kieran's camp went.

If you can save yourself, don't wait. Being on the run gives you better odds than being locked in a box.

Daisy nodded as Zorn's words faded from her mind.

She needed to free herself. If anyone could find her, it was Kieran—he was wicked smart, cunning, and extremely knowledgeable—but what if Kieran had flipped on them? What if he'd realized leading a territory would be easier if he took a page from his father's book? Daisy wouldn't put it past him. Men often lost themselves to greed and power. Hell, all the human kings in *Lord of the Rings* had become Ring Wraiths. J.R.R. Tolkien had known what was up.

And yet...she found herself thinking of Jack's strange, jerky movements. The way he'd dropped her. The woman who'd scooped her up had moved like that too, in jerks and jolts, as though she weren't totally in charge of her body.

Daisy shook her head and gritted her teeth against the dull agony of her wrist while she worked her left hand within the holds. None of that mattered right now. She didn't have enough information to piece everything together. She had one purpose: get free and get out.

MAGNUS

"SIR, WE HAVE news and a possible situation."

Magnus looked away from his computer screen. Gracie stood in his doorway with a severe expression.

"What is it?" He clasped his fingers.

She crossed the room and stood behind the chairs in front of his desk. "Aaron made his move, and it was just as blunt and shortsighted as we suspected it would be."

Magnus listened in silence until Gracie had finished, giving him a moment to process.

"He thinks nothing of the child Demigod," Magnus surmised, leaning back in his seat. "He thinks the child tearing down his father was a fluke."

"Many do, sir, as you know," Gracie said, tapping her fingers against the top of a chair. "They think Valens was too close to the situation to properly judge it."

"Which is undoubtedly true, to some extent, but Valens was not a trusting man. He kept his son on a very tight leash." Magnus allowed himself a smile. "This is excellent. We can see, firsthand, how the child deals with the situation. If he moves to strike quickly and harshly, as I am sure he will want to, he'll get flagged by the Directorate. I'll personally push for his...removal. That would solve many of my problems."

Gracie knew enough about the Directorate, a secret

society of Demigods that monitored the magical world and worked to maintain its balance, to know removal would mean demise. The Directorate was small and hand-selected, and not even the leaders who attended the Summits knew of its existence. If any one ruler stepped too far out of line, pushing for the grandeur of world domination as in times of old, the Directorate would swiftly and silently tear that ruler down. They'd been watching the child closely, understanding of the situation with his father but ready to block him should he attempt to expand his territory.

"And if he does nothing?" Gracie asked.

"Then I will know he is thinking of the long game, and I will need to continue with the plan we currently have in place. Either way, he will need to be removed from his position. I need access to the girl. Too bad. If he were to remove Aaron, it would help me out greatly. I'm sure no one would bat an eye if Patricia took over as sole ruler. She already handles all the details in their territory."

A little smile slid across Gracie's lips. She knew Patricia was fond of Magnus. Too fond. She welcomed his opinion and his roaming hands. It would make for a great alliance and possible merging of territories. Patricia certainly didn't mind looking the other way when her husband found lovers, as long as she was kept in a certain lifestyle. Magnus liked to spoil his women.

Win-win.

"Now for the stickier situation, sir," Gracie said, and her humor fled. "Amos slipped into one of the child's men during Aaron's attack. His goal was to get the child killed in a way that would put the blame squarely on Aaron. But no one expected the Spirit Walker would be on the front lines of the battle. He had to improvise, so he decided to drag the wards out into the battle and ensure they were killed. The Spirit Walker is partial to those kids, and as we know, the child is partial to her. It would've escalated the retaliation and created chaos that Amos could later exploit."

"Yes, sound planning. What happened?"

"The wards fought back more than expected. Amos had to kill one of them, and he was dragging the other out, intending to use the back door and slip into the battle from the rear, when he ran into one of Aaron's staff. She apparently did a number on the body he was using, so he had to jump to her, something that really taxed his energy."

Magnus scrubbed his fingers through his shoulder-length hair. "Aaron is a fool. Did he not study the situation at all before bumbling into it?"

"No, it doesn't seem so, sir. Nothing besides a few Google searches and visiting in spirit."

"So where does that leave us?"

"Unfortunately, the severe energy drain meant he

couldn't maintain real-looking movement in the possessed body. He didn't have stealth on his side. He also needed to get back to his body without using much energy. He didn't have a lot left, apparently. He decided to take the ward with him."

"He decided the best use of his time was to kidnap the wrong person," Magnus said slowly.

"Yes, sir. He didn't want to leave Aaron's staffer alive because she'd likely know she'd been possessed, and you're the only one who has both a horse in this race and access to a Possessor strong enough to manage this. Except, before he could make her kill herself, he had to flee the body or risk his energy depleting so much that he wouldn't make it back."

It took every ounce of Magnus's self-control not to throw something against the wall. "I had Nancy place that Defalcator so he could get objects from the child's staff. Amos doesn't have anything belonging to Aaron's staffer, does he? Or the kid he took?"

"No, sir."

"So how the hell is Amos going to get back to her or the kid? He's going to lead Aaron right to me, and the child with him."

"Amos will drive there, sir. He knows the location, so he'll physically go. It's one of Aaron's spy shacks, as he calls them. There was paperwork in the car with directions and enough info that we'll be able to link

Aaron's name to the kidnapping. It's located in the non-magical zone and didn't appear to have been used in a long time, which was why Valens probably didn't know about it. It's not too far away, though. The child is already searching for the ward, in both zones, so the woman's in a bad position. She either needs to leave the ward behind or stay put. She can't risk being spotted with the kid. That gives Amos time."

Magnus laughed, incredulous. He slammed his fist against the desk. "Tell him to hurry. I can't have the child finding Aaron's staffer or the girl alive. He'll need to kill them in a way that makes it look like they killed each other. Or that the staffer had wounds from the battle that bled out. Whatever. After that, tell Amos to wait. Lie low. We'll see what kind of damage this does. If a Possessor is not suspected, *only then* should he re-engage. In the meantime, make sure we have everything we need to pin this on Aaron."

Gracie stood back from the chair. "Yes, sir. I'll tell Amos right away."

Magnus waited for a beat, feeling his anger wrap around him. He couldn't believe how shortsighted and stupid Amos had been. Magnus knew that, under duress, a Possessor was at risk of taking on the host's desires and goals, but Amos should've been past that by now.

Then again, when was the last time Amos had been

in such a stressful situation? The position of a Demigod wasn't what it used to be. These days, important things were usually decided with whispers in dark rooms, maneuvering and manipulating. There were fewer out-and-out wars. Less blades and blood.

It seemed the child upstart was skewing things back toward the old ways. Magnus had to admit that it was a little refreshing. He hated hiding behind smoke and mirrors. He had always much preferred to look in a man's face as he shoved his blade into his gut.

But he was getting ahead of himself. The child was on shaky ground. The members of the Directorate were watching, not to mention the much larger pool of world leaders, magical and not, and the last thing Magnus needed was to be implicated in any way. That was a sure way to get his vote muted if something should come to pass.

He had to make sure Aaron's staffer and the kid were wiped out, along with any evidence implicating Magnus. If he could eliminate the witnesses before Aaron or the child arrived on scene, there would be more questions than answers. Only a great fool would move on another ruling Demigod with nothing but a hunch.

Chapter 24

ALEXIS

"**H**EY."

Bleary-eyed, I looked up in time for Bria to come around the island. Dark circles lined her tight eyes. She squinted in the midmorning sun streaming through the open kitchen windows.

"Hey," I replied, my gut churning with worry, hating that I was just sitting around, doing nothing, when Daisy needed me.

Kieran and the guys were at the government office, checking in with police and looking at footage from traffic cams, trying to find a trace of the car and the kidnapper. They were also getting more information on Aaron and his people. It was unanimously agreed that I needed to stay home with Mordecai, out of sight, or else risk alerting everyone that laid eyes on me that something was wrong. Kieran didn't want this in the papers, fearing it might freak the kidnapper out enough to kill Daisy and make a run for it.

"Where's Red and Aubri with an *I*?" Bria asked,

grabbing the coffee pot.

"I accidentally on purpose told them to fuck off. Red only did so because I forced her to leave with my magic. I don't think that woman is used to getting scared. I guess this'll put manners in her."

"Doubtful. So hey, I'm just going to break it to you. We've got nothing yet." Bria filled a coffee cup before sliding it my way. Liquid sloshed over the side. "But nothing is not nothing. It means the wench is staying put. Kieran is hoping to hear about a trade."

"Or else they got on a plane and are no longer in the area."

Bria shook her head, pouring herself a cup of coffee. "Henry was in charge of looking into that possibility, and he does not fail. She's in the area. Somewhere. We just need to find out where. How's Mordecai?"

"He's Mordecai. That guy has been on the brink of death more times than you'd care to hear. He's crawling his way back to health." I pushed my cup away and dropped my face into my hands. "I brought this on them. I'm the reason these kids can't catch a break. I'm the only reason they were in any danger at all."

"Nah. They were in danger because of Kieran. If you are going to lay danger at someone's feet, you might as well choose the right pair."

"Something is going on outside, Lexi," Jack said quietly, waiting in the corner. His eyes were solemn, his voice subdued—I knew he was responding to the loss of himself. Of his life. The dead mourned, too, maybe more than the living.

I'd offered to push him over the Line, but he felt responsible for Daisy. He wanted to hang around and help. He just didn't know how.

I turned to find Frank on the grass, his hands on his hips, arguing. He flung his hand at the window, as though talking about someone inside.

"Want me to go sort it out?" Jack asked, and I knew he didn't want to. That would be admitting he had more in common with Frank than he did with us. The guy was dead; he didn't need to be depressed too.

"No, it's fine. Frank only listens to Kieran and me," I said, sliding off the stool. "You'd just be annoyed."

A glimmer sparkled in his eye. He stepped forward, flexing his spectral muscles. "We'll see about that."

I stopped from huffing. I should've used a different excuse. Jack was going through a post-living crisis, but he was still Jack, and he didn't like being told someone wouldn't listen to him. Now I would have to pull off the spirit repellent then quickly reapply it before Frank caught wind of the change and decided to make himself at home. The whole exercise still required a lot of effort.

We got outside in time to hear Frank yell, "You don't belong here, that's why."

The other Spirit Walker stood in front of him in

human form, his sideburns accenting his strong jaw, his hair pleasantly tousled, and his lips pulled up in a grin. "And I suppose you do?"

"Yeah. That's right. I *do*. Her mother asked me to watch out for her." Frank spread his arms.

"And how have you been doing that, exactly? By yelling at the good guys and running away from the baddies?"

"What's going on?" I asked. Jack stood at my side, his hands on his hips, flaring his huge biceps.

The Spirit Walker chuckled softly. "Not a thing. I was just waiting patiently for you to stop doing nothing and ask how you could help your kid. Frank was keeping me company."

"He's a smug jackass," Frank said, scowling.

"Kieran can't be thrilled with how suave and attractive this guy is," Jack murmured.

The Spirit Walker's smile intensified. "It's as if you don't think I hear you."

"I wish I didn't hear you," Frank replied.

"What did you say about helping my kid?" I asked, motioning for the other two to shut it.

"I said you should ask how you could." The Spirit Walker slipped his hands into his pockets. "Instead, you've been letting your Demigod do all the heavy lifting. He's making strides—I checked up on him. But he's not working fast enough. You're the key to finding her in time, not him."

"Finding her in time…" I struggled to breathe. I felt a spirit hand on my shoulder, and I didn't have the heart to tell Jack about the no-touching rule.

"Oops. You're not gonna wanna do that, haus." The Spirit Walker made a motion, and even though he didn't actually touch Jack, Jack pulled his hand away as if he'd been burned. "You're unintentionally greedy when you just lose your body. You'll suck up all her energy, and then she can't go and fix your mistake."

"It wasn't his fault," I said automatically, seeing Jack's face fall.

"Eh." The Spirit Walker waggled his hand. "Fifty-fifty. Which is something we need to go over, Lexi—I can call you Lexi, right? I feel like we're close enough now. You need to learn how to protect yourself from Hades's minions. But first, there are more important things. Like being a hero."

"A *really* smug jackass," Frank grumbled.

"How?" I asked, ignoring Frank. "And why couldn't you tell me all this sooner in cat form?"

The Spirit Walker looked around. "Because the damn thing keeps running off on me. I should've picked a dog. They aim to please. A big dog, so it'd be easier to find in the jungle you got around here. Anyway, you have a missing person on your hands. I can show you how to locate her."

"How?" I asked again, blinking away moisture.

"Are you ready for your next lesson?"

I didn't get a chance to answer before he started walking. At the back of the house, he sat down on the grass and crossed his legs. I followed, my heart pinging around my ribcage. Jack stood off a ways, his arms crossed, with Frank a little behind him, apparently giving him backup. I felt Bria starting out of the house, working her way around to us.

"Is this a trick?" I asked softly.

"That question only applies if I have a body and there is a bed nearby. Look, it's real simple. You're able to call spirits from across the Line, right?"

I clasped my shaking hands and nodded. "When I have an item, yes. A personal item, like when I called you."

"Right...mostly. You don't actually need an item when you know the soul, but that's a lesson for another day." He stretched out on his side and braced his head on his fist—getting a little too comfortable, if you asked me. "You're also able to call spirits to you on this side of the Line, correct? You can even call them on behalf of other people. You think about them hard enough, and they drift to you."

I nodded slowly. "But those are spirits. They're not living people."

"They're souls."

"Right. But souls without a body that keeps them put."

"Exactly. They are souls with no anchor, but they are still souls. Souls that you can feel. Souls whose signature you can recognize. The woman wandering this way right now, for example, is your friend. The kid out near the cliff is probably high and a stranger. One of them you recognize, and judging by the sudden anxious look on your face, one you didn't know was there. You need to do some serious exercising in magical reach."

Bria cleared the corner of the house before drifting to one of the patio chairs to watch. She was clearly checking up on me.

He was right—I could find souls beyond the Line *and* in our world. The latter I called to me because they were easier to reel in. When a soul was over the Line, though, I had to slip into a trance to call them, and if they were powerful, I sometimes had to meet them halfway. Or, in the Spirit Walker's case, go and get him.

"Okay, assuming I can track her soul down in the world of the living...somehow, then what? She *does* have an anchor." Fear choked me. "God, I hope she still has an anchor."

"She does, Lexi," Jack interjected. "She does. That little gremlin isn't one to give up. She's not one to say die. She's alive."

"That's right. She can't come to you...but you can

go to her," the Spirit Walker said.

I tried to fit this into what I knew about my magic, but the pieces just weren't connecting.

"The world of the living operates differently than the spirit realm," I said. "I can't be mobile and in a trance at the same time, even if Bria were driving me. I don't have spatial awareness when I'm finding the souls. It's just—" I shook my head in frustration.

"You need to think *outside* of the body. Outside the constructs of the living. You'll be leaving your body behind."

Tingles washed over me. Jack shifted his weight from side to side, but didn't say anything. I repeated what the Spirit Walker had said for Bria.

She nodded slowly. "This is the training no one else but a Demigod or a Spirit Walker could give you," she said, her voice a low murmur, like she was uncomfortable. It was happening a lot lately, and it made me nervous. It took a lot to make her uncomfortable. "It's your magic."

"It's dangerous," Jack said.

"How do you know?" the Spirit Walker replied.

Jack spread his hands. "How do you think I know? I'm fucking dead, aren't I? She has the magic, sure, but if she doesn't use it right, there'll be two of us making the boss jump when we enter a room. He doesn't need that shit. *I* don't need that shit."

I relayed all that was being said for Bria, not getting a chance to offer any kind of response before the Spirit Walker replied, "Then scamper across the Line."

Jack's jaw set. "I need to see this through first."

"So what you're saying is…" I took a deep breath. "I can find a soul anywhere, but since she has a body, I will need to let go of my body and travel through spirit to find her. Then, once I'm there…" I thought about it a moment. "Once I'm there, I'll look around, get a lock on the location somehow, and return to my body so I can direct the cavalry?"

"Bingo," the Spirit Walker replied.

"This isn't a trick?"

"I'm not going to lie—I'd really like to have a body and a bed. You're incredibly smart and sexy as hell. I barely need to train you; I just have to explain the basic rules and you do all the work." He winked. "I like a woman who does all the work."

I shook my head as urgency coursed through me. "Let me go get—"

"You don't need to get something of Daisy's to focus on. You already know her well enough." He draped his arm over his waist. "Just lie back, close your eyes, and join me in spirit. I'll guide you until you get your bearings. It won't take long, not with your kid counting on you."

I hesitated, and his eyes increased in intensity.

"Think," he said, his voice low, his tone sending shivers across my body. "This isn't your first time doing this. This is just the first time you've started from a wakeful state. It's harder, but you have a good reason to make this trip successful."

"What's he saying?" Bria asked, leaning forward, but I ignored her.

Memories jostled for position. Dreams and the feeling of intimacy. Of lust. The feeling of a shadowy hand holding mine, escorting me across the Line. Showing me the other plane.

"A body and a bed, indeed," I said, my breath catching in my throat.

"What does that mean?" Jack asked, stepping forward. Frank shadowed him, clearly with no clue why.

A sly smile curled the Spirit Walker's lips. "Well. Maybe I don't always need a body, no. What can I say? When I got word there was another Spirit Walker roaming around, I had to have a closer look. I liked what I found."

I remembered the feeling of being helped when working on Will Green's spirit box, of the shadowy form that helped with Valens. I hadn't felt the same intimacy with those. If anything, the spirit guide in those situations had been gruff, pushy but acting in my best interest, mostly non-violent. They didn't seem like this guy at all.

I shook my head. None of this felt like it was adding up. "I had to travel really far across the Line to make contact with you."

"I know, right? Without any training. That was truly exemplary."

"And you attacked me."

He shrugged. "What can I say? I wanted to make you earn it. I wanted to see how determined you were."

His grin pissed me off. I pushed it aside as Bria stood, expressionless. It meant she was trying to keep from influencing me. She was out of her depth.

That makes two of us.

"What if I can't figure out where she is from the setting?" I asked. "Is there another way to get her location?"

"Eventually you'll develop a sort of inner guidance. A spirit GPS, if you will. For now, however, you'll have to look for street signs. Peek in mailboxes—whatever you can do to tack the location on a map. It's not like this is in the Beyond, which is much more complex. That will take a lot more training. A lot of late-night walks, hand in hand."

Which, apparently, we'd already done.

"Can I rip someone's arms off in spirit land?" Jack asked, taking a big step toward me. Frank followed, scowling.

"My, my, you do have a lot of bodyguards." It didn't

seem to bother the Spirit Walker. "Rest assured, with guidance, this will be easier than leaving your body to cross the Line."

"So why didn't you take this approach before?"

He shrugged. "The Beyond is more intimate in certain ways. I wanted to see how attached you are to your Demigod. Annoyingly so, I found out."

"What's going on?" Bria asked, walking closer.

I quickly explained what the Spirit Walker had said, what I would probably do, and who had been behind those walks in spirit, which were apparently not dreams at all.

She sat down cross-legged next to me. "With enough time, Kieran and his team will find her. Of that, I have no doubt. With enough time, Zorn will pull her out of whatever situation she is in. He's not holding together much better than you are; he just doesn't show it. He feels responsible."

We all did, so I didn't argue.

"But with enough time, she could be dead," Bria finished, hitting the nail on the head. "I should mention that Kieran would be against you doing this on your own with a guide like that."

"Yes, he would," the Spirit Walker said, clearly tickled.

"He certainly would," Jack agreed.

"Young women shouldn't be discussing their bodies

like they're sacks of skin," Frank mused. "It's unseemly."

"Thanks, Frank," I said dryly. "But it's not like Kieran can chaperone, so I don't know what other choice we have."

"To not go right now, and to train in smaller increments," the Spirit Walker said, completely at ease. He clearly didn't care one way or the other. That actually made me feel better about the situation.

"Could I get lost?" I asked him, adrenaline coursing through my body.

"On your own, yes," he answered, and his smile dripped off. "Your Demigod is your anchor. That's part of what a soul link does. You latched on to him when there was a fear of you getting lost in the Beyond. Your connection was strong enough to pull you toward the world of the living, and you found your way from there. But this time you'll already be in the world of the living, so if you get lost, you'll pull yourself right back to him. Directly to him. If he is not next to your body, there's a good chance you'll just get yourself turned around and lost again. Enough time passes, and your body will die without its soul.

"In this situation, however, I'll be guiding you. There is no fear of me getting lost." Absolute certainty rang through his tone. His body, still loose and relaxed, somehow conveyed his unyielding confidence. "You will get us to your ward, and I can easily get us back. Hopefully in time to meet that cat and hitch a ride again."

I blew out a breath, trying to stay cautious, to remember that I didn't really know this guy, and now I had proof he wasn't trustworthy. He'd been hanging around a while, and at any time he could've been training me. At any time he could've made a real impact in my life. Instead, he'd chosen to play mind games.

He still might be playing mind games.

The smart thing to do would be to wait for my anchor, ensure Kieran was waiting beside my body.

Except…if I pulled Kieran away from trying to find Daisy, and this didn't work…

With enough time, she could be dead.

"Okay." I lay down on the grass. "I'm going to try to find her."

Bria put out her hands like she should be doing something. "Do you need…incense or bells or anything?"

"For the love of the Great Mountain, no bells," the Spirit Walker said.

After I relayed the info, she paused, then said, "I'll get the incense. Maybe I can see what's going on."

"She is tenacious. I like that in a woman." The Spirit Walker scooted closer to me and lay down on his back. His spirit arm brushed mine, and I scooted away.

"Don't worry. I'm not hungry for your energy. Just you."

"Will you take this seriously? My kid's life is on the line."

"Close your eyes," he said softly, and something in his voice changed. It reduced down to a whisper that seemed as old as time, drifting in with the breeze from the Line. "Get into the headspace to find a soul."

I sank into a light trance, feeling the spirit around me, feeling the pulse of power.

"Deeper. You're clinging to the living world. Clinging to your body. You need to set those things free. You need to step out."

Fear wormed through me, but I went deeper, thinking of Daisy's soul, bright and beautiful, full of energy and light. Full of love hidden behind sulks and sharp knives. Deeper I went, knowing she was worth the risk. She was worth me trusting this character. Whatever else his flaws, he clearly knew what he was doing.

"There you go." This time, his voice wasn't a whisper at all. It was wordless, moving through me. I understood without knowing how, confident it was him but unsure why. "With your soul, just like in the dream walks, rise."

He held out his hand, less like a shadow than it had ever been. I lifted my hand to take it, and my skin fell away. My soul jiggled free of my frame, suddenly loose and free of gravity.

Fear accosted me, and I slammed back into my shell. My soul clutched on, and I could feel it docking. Reality rushed back in, and suddenly I was sitting up, gasping for breath.

Chapter 25

ALEXIS

"FEAR IS SUCH a tricky devil, isn't it?" The Spirit Walker was smiling at me teasingly.

"What's your name?" I asked, suddenly needing to know who I was trusting with my life.

He studied me for a moment. "Harding."

I repeated it for Bria.

"That's the last Spirit Walker's birth name," Bria said.

So not the nickname he'd created for himself when he was high on power, or the one he'd been given after being turned into a killing machine. He'd chosen the name he used when he was just a regular guy. Well, a regular guy who could pull souls out of bodies. That had to be good, right?

I didn't actually say any of that out loud. He'd probably set me straight, and I didn't want to hear it.

The grass was plush and welcoming. The cool breeze carrying the salty ocean flavor was relaxing. Drifting back down into a deep trance, I felt my soul swish around like it wanted to float up.

It was still downright terrifying.

"Easy does it," came that voice, melodic and entrancing. Not real. "Don't rush this. Just ease into it. You'll learn to love this part, when you become weightless. When you feel what it must be like to fly."

I focused on that description. Flying. Lifting up out of my skin.

My heart hammered. My limbs tingled. I gritted my teeth.

Then I no longer had teeth. Or limbs. Or a heart. I was walking into spirit, Harding beside me.

"It's okay. I would sooner start a war than let anything happen to you," he said, the voice reverberating around me, sliding against my skin and tickling fingers I no longer had. "You must train your consciousness to let go. It will reach for your body. You must not let it, or you will be jarred off course."

He stood next to me in a world painted with grays and violets, outlined in deep blues, throbbing with peripheral color. I could no longer see my body or the house.

"If you focus, you can change the colors to something a little more normal for you." He smiled without lips. Without a face.

How did I know he was smiling?

"You can feel me." The answer reverberated off the

inside of... Not my skull. I didn't have one. Just a shadowy orb, like the guy next to me.

My reality wobbled with the fear of this strange place.

He held out a hand, and regardless of any lustful trickery, I reached out to take it. Thankfully, his shadow touch was nothing but comforting.

"There are different rules here," he said. "Different everything, but once you are familiar with it, it'll seem natural. Beyond the Line, in front of it, within it—it'll all seem as natural as the world of the living. That's your gift, Spirit Walker. Only a Demigod of Hades can maneuver it as well as you."

"I don't feel like I'm maneuvering at all." I stuck out my leg, remembered I didn't have a leg, just the shadowy equivalent that didn't feel like anything at all, and wondered how I was moving without muscles. Reality wobbled again.

"Don't think in terms of gravity and moving parts. No legs. No ground. Just feelings."

A sudden rush of sensation, as powerful as any orgasm, stole my breath. I couldn't even stop to remember I didn't have breath, lost as I was in utter bliss.

When it cleared, there was only his amusement. "It's not just your Demigod who can inspire lust without touching."

Anger infused me. "Do that again, and I'll..."

He laughed, giving me space, though he kept hold of my hand. "One day you'll have something to threaten me with, yes. For now, let's begin. Think of Daisy's soul. Nothing else, just her soul. How it feels when she comes into the room. When she leaves. What it looks like in your mind's eye…"

I pushed everything else away—the weird place, my mind's attempts to stray, the oddness of not having a real body. I centered myself and did just what he said, desperate to feel her soul enter a room again. Bright and beautiful and Daisy.

"Now call it to you."

"But it—"

"Do as I say. Call it to you."

I closed my eyes—surprised I could still do that, given I had no eyes—and did as he'd said, focusing on her soul, pulling it near as I had with so many other spirits. As expected, nothing happened. I said as much.

"Are you sure?"

I opened my eyes, annoyed with his teasing tone. The same bruise-like colors greeted me, and out of annoyance, I swapped them. Replaced them. Hell, I didn't even know what to call it, just that they weren't right, it was stupid, and I wanted them to look more like the world of the living.

Like a lamp had flickered on, the darker colors lightened. The midnight blues and violets morphed into bright green grass and blue sky. The gray still hovered, permeating everything like a fog, but beyond it, within it, I could see the world where my body lived. I could see my body lying on the ground, Bria's fingers on my vitals and a phone trapped between her ear and her shoulder. She was probably filling Kieran in. She was fine with flouting the rules when she was in her element, but not when the situation was knee-deep in crazy not of her own making. Or neck-deep, in this case.

"Very good." The disembodied voice sounded much too close to my ear. I shrugged it away. "Even better. You are creating your own spatial parameters. That is necessary when you traverse places with souls that…haven't gotten out in a while, shall we say. You are the natural your magic promises. Now, pull again, and *feel* what it is you are doing."

Frustration overcame me, but I did as he said, trying my damnedest, envisioning Daisy's soul and yanking with everything I had.

"There is no way. My body is keeping me grounded," I said, exhausted from my efforts.

"Yes, it is. But you can pull free. You just have to get a fix on Daisy's soul and grab it."

A light bulb clicked on, and I immediately saw Daisy's soul glittering and shining in my mind's eye. In this realm. It was in her body, I could feel that, but…

"Look down," he murmured.

A little string glittered in my hand, twinkling and shining just like her soul—connecting me to her, and her to me. All I had to do was pull, but this time, it wouldn't be her coming to me, it would be me pulling my way through this place to get to her.

"Exactly," he said, and I could hear the pride in his voice. "Now, close your eyes, focus on her soul, and pull yourself toward it. Just like when you pulled yourself through the Beyond, back to your Demigod. Pull yourself along, and bring me with you."

I couldn't even think enough to be scared. I wouldn't fear myself back into my body even if I tried, not when I had a line on Daisy and could potentially find out where she was being kept.

Spirit moved around me. In another setting, I would've been grinning. It *did* feel like I was flying. But now all I could think about was moving faster, getting there and getting back.

Getting to Daisy in the physical world.

I felt my soul draw closer to hers, strong and bright, just like I'd left it, closer and closer until it felt like we were in the same room. Like her soul was blaring right next to mine.

I slammed to a sudden stop and "heard" a grunt from Harding. He squeezed my hand, and I opened my eyes.

I hung suspended in the air, upside down, my shadow head nearly bumping the ground. Colors flickered around me, dark then light, pinks and oranges fading in. Reality wobbled around me in the small room, threatening to send me careening out of this plane.

"It's okay." His voice was silky and smooth. Comforting, like his hand holding mine. "That was a lightning-fast transition. Give yourself a moment to adjust. Maybe close your eyes again. I'll right us. It's a great distance to go your first time."

I did close my eyes and take a moment. Despite the situation, and finding Daisy—I'd found Daisy!—I needed to center myself.

Harding's tug moved us further away, and then a pull had me swinging, my feet moving through the air until they bumped against something solid. The ground.

I opened my eyes, two feet from a stucco wall covered in dirt. We were outside. He was clearly giving me a chance to get my bearings before I got down to business. I blinked, forced away the urge to rush to my ward, and took precious seconds to get my bearings. One misstep, and I'd go running back to my body without being able to help myself. I couldn't let that happen, not when I was so close to my ward.

I brought up my hands, wiggling my fingers. Much of the shadowy fog had burned away, and my body felt like it had some weight. This wasn't reality, but it mostly looked like it, which made it easier for me to wrap my head around the situation.

"I'm like a spirit now instead of a shadow…"

"As I said, only a Demigod of Hades can walk through spirit as well as we can. I know you've only seen the Demigods as shadowy forms, but that's because they're worried about keeping their identities secret. Otherwise, they would have manifested like this. They would've looked like any other spirits, and had more power to work with. Then again, you would've been able to grab a hold of their vitals, so…"

"But how did you do this? How did *you* change me?" I lifted a foot and put it back down, feeling the urgency to get to Daisy, or to look around, but knowing I didn't have my head on straight yet. Harding wasn't holding on to me anymore—I didn't want to jerk myself into the never-never and get lost.

"By leaning on spirit a certain way and forcing your soul to show itself. It's advanced. You're not there yet. You're barely *here* yet."

"Why didn't you tell me this when we started? Or one of those times you dragged me out of my bed and marshaled me into the Beyond, as you call it?"

I took a step back and then quickly breathed through the flip-flopping of my stomach. Gravity was still weird, like it wasn't holding me properly. I imagined this was what astronauts felt like, except they'd trained for it. And also, they were in a whole different place. It was a trip to feel this way somewhere that looked like the real world.

"It takes a lot of energy to hold this form. I know you're determined and powerful, but most people freak out the first few times they leave their bodies. If you'd needed a few more stops and starts, you might not have had the energy to make the trip. But your courage continually surprises me. You only balked once. So far."

I nodded, because that made sense, ignored his teasing, and definitely ignored the glow of approval. He wasn't the sort of guy I should let charm me. The fact that he was incredibly good at it was proof enough.

Dirt and a few rocks didn't scrape underfoot as I pivoted, looking around the small parking lot, deserted except for one shiny red Honda. All around, buildings rose into the sky, mostly newer condos and some older office buildings. Shiny glass reflected rays of sunlight down onto this little forgotten hovel, three stories high and badly in need of an update.

The tides pulled at me from a distance, and though I could smell the ocean's influence in the air, I could not hear it. The natural environment had all been paved or covered over with landscaping. No street signs rose in my line of sight.

I had no idea where I was.

"Okay," I said to myself. "First things first. Make sure Daisy is okay."

I felt her soul, strong and sure, and walked toward the corner of the building in search of a door.

"What are you doing?" Harding asked.

I paused. That's right, I couldn't open doors. Or, if I could, it would take an insane amount of energy.

I stared at the wall instead, and my reality wobbled. Suddenly I felt like I was in a dream, and if I thought too hard about it, I would go scurrying for reality. Except I couldn't just wake up from this. And if I did, I'd have to find my way back here anyway. Daisy was counting on me. I had to *get a grip*.

"I can go through that, because I am not real," I said to myself, stepping up to it.

"Close your eyes and walk through," Harding said. "Or close your eyes and I'll move you through."

"Look, if you'd just trained me in the first place rather than hijacking my sleep, I wouldn't freak out so much."

"You work better when you're under duress."

I gritted my teeth. Bria said that all the time.

Steeling myself, I closed my eyes and walked forward. Spirit swished and moved around me—until it reached a thin line of nothingness up ahead. That had to be the wall. Spirit couldn't penetrate the solid object.

Once we made it through the wall, I opened my eyes

and immediately felt a pang in my gut. Daisy sat in the middle of a bare room, her face a mess of bruises and blood, tears streaming down her cheeks, and her grunts sounding more like whimpers.

"Oh my God," I said, bending toward her.

Harding's hand and clipped "no" froze me.

"You as a spirit need to learn not to suction energy. She needs all the energy she can get. Do not touch her."

I yanked my hands away, agony throbbing in my middle. I walked around to the back of her and gasped. Her right wrist was black and blue, swollen to epic portions, very badly sprained or broken. Rope burn had made a red line right above it, and her left wrist was bleeding. She'd ripped and torn her skin trying to loosen the ropes. Despite the obvious pain she was in, she was still going, the clumsy fingers of her left hand working that badly tied knot.

"She's close," Harding said. "She's almost there. She's a fighter."

Tears would've overflowed if I had a physical body capable of crying. "She's had a mostly shitty life."

"Thank the heavens, huh? Or else she'd just sit there, in pain, waiting to be saved. No worse pastime than that."

I wiped my nose—force of habit when it felt like I was crying—and moved around to her front, bending so I could see her face. Her swollen face, which looked like it had been smashed against something.

"Jack would never do this," I said, straightening again. I wasn't helping her by staring. I had to get moving. "He said he didn't remember, and I know he wasn't lying. Who could have—"

Jack drifted in through the wall beside me. He looked around, his gaze coming to land on me. "What the fuck? Where am I?"

Harding started laughing. It was anything but funny.

"Crap, sorry. I must've pulled you here by thinking about you. I'm all screwed up in this plane." I walked to the door and held out a hand on impulse. "If people can sense my soul as I am now, would it be better for me to return to that shadowy body to see if anyone's in this room?"

"Very few magical people can feel souls the way you do, even those who possess others or use others to travel through spirit," Harding said. "And no one in the world right now can rip a soul out of a body the way you can. Trust me, I've been looking. Spirit Walkers don't come often, and they don't seem to last long with the violence that surrounds them—as you're learning. You're safe for now."

"Look what I did." The words were like a tire leaking. Guilt lined Jack's face. He bent down to Daisy. "I'll never be able to say I'm sorry. I'll never be able to explain, or beg for forgiveness. I won't be able to let her get revenge."

"She'll get revenge," I said, readying myself to walk through another wall. "I'll make sure of it."

I pushed into the next room, my determination stronger than the strangeness of walking through walls. This room was nearly as bare but for a desk with no chair and a couch with a mess of papers on one cushion pushed against the far wall. A closed door led out to what I suspected was a hall in a small-scale business building. Judging by the lack of cars, an unused small-scale business building.

A woman stood in the corner holding a laptop, her body bowed with fatigue and her hair a messy halo tucked into a ponytail. A white cord ran from the computer to the headphones she wore. The man on the screen was a stern-faced stranger, with red cheeks and a bulbous nose.

"Yes, sir, I know that. I do," the woman said. "But when I came to, I was already at the rendezvous point and confused as all hell. It was too late to dump the body and reconvene."

The man spoke in what seemed like short bursts, his head bobbing with whatever points he was making. Her shoulders tightened and she jammed her left hand onto her hip. She was clearly frustrated with whatever she was hearing.

"As I told the others, I have a black spot in my memory from the time I took down the Kraken to when I ended up here. I came to standing in the middle of the room, staring down at my phone crushed under my foot." The man barked out some words. "Yes, sir, but as you recall from what I just said, I didn't have a phone with which to call. It was crushed."

I headed to the desk, hoping there was any info on it about where we were. My spectral limbs dragged, getting tired. I pulled power from the Line and the spirit around me to keep me going, but time was running out, I could feel it. I'd need to head back and recharge.

"Yes, sir, as you see. But it took a while to get the Wi-Fi working. I had to hack into a local business, and I only have a basic understanding of computers. I'm not typically a field operative without support."

"Alexis." Jack shivered before looking back at the wall. "I hate that feeling." He spotted the woman in the corner. His eyes turned to slits. "That bitch is the one that took me down."

"Yeah, I know." I couldn't get into any of the drawers, but there likely wasn't anything in them anyway. This place was a shell. I hurried to the couch, looking down at the papers. Code and computer gobbledygook. I had no idea what any of it meant, but regardless, it wasn't the location. "She had a memory blackout, too. Sounds like you two were hoodwinked somehow."

"Magic," Jack said.

"Well, yes, that is what your whole world runs on," Harding said. "Some spirits get a case of the stupids when they lose their bodies, but this is ridiculous."

"I was just thinking about what kind of magic it could be, dumb shit," Jack retorted.

"Yeah. I'm the dumb shit," Harding said, looking out the window. "I gave you a hint and still you are in the dark."

"What?" I asked, jogging toward the door. "What hint? What do you know?"

Harding put up his hands. "Here's what I don't know—where we are. Anything else is unimportant right now. You're running out of steam."

He was right. I needed to get the show on the road.

"How come I'm not running out of steam?" Jack asked.

"Because you don't have a body, and she is acting as your anchor." Harding crossed his arms, not as helpful in all this as I would've hoped.

"Okay, I'll just pop outside and…find some street signs. Jack, go look through that red car. Maybe there is an address. Harding…come with me, just in case…"

Before I could dash through the door, the woman said, "Yes, sir. What should I do with the body? I've heard the new Demigod of San Francisco is smart. If they find the body here, they can probably trace—" The man cut her off before the screen went dark. She huffed, clicked the computer closed, yanked the earbuds from her ears, and tossed the whole lot onto the couch. "Sure, transport a bleeding dead body in a trunk with nothing to wrap it in. Great." She rolled her neck and stretched. "Fuck it, I can just strangle her and dump the car." She looked around before throwing up her hands. "But what the hell do I wipe the car down with? My bra? This is bullshit. How the hell do they expect me to work like this and actually pull off the job?"

She turned toward the door leading to Daisy's prison, then hesitated and glanced back at the one leading to a hall. She wasn't sure what to do first, kill Daisy or get the car ready.

Terror choked me. I had to do something, but what?

"You might switch to your shadow form to conserve energy," Harding said with a feigned nonchalance that rang false. Teamed with the way he'd mentioned hints a moment ago…

Why he didn't want to openly help me, I didn't know, but I'd take what I could get.

Energy.

I closed the distance as she pivoted, heading toward Daisy's door, and slapped a hand onto her shoulder. She startled and swiped at my hand, clearly feeling a presence and thinking it was as harmless as a spider. I bore down, sucking energy from her as hard as I could.

She blew out a breath and wiped her forehead, feeling the drain. My own tanks were filling up, but I kept going. Her body bowed slowly as she took her first step. She was moving slowly, haltingly, but she'd nearly made it to the door.

"I should grab that trail mix," she muttered, her eyes drooping. She leaned forward and braced a palm against the doorjamb as Jack rushed back into the room. She shook her head and straightened up, trying to push through it.

"Jack, hurry," I cried, sucking energy with everything I had.

Seeing what was happening, he wasted no time. He was at the woman's side in a moment, both hands on her upper arm.

"What's your story, bro?" Jack asked Harding. "You can't help?"

Harding leaned against the wall. "I *could*, but I won't. She needs to learn to fight her own battles. I'm merely the guide."

I couldn't tell what Jack muttered, but it didn't matter. The woman swayed, her side brushing Jack's. Mumbling, she staggered toward the couch, our hands still on her, still pulling energy until she spread out, her arm thrown over the couch arm, her head lolling to the side.

I stood back, high on energy yet out of breath. "How long will she be out?" I asked Harding.

He stared at me for a long moment. "If you'd been

properly trained…forever. You are a Spirit Walker. You don't need to be physically present to dislodge someone's soul. It's why your kind make the absolute best assassins. It's why you are so sought after."

"That'll never be her fate," Jack said, crossing his arms. "Kieran will never let that happen."

Harding's eyes sparkled. "One hopes so. But it's really such a waste."

I looked down at the woman, then used my magic to reach into her chest. Her spirit box greeted me, hard and unyielding. I changed tactics and soaked down into it, feeling the prongs holding her soul in place. All I really had to do was break those suckers. She probably didn't have enough energy left to bounce back.

The first felt like aluminum, bending before I finally managed to twist and turn it into breaking. The second was harder still, resisting. The third might've been iron for all I could handle it.

Out of breath, I shook my head. "Too hard."

Harding smiled. "As I said, you need more training. So…I'd give her forty-five minutes, maybe an hour. But do you know where we are?"

"Berkeley." Jack nodded at me. "We're in Berkeley. I couldn't figure out how to move a piece of paper out of the way, but I saw the city and zip. That'll be enough to get us here."

But would it be enough to get us here in time?

Chapter 26

KIERAN

"SIR." ZORN STALKED into Kieran's office with hollow eyes. He'd taken Daisy's kidnapping hard. The man was loyal to a fault. If you were lucky enough to have him on your side, he would tear down the world for you. He'd taken Daisy under his wing, promised her safety, and now felt like he had failed to deliver. He would never rest until he righted this wrong. Whoever had ultimately been responsible for her abduction had created a savage enemy, not least because Kieran wouldn't stop until he made sure Zorn got his vengeance.

Zorn held up his phone.

"Bria wasn't sure if she should call you. Alexis has gone into the spirit world with the Spirit Walker to track Daisy."

Kieran stood from his chair. He'd sensed Alexis had gone into the other plane—her presence had disappeared from his radar—but it had bleeped back before he could react. It felt distant, though, further away than when she'd left. She'd been doing it so often lately, including during sleep, that he'd been taking pains to study the patterns.

"Was she successful?"

Zorn's brow furrowed, probably because of how calmly Kieran was taking the news. He couldn't prevent her from learning her magic, and he didn't want to suffocate her. If she didn't think she needed him, he had to respect that—while preparing to help at a moment's notice in case something went wrong.

"Bria doesn't know. She's still…out."

"What do you mean?" Kieran asked, getting a jolt of alarm. "She's still in the trance?"

"Sir." Red stepped into the room with someone Kieran couldn't see at her back. "The Defalcator is here—"

"Nester," came the disembodied voice.

Red barely paused. "The Defalcator is wondering when he might tutor his new pupil."

Kieran heard a sniff.

"That guy has taken residence in this office since he showed up," Zorn said, annoyance in his voice. "He was told we'd get in contact. Yet…"

It was clear Zorn thought Nester was snooping. Given what had happened last night, there was no doubt he was right.

"Show him in." Kieran took a couple of steps to

clear himself of the desk. A kaleidoscope of emotions pulsed through the soul link. The clearest was pain.

The slight man with bony shoulders stepped into the room. Medium height, bland face, no discerning characteristics whatsoever. The eye wanted to slide right past him. That alone set him up to be an excellent pickpocket. Good thing they had nothing of value around the office.

"Sir, yes." Nester bowed slightly before pulling his hands behind his back. "I was just wondering when I might be of use."

"Thank you, Nester, yes. It was good of Demigod Nancy to recommend you. At present, Alexis is exploring other avenues. Just as soon as she is ready, she'd be happy to entertain you. Until then, please enjoy the city, on me. San Francisco is an absolutely lovely place to visit. I'll set you up with a driver and an itinerary."

Nester opened his mouth to argue.

"And of course I'll make sure Nancy knows the delay is at my discretion," Kieran said.

The Defalcator closed his mouth. Kieran had stolen his only defense. Nester nodded briskly. "Of course, yes. How good of you."

"Red, see that he's taken care of," Kieran said, clearing his throat when sadness and then fierce determination radiated through the link.

Henry turned sideways, slipping in past the exiting

K . F . B R E E N E

Nester. He closed the door behind him, drawing attention to the papers in his hand.

"You're sure she's still in the trance?" Kieran asked Zorn, staring out the window. Zorn had probably hoped the news would drive Kieran from the building. Zorn was more useful in the field.

"When Bria called, yes." Zorn tapped his phone then lifted it to his ear. "I'll double-check."

"Sir." Henry dropped the papers onto Kieran's desk. "I have information. We have the car narrowed down."

Zorn turned back, his eyes hungry.

Henry spread the half-dozen pictures out on the desk, all different colors and makes. "We're still trying to hack into the satellite owned by the Chester government, but this is what we have so far. Each of these were seen leaving the area in the correct window of time. In addition, most had an entry time stamp that would make sense with the battle. Now, this might not be all of them. We are relying on a few traffic cameras and a couple of gas station cameras that look out on the street. If the perpetrator knew to watch out for these cameras, there are two ways to get around them. But this is a start. We are working on getting the various records and checking out the drivers."

"She's still out, sir," Zorn called from the back of the room. "Lying still as a stone. Jack has disappeared from the area too. Bria felt his soul take off. She has no idea where, obviously."

Kieran nodded to Zorn, forcing himself not to react to the gut punch, as Henry continued.

"I researched the types of magics that can control another person's actions. Most of them are more persuasive. The magical user convinces the victim what to do. Almost always, the victim remembers what happened, but there are a couple of instances where the magic causes a blackout, like Jack experienced. One is dark fae magic, and the other, which makes more sense, stems from Hades. I checked them both out, of course."

"Hades," Kieran said, knowing it was rare for dark fae to work for Demigods or anyone else. They had their own lands and their own established royalty. Their lineage didn't stem from the Olympian gods, nor did they believe in the various human gods. They were an independent people, embroiled in their own cutthroat society. Their magic was potent and dangerous, and Kieran was glad this didn't seem like something they'd be interested in.

"That's the conclusion I've come to," Henry said. "A Possessor. Someone that can take over a person for an hour or two. He grabbed Daisy using Jack. But here is where it gets fuzzy: why grab Daisy in the house instead of Alexis in the battlefield?"

"Alexis would've ripped the soul right out of him," Zorn said, back to staring out the window. "It would be asinine for anyone to try grabbing her without drugging her first."

"Unless they underestimate her. Everyone knows she's untrained," Henry replied.

Zorn shrugged. "So he grabbed Daisy, fine. Handed her off like a baton. What now? It's been nearly twenty-four hours and no ransom call. No offer to trade. No gloating from Aaron or anyone. Something isn't adding up."

"No, it isn't," Kieran said, staring at his computer, thinking beyond it. "Does Aaron have a Possessor?"

"No," Henry said. "His databases barely have a fire-wall, they are so open. He has no secrets from us. As for who does... Well, we're checking."

"Check the other Hades Demigods first."

"Already on it. They both have their systems locked up tight, but it's nothing we can't get through. One thing of note—Possessors can hop small distances. Very small. Like from Jack to the woman he ran into."

Kieran slipped his hands into his pockets and turned to the window, looking at the glittering blue waves. They weren't doing much for his turbulent mood, emotions that matched Alexis's feelings at present. She wasn't liking whatever she was finding.

"Sounds like a third party," Zorn said. "They grabbed the kid, but they didn't get to do whatever they were planning. They had to pivot when the woman confronted them. So they switched bodies and made use of the woman's getaway car. Any idiot would've found the car—the woman was moving from that direction. Her plans were probably in the car, on her phone, whatever. A Possessor this skilled in working under the radar would've had all he needed to pull this off."

Henry and Kieran nodded. But one thing still didn't add up.

Until Zorn completed the puzzle.

"Kill the kid, blame the woman from Aaron's staff, create a distraction as we figure out how to deal with a call to war…all of this is to open a door to this person's true purpose."

"Maybe the third party plans to use Daisy as a lure and is getting everything in order," Henry said.

"Any third party operating under the radar doesn't use a lure," Zorn replied, his tone gruff. "The person pulling these strings is sly. Savvy. He might not even be after Alexis. Or be of Hades lineage. He might just want to see how Kieran reacts when someone gets personal. Without knowing who is behind this, we have no idea what their end game might be."

Kieran had to agree with Zorn. Daisy was collateral damage. "Henry, if you can figure out who the Possessor is, get his ID. We can run him through the facial tracker in the city and see if anything comes up. He has to be on scene. I don't know how far away a Possessor can be, but I know it isn't across oceans. He's here, somewhere. If we can grab his body, we own his magic."

A swirl of emotion ran through his middle. He paused for a moment to catch his breath. Zorn's phone rang.

Time to go.

Chapter 27

ALEXIS

"**I** CAN'T USE my fucking hands!" Jack tried to slam his fist against the laptop on the kitchen table. His hand went straight through both the computer and the table. "What the hell use am I if I can't use my hands?"

Bria slid into the chair he was lurking in, then jumped back out. "That was cold. Jack, move. I can feel your soul."

"This is a nightmare." Jack turned away, dodging around the cat that once again housed Harding's spirit. I'd put the spirit trapper/repellent back up, mostly to keep Frank out, but also as a little protection in case one of the Demigods sent spirits to spy. "How the hell am I going to find the place without going online?" The cat jumped up onto the island, and Jack bent over it. "Can't you figure out some sort of spirit information infrastructure?"

"They can always put you in a body," the cat said, eyeing a hairbrush Aubri had left out on her last visit. "You know, in case you still have the stupids and didn't think about a Necromancer using her craft on you."

I motioned Bria back into the seat. "He said it's in Berkeley."

"Berkeley is a big place. Care to narrow it down?" Her phone vibrated and she glanced at it. "The guys are all en route except for Henry. He's going to stay and look for more intel. Zorn is asking how Mordecai is." She resumed looking at the laptop, preparing to type.

"Good. Just checked on him," Jack said. "I can at least look and report. That's about all I'm good—"

"Enough." I slashed my hand through the air and accidentally put a little magic behind it. Jack jerked back, and the cat jumped and twisted at the same time, yowling. It landed on its feet and zipped away, Harding clearly not in control of that one. "Jack, I know this is traumatic for you, but Daisy is still alive. Right now, she is still alive, but we only have fifty minutes *if we are lucky* to get to her—"

"We're lucky," Bria said, nodding. "We're lucky. We'll get her."

"So I need you to cut it out with the self-pity and get on board," I continued. "Where is she being held?"

He took a deep breath and nodded before positioning himself to see over Bria's shoulder. I saw goosebumps rise on her flesh, but she didn't comment.

As I felt Kieran drawing closer, I relayed Jack's instructions for a Google search. After five minutes of futzing around on street maps, we had an address in the non-magical zone, which I scrawled down on a sheet of paper.

It would take us over an hour to get there without traffic. The Bay Area, magical or otherwise, always had traffic.

"Move Mordecai into the panic room," I told Bria, my hands shaking, tears threatening. Panic clouded my mind. "Think, think." I took a deep breath. "If we get a police escort, there won't be traffic. We could make it. Except it would take time to arrange all that."

"Use the helicopter," Jack said, watching my face.

I widened my eyes. "What helicopter?"

"Valens's helicopter that is now Kieran's. It's...not close to here. We aren't exactly central."

I tapped my fingers against the kitchen island. "The ocean! I can't swim that fast, but Kieran can. Maybe he could—"

Bria raced back into the room, and the cat darted behind her and then winged out to the side. The thing was on crack and Harding was going for a helluva ride. She held out her hands.

"What the hell are we doing standing there? Let's meet Kieran on the way," she said.

"And what? Hang out in traffic? Even with an escort, getting through the city and across the bridge will take ages. Cars can't get out of the way if they don't have somewhere to get out of the way *to*. We don't have time! No, the ocean is the fastest. It has to be."

Bria gestured for me to follow her out of the house, which I did, bringing the address with me even though I knew it by heart.

"Meeting him would be out of our way, anyway." I hopped up and down to expel some frantic, worried energy as the cat raced out of the open door.

Harding flew up out of it with his arms windmilling, landing on his butt. "That devil does not like co-existing," he said, pushing himself to standing.

Kieran's red Ferrari tore down the street, followed by two black BMWs and the pink Corvette from the other day. Given Aubri wouldn't be called on to do my makeup in a crisis, Red must've owned it. It was like Valentine's Day on wheels with a hockey-mask-wearing driver. How confusing.

Tires skidded against pavement and smoke drifted into the sky as they all stopped in front of my house. Kieran hopped out and jogged over, his eyebrows up.

"Over an hour away, not including traffic," I said, handing him the paper with the address. "Apparently you have a helicopter, but Jack says we can't get there in time, and Daisy only has forty-five minutes *max*. More like less than thirty." Tears clouded my vision again. "I was thinking the ocean. How fast can you travel in the ocean? If at least one of us gets there…"

"Where is she?"

"Berkeley." Bria said. "Not horribly far from the ocean."

Zorn stepped up beside Kieran. I'd forgotten Zorn was a Marid Djinn, his magic originating from dark sea spirits. He, too, was at home in the water.

"We can manage this," Zorn said, muscles popping out along his frame as he braced for what was to come. "We can get there in time, and we can drag Lexi behind us. We won't want to be without her."

"It's just a woman who's holding her. You don't need me—"

"Let them take you," Harding cut in.

Kieran zeroed in on Harding for a moment, as if he was reading into those words. I didn't have time to wonder what game he was playing now.

"Fine. Drag me along, but only if we make it in time," I said. With my blood bond to Kieran, I could survive underwater for a long time.

"Thane, grab a rope," Kieran instructed, glancing behind him as his people jogged up. "Red, clear the train lines. That's the second fastest way to Berkeley at this point. Get a train ready and meet us there as fast as you can."

"Yes, sir," Red said. "But where is *there*?"

Kieran handed off the piece of paper. "It's not far from BART in the non-magical area."

Red pulled out her phone as Thane ran from around the garage side of the house holding an ordinary rope I hadn't realized was in my possession.

"We'll be cutting through the water fast," Kieran was saying, grabbing the rope from Thane and wrapping it around my waist. "I'll be manipulating currents and the water itself, so it won't feel natural."

"Deep-sea swimming will never feel natural," I said, lifting my arms.

He grinned at me. "Someday it might. Plug your nose, close your eyes, and hold your breath, okay?" He wrapped the rope around my shoulders and between my legs, and then used an impressive knot to tie it all into place at my stomach. "Maybe even cover your face."

"Remember that you can hold your breath for more than an hour," Zorn said, taking a black bag from Donovan, who unknowingly stood beside an eager Jack, and stowed a gun in it. He then peeled off his shirt, exposing thick slabs of muscle crisscrossed with silvery streaks of scars. "Just let Kieran drag you and *do not* think about gasping for breath, even if you crest the surface for a moment."

Kieran leaned down a little so his beautiful blue eyes, stormy with emotion, connected with mine. He took hold of my upper arms. "I'll tie myself to you in the water. Then do as we say and just hang on, okay?" He waited for me to nod before straightening and turning to Donovan. "Once you get off the train, get a car to meet us at the closest point. Zorn, do you know where that address is?"

"Yeah," Zorn answered.

Kieran nodded and looked at everyone. "Watch each other. A Possessor took over Jack. I'm guessing the differences were subtle, mostly missed…"

"Very good," Harding said, and his words from before filtered through my head.

Very few can feel souls the way you do, even those who possess others or use others to travel through spirit.

…even those who possess others…

That bastard had known all along, but he'd played Sherlock Holmes with the information. I'd be mad later.

"The Possessor took over the woman who grabbed Daisy," I said before Kieran went on. I quickly went over the things I'd heard.

"Bria, get that information to Henry," Kieran said. She nodded but didn't immediately lift her phone to her ear, waiting for Kieran to finish. "If someone is acting different, ask them what we call Daisy. If you are asked, and you are yourself, answer *princess.*"

"But—"

Kieran held up his hand. "There is a chance others know that we call Daisy a little gremlin. But we have never called her princess, for fear of our lives. So that's the code we'll use, got it?"

Everyone nodded except for Harding, who was looking around at our faces.

"Good. Let's go." Kieran motioned me toward the cliffs and the groups broke off, the non-seafaring folk running to the cars as Red barked on the phone. Zorn and Jack followed us.

At the end of the street, trees dotted the way. The end of the rope bounced and swung behind me, snagging in the weeds. I pushed a tree branch aside before getting smacked by another. Brittle grass crunched under my feet.

"This is such a terrible idea" I said, adrenaline coursing through me. The salty air whipped my hair, and Kieran's invigoration coursed through me. Suddenly I was running out to the edge of a cliff ending in sharp rocks below.

Harding appeared next to the very edge, a grin on his face and his arms crossed. "A woman of Hades and a man of Poseidon. This is what happens when the worlds collide."

"We are stronger when we band together," Kieran said, stopping beside Harding, on the very edge of the cliff. He had absolutely no fear he would slip and fall to his death. I did not know how.

"No doubt. I see the evidence everywhere," Harding said. "And thankfully, you have plenty of money to buy underwear every time one of you shits himself."

"It's the ocean. You don't need underwear," Zorn said after I relayed what Harding said, pushing off his pants and then tucking them into the black bag now tied around his waist. He wasn't kidding about that. The guy apparently went commando.

"Oh, but your Demigod will certainly need them the first time his body is left behind, and his soul is dragged through spirit." Harding stepped out of the way of Zorn's preparations. "Or doesn't he know soul mates go both ways, and his Hades queen can yank her cheapie king into the Beyond with her?"

Zorn put out his hand to me, so I took it, edging closer to the cliff face.

He dropped my hand. "Clothes. Demigod Kieran will be able to wring the water from his clothes. He doesn't need to waste energy on yours."

"Chivalrous," Harding said with a teasing smile.

"Zorn, leave it," Kieran said, lifting his hands into the air.

I edged a little closer and watched the water beneath us as it surged over the rocks and rose up the side of the cliff. The chaotic currents within it pulled at me, thrashing and yanking.

"I'll tie you to me once we're in the water," Kieran repeated, his power throbbing around us. "Then you'll just hang on."

"Right." I licked my lips, staring down at the torrid waters still far below. If I jumped in now, I'd be swallowed in the surge, churned into butter within the white foam.

Kieran dropped his hands before turning and running a thumb across my jaw. "Love you. See you in there."

"Wha—"

He dove off the side of the cliff, his arms stretched wide, his shirt clinging to the muscles across his back. At the last moment he turned the movement into a perfect swan dive, cutting through the mist and disappearing beneath the crashing foam.

"There's nothing to this, Alexis. You'll be safe." Zorn nodded at me, as if that was any sort of pep talk, and followed Kieran. The sun glinted off the mess of scars along his back.

"That guy has obviously been through the stink, huh?" Harding said, watching.

"Come on, Lexi, you got this!" Jack ran and jumped a moment later, hitting the waters a second before changing form. Great spirit tentacles rose from the water before splashing down, no longer creating a disturbance on the surface.

"Man, I'm glad I'm not you. There's a reason Poseidon was sequestered to the ocean," said Harding, who'd taken a step back. "I mean, besides being too cheap to build much in the way of accommodations. This is…not great."

"Yeah, thanks, man." My heart thumped so hard that it felt like it was rocking my whole chest. Fear clawed at me—the fear of drowning, the fear of being bashed against the rocks…

"Without fear, there is no courage," I murmured. "It is inaction that breeds fear. Be action. Be confidence. Fuuuuck meeeeeee—"

I took two fast steps and jumped, suddenly weightless, but not because I'd stepped into spirit. No, this was totally, completely, horribly real. I was really plummeting into the churning waters of a death machine. Suddenly the spirit world I'd walked earlier didn't seem so scary. Not compared to this.

The deep chill enveloped me, sliding across my body and over my face. The current ripped at me immediately. The waters threatened to throw me into the solid rock of the cliff wall.

A strong hand grabbed my arm, and suddenly I was being pulled away. The current shifted, now rushing past me back out to the ocean. Frigid bubbles whizzed by my body. My head broke the surface, but still I held my breath, my eyes shut.

"You're good, babe. I just need to tie you up. You can open your eyes. Breathe."

I blinked into the wet face of Kieran, water clinging

to his eyebrows and lashes. The surface of the water had calmed around us, with Zorn waiting not far away. Beyond us, though, huge waves rose into the sky, cutting into my visibility.

I treaded water, realizing why no one else from the Six had accompanied us. We were all strong swimmers thanks to Kieran's blood bond, but this was ridiculous.

The rope tugged at my middle. Kieran stilled, confidence pumping through him.

"We're going to make it," he told me, his lips just above the water line. "She's going to be fine, okay? We'll get there in time. Just take a deep breath, close your eyes, and *hold your breath*. Don't breathe, whatever you do. If something happens, send a shock of terror through the link and I'll stop. Okay? Don't die back here without letting me know."

"That's not funny," I said, the situation making me shiver even if the cold did not. My clothes pulled at me, wanting to drag me down.

A small knot formed between his brows. "It wasn't meant to be. Zorn, stay at her level. Watch her until we're in the area. Then you can take over leading. We'll move as fast as we can."

Chapter 28

DAISY

DAISY FROZE AS something thumped in the outer room. It had been lovely and quiet for a while, giving her time to work at the coarse rope with her nondominant hand. Fatigue dragged at her and pain dulled her mind, but she'd nearly gotten it. Just a little yanking and she could shrug out of it. But now she could hear movement. Was that…sliding?

She glanced at the high, dingy window to her right. If someone was blocking the door with the intention of setting fire to the place, she had a way out. It would hurt like hell, sure, but pain had been her life for…however long she'd been in this damn chair.

Footsteps made their way toward her, heavier than before the surprising reprieve. It was either someone else, or the woman who'd grabbed her was as exhausted as Daisy was and not handling it any better.

Daisy's heart sped up, but she controlled her reaction. She breathed deeply, focusing on the rope, on her goal of getting out. Hurrying would reduce her efficiency and end up delaying her. Same with panic. She didn't work well when overly keyed up. It was one of the first things Zorn had identified. She had to be calm. Had to focus on the problem.

The problem was that the fucking knot would not fucking come loose and made her fucking pick at it like the motherfucking invalid she was.

That was not the way to remain calm.

The door handle jiggled. Breathing through her nose, she pulled her hurt arm up to loosen the binding. Pain blasted through her, making her dizzy. She cried through the pain, no shame, barely able to feel with her good fingers over the pounding in her head.

The door swung open, revealing her kidnapper—a heavy-lidded woman with frizzy hair and sluggish limbs. A knife was in a holster at her belt, and she flexed her hands, her fingers momentarily looking like claws.

Daisy kept her feet utterly still and pushed back against the chair legs as though they were tied. Why they hadn't been, Daisy didn't know. Probably an oversight. Whatever the reason, she didn't plan on pointing it out until the last moment—until she could use them.

"So. What's on the docket for today?" Daisy asked, not sure which path to choose here. She could look miserable and vulnerable at a drop of a hat, especially with her glassy eyes and tear-stained face. Guys responded best to that, though women with children also reacted to waterworks. At least, that was what Zorn had said. It certainly hadn't ever helped her in the foster homes when she was getting slapped around.

Or should she sink into a state of calm, something that would invariably help her? Maybe the woman would think Daisy had something up her sleeve, like magic that might actually help.

"You got unlucky, kid," the woman said, stopping in front of her. "I was supposed to grab the Soul Stealer, not her kid. You were probably part of someone else's plan that went tits up. Unfortunately, that leaves me to clean up the mess."

Daisy yanked at the rope, getting the knot a little looser. She whimpered with the pain, letting more tears fall. At this point, it really couldn't hurt. This woman was about business.

"Yeah. That big guy messed you up, huh?" The woman glanced behind the chair and then grimaced. "That looks like it hurts. This isn't going to feel too good either, but at least it has an ending, huh?" She curled her blunt fingers around Daisy's neck. "It won't hurt forever, though, I promise, okay? Just let yourself experience it, don't fight, and it'll be over really quick."

"What do you want, money?" Daisy asked, stalling for time. She twisted and turned to pretend she was trying to get out of the woman's grasp while she picked at the knot. Almost there. "I got money. I'm the Demigod's girlfriend's ward. I'm worth a lot. They'll pay you, I'm certain. Demigod Kieran is great at covering trails, too. He fooled Valens, and *no one* fools Valens. He can set you up somewhere nice. You'll never have to work again."

"Why would I want to become a pawn between Demigods when I got plenty of money of my own? Not to mention the status that goes with it. A couple bad jobs doesn't make a shitty life, know what I mean, kid?"

"I'm fourteen, did they tell you that? I'm not even old enough for a job. I'm not even magical!" The hands tightened on her throat. The stubborn knot held tight. "I don't know who you are," she said, wheezing. "I won't—"

Her air was cut off, silencing her. Her vision sparkled with red and black spots. Another wave of adrenaline washed into her. She stilled, closing her eyes.

"There you go. Just let it come," the woman whispered like a lullaby.

Zorn had trained her for this, though he had also tied her feet. Mordecai had thought it barbaric. Thought it too much.

Her heart hurt as much as her neck. As much as her wrist. All she wanted was to run back to Mordecai, hug him, and tell him that he was wrong and she was right. *Na-na-na-na-na.*

A tear leaked out of her eye. The pain flared from her wrist as she pulled again. It was now or never. Clumsy left hand or no, it was time to get that knot free. It was time to survive.

She scrabbled at it, disappearing into her head, cutting out the pain. Her mind might be fuzzy around the edges, not far from dying, but she wouldn't let it get to her. She could do this. She could get out of this.

The rope came free in her left hand. It slid off her right arm and dropped to the floor. Her hands were free.

She thrashed her shoulders, taking the focus from her lower half, acting like she was trying to get out.

"Almost there now," the woman said. "Almost there."

"You're going...straight...to hell," Daisy mouthed, no breath to let the woman know what was coming.

She kicked her feet out, separating them at the last moment to hit the insides of the woman's knees, as she jammed her left hand into the neck of her shirt. The woman's hands tightened even more around Daisy's neck. Blackness encroached on her vision.

Daisy wrapped her hand around the hilt of the knife in her bra. Before the woman could stop her, she yanked the blade out, slicing her would-be strangler's arm as it passed by.

The woman jerked back and turned, immediately

going into defensive mode. It was too late. Daisy was already moving, thankful for the proximity, since she had to use her nondominant hand. She surged forward and rammed the blade into the woman's gut. Before the woman could fully pull her hands away from Daisy's neck, Daisy pulled her blade out and slammed it in again, this time slipping it between the ribs. Lucky shot. One more for the kidney, which she missed, slicing the woman's side instead. She really needed to work on this hand.

The woman grunted, unreally quiet despite the onslaught, and staggered forward. Daisy tried to get out of the way, but she got twisted up with the chair and went down. Her bad wrist hit first and she cried out.

The chair tumbled out of the way. The woman, blood running onto the floor, grabbed for Daisy. Daisy rolled away, the room spinning.

She forced herself through it, knowing this was life or death, and scrambled up, her wrist held down at her side. It would feel better if she cradled it against her body, but it was out of the way in case the woman surprised her with a body kick or punch.

The woman rolled onto her side, trying to get up, giving Daisy an opportunity to kick her in the stomach, right in her wound. The woman screamed, curling in on herself. Daisy dropped and stabbed the knife through the woman's throat.

"You don't fuck with my family and get to live," Daisy said, straightening up. She wiped the drool from her mouth and stepped back slowly, watching, waiting. If the enemy was good, she'd feign a mortal wound to bring the attacker closer, greedy for a kill.

One must never be greedy for a kill.

If the enemy was good, she would see the attacker backing off, assured of victory, and become the attacker herself.

One must never let down her guard, even when the enemy is on the very brink of death.

So when did one finish things up, or was Daisy supposed to wait here all day for the woman to bleed out? She wished she'd known to ask during Zorn's instruction.

Daisy waited for the remorse to come, for the cacophony of emotion following a kill, especially her first personal kill. Zorn had warned her to be ready for it. To be ready to talk herself around it if there was no one there to help her.

None came.

She felt no remorse whatsoever. Not for this woman, who had intended to kill her. Not for her partner in crime, who had killed Mordecai...

The sorrow nearly stole her breath.

Okay, fine, she did feel pain for Jack. Clawing betrayal. She wasn't dead inside, after all. She'd need help dealing with Jack. But not this woman. Not this asshole, who'd tried to kill a kid in cold blood, whispering lullabies and calling the situation a mess.

"Look who's the mess now, motherfucker," she whispered. "And you better bleed out before you can tell Alexis I swore."

✕   ✕   ✕

AMOS

AMOS PARKED ALONG the street in the plain brown Dodge he'd stolen from his hotel parking lot. The afternoon sun beat down on the corner lot, the weathered and beaten building hunkering among the newer condos and buzzing office buildings. He could barely see the red car sitting idle in the parking lot.

Aaron's staffer was still there.

Amos let his lungs slowly deflate. That was a relief. Demigod Magnus didn't tolerate failure. Amos wasn't the only Possessor in the world, and he wasn't even the best—he didn't want the boss to think about replacing him.

He grabbed his bag from the front seat. The various items within tinkled as they fell against one another. He strung the strap over his shoulder and stepped out of the car, dressed in business casual with his hair slicked to one side. There was less of a chance people would notice him if he fit into the surroundings.

A soft breeze carrying the salt from the distant sea floated through the trees, waving the branches. He made his way down the sidewalk, not used to doing this in person. Usually his body was stored away in a safe place, always available if things went wrong. Always welcoming.

His shoulders bunched against his ears and then relaxed, a nervous tic. He felt completely exposed. Absolutely vulnerable. A knife in the ribs could only hurt him, not kill or even wound him, if he was in someone else's body. But here, in the flesh, that knife could be the end of him.

Had that been Magnus's plan? You could never know with that Demigod. Magnus was tricky. He laid plans sometimes years out, working each little thread like a spider until his desired outcome came to pass. It was better to go into service to the less political Demigods, the ones without such rich and influential territories. You wouldn't get paid as much, but on average you lasted longer.

Given Amos's magic, he hadn't thought it would be a problem. With his body safe, he usually didn't have to worry about *lasting*. Following orders and, when he couldn't, doing a good job had always been enough.

It was fine. He'd just hop into the body of Aaron's staffer, take out the girl, arrange everything, kill the host, and be back out, lickety-split. The girl was tied up

with a broken wrist. She had no weapons—Amos had
checked her himself. He could just slit her throat and
move on.

Down the way, a car sped around the corner and
pulled up across from the dingy building. It then swung
into the parking lot and parked at a diagonal, close to
the red car. Three people hurriedly stepped out, walking
around the front to convene. Two well-built men and a
woman, from the look of it. Amos was too far away to
see their faces. They were dressed well, which bespoke
the area, but they moved differently than Chesters.
Non-magical folk had a tendency toward jerky, bumbling movements, but these three moved like they were
prowling, sleek and graceful. And they were moving
quickly. Nearly jogging.

Amos slowed.

The taller, dark-haired one put out an arm to keep
the woman back while he took the place in. The other
man, standing in a way that reminded Amos of death
incarnate, scanned the area. Though Amos couldn't
make out the man's features, he *knew* those eyes were
sussing him out, analyzing him as he continued to
amble along.

Thank mighty Hades that Amos had chosen to fit
in.

The man in the lead started forward, the woman
hurrying to follow. Amos continued toward the build-

ing, watching them from afar. As he got a little closer, excitement coursed through him.

The Demigod! The Soul Stealer! And one of the Six, Amos was sure.

With a grin, Amos about-faced and stalked right back to his car. He slid into the passenger seat, locked the doors, and leaned his seat all the way back. Once there, he pulled his bag closer.

From the distance, he couldn't be sure which of the Six that had been. Or, he should say, which of the five. He'd already shaved down one of their number. This Demigod would soon learn why all the other Demigods had such large staffs.

He pulled out the little charms the spirit thief had nicked, nasty little cretin. That plain fellow gave the Hades lineage a bad name. Any Chester could basically do what he did, after all. Still, he'd been useful. The tokens all glittered in Amos's hands: a pen with the writing worn off from heavy use, a cuff link that had lost its shine, a button from a favorite jacket—all stuff that had been around the owner for a good length of time. All easily nabbed from desks or office floors.

Amos wiggled to get comfortable and settled in. He'd studied up on the Six. As soon as he found the right body, he'd know which magic lay at his fingertips. He'd let everyone else deal with the crying girl and Aaron's staffer. The chaos would prove excellent cover to take out the Demigod.

Chapter 29

BRIA

B RIA TURNED AND stared down a filthy man in raggedy clothes with an open plastic bag full of cans. A few cans had broken free and were now rattling around his feet.

Boman checked his watch, standing beside Thane and Donovan near the door at the other end of the car. "Twelve minutes."

Red nodded tersely. She stood next to Bria beside the car's second exit, close to Can Man.

"Hey, bud," Bria said to the man. All the other patrons on the train had been cleared. Every single one...except this stubborn asshole. He'd refused to budge, insisting it wasn't constitutional. "Mind picking up your cans? They're driving me crazy."

"I gotta right to be here," the man yelled. "This is the U-S-of-A, damnit. I have a right to be here, and I have a right to these cans. You can't stop me."

Bria checked her phone, the desire for action pumping through her. "Donovan, do something about those cans, would ya?"

"Anything yet?" Boman asked her.

She didn't respond. Zorn had called when they hit the shore. They were going to grab a car and head to the building. That had been seven minutes ago. Zorn had reckoned it was a six-minute trip.

"Donovan!" she barked.

The fallen cans lifted into the air, three of them tucking into the plastic bag. The fourth fell back to the ground.

"The devil!" the man shouted, ducking from some unseen force. "Witches!" He straightened up and pointed at Bria. "Witch!"

"Sexist," she said. The train went around a bend in the track. The can rattled across the floor and bumped up against the side. "Donovan."

"What?"

She turned at him, annoyed. "What do you mean wh..."

His eyebrows were raised. His shoulders twitched upward.

"What do we call Daisy?" she asked him, butterflies swarming her stomach.

Everyone else froze, a terribly obvious reaction to what was happening.

Donovan wiggled his finger in his ear and then stopped moving. He blinked, took his hand down, and stared blankly at his finger.

"Donovan, what do we call Daisy?" Bria repeated, then held up her hand as an *oh shit* expression crossed his face. "Wait, never mind. I remember now…"

Thane jerked and then reached for the bar next to him to stabilize himself.

Thane liked challenging his balance. Always. He was no longer himself. The Possessor was moving through heads, looking for someone. Probably Lexi.

Would Lexi be able to resist him? Was that possible with her magic?

"I heard a joke the other day." Bria walked over and picked up the can.

"Filthy witch," the homeless man shouted at her.

Thane swung his head around to look at the homeless man, clearly confused.

She resumed her position, holding the can in her outstretched hand.

"Knock, knock," Bria said. "Boman, knock, knock."

Boman was staring at the back of Thane's head. He started buttoning his pockets. He was preparing in case he was next. He wanted to make it harder for the Possessor to get to his weapons, easier for the others to take him down. He was prepared to die to keep someone from using him to kill one of the others.

"Who's there?" Boman replied.

Thane leaned back, shaking his head, then stepped

away from the pole. Bria thought she heard him swear—not usual for him.

"Banana."

"Banana who?" Boman asked, backing up into the corner and putting his hands on the walls. Donovan tucked his hands into his pockets.

"Knock, knock," Bria said, starting over, still holding that can, wondering who would be next. If they would be in the train.

The train jerked on the track, then curved right. Henry staggered backward and fell between the thread-bare cushioned seats.

"Uh-oh." Thane turned to help him.

"Who's there?" Boman asked, his palms still on the walls.

"You okay, buddy?" Thane was standing in Henry's way, making it awkward for him to climb out of the seats to standing.

"Banana."

"Banana…" Boman took his hands away from the walls before he jerkily put them back on. "Uhm…"

"He's not being subtle," Red murmured, ignoring the shouting from the homeless man and looking out through the window. "He's not after someone in this train."

"I know."

"He thinks the job will be done by the time we reach

the others."

"I know."

"What's the job?"

"Whatever it is, we have"—she checked her phone—"ten minutes to save the day."

Chapter 30

ALEXIS

T HE PEELING WOOD door of the small office building felt warm under my hand. One soul pulsed inside, big and bright. Tears clouded my vision and I wondered if I'd ever stop crying.

"Just her." I tried the handle. It was locked. "It's just Daisy in there."

Jack slipped through the door, and Kieran nearly took a step back. Jack, thankfully, didn't notice. A moment later, he was back.

"Daisy took that chick out." Jack said it so exuberantly that he would have sprayed spit had he been alive. "She took her out! How the hell…"

Zorn gently moved me to the side and proceeded to ram his shoulder into the door. Wood on the frame broke. The door swung inward.

"Where?" Zorn asked, stopping in a sort of seventies lobby area.

I jogged down the hall, pointing toward the small office on the left. The black letters on the door were peeling off and illegible, but there was a plaque bearing the number 101 beside it. Zorn busted into that room, too, the door breaking free from one of the hinges and swinging.

The sparse area I'd seen in the spirit world greeted us. To the side, the door leading to the supply closet in which Daisy had been held captive stood open. Daisy's soul gleamed in there, and I jogged to the door quickly, gasping when I stood at the mouth of it.

The woman I'd seen earlier lay on her stomach with her face to the side, blood pooling around her on the floor. Her spirit had already taken off.

Daisy stood against the wall, a bloody knife in her left hand, and her badly bruised right wrist tucked up against her middle. Her face was paler than I'd ever seen it.

Zorn stepped in front of her and turned so the carnage was at his back. So he was blocking it. He lowered his head to her. "You okay?"

Her luminous eyes had been dulled, and I couldn't tell if it was because of the pain or what she'd done. She blinked a few times and her pupils constricted. Tears filled her eyes when she saw me.

"You came."

"Of course we came." I rushed to her, hugging her tightly. Her cry made me step back and look down at her hurt wrist. "Sorry! I'm sorry." I smoothed her hair, tears dripping down my face. Guilt consumed me. We wouldn't have been in time. She'd had to save herself. "I'm so sorry," I said again, and not because of her wrist this time.

"You okay?" Zorn asked again, scanning her face.

She seemed to know what he was asking. "Not about Jack." More tears dripped down. "I'm not okay about Jack. He did this. He k-kill—" Daisy shook her head, unable to say the words.

"Tell her, Lexi, please." Jack squeezed in. "Please tell her I'd never hurt her. Not if I was in my right mind. Please."

"Zorn, give them a second," Kieran said, his voice a whip crack of command. "Alexis, go ahead and act as the bridge between Jack and Daisy. They both need closure."

Zorn stiffened, and I wasn't sure if it was because he didn't want to leave his charge, or because Jack was in the room, before stepping aside.

"She's okay, but our work isn't done," Kieran murmured to him. "Find out who owns this place. How long it has been here. Let's make sure we have all our eggs in the basket. Call the others to tell them she's safe. Then we need to find out more about that Possessor."

They moved into the larger room as I explained the whole Possessor situation to Daisy, telling her that both Jack and the woman who'd kidnapped her had been possessed.

"But Mordie made it," I finished, tears in my eyes. "He'll be okay."

"Wait." She grabbed my upper arm with her good hand. "Is…" She swallowed. "He's…?"

I nodded at her, smiling with the relief I'd felt. "He's okay. He'll be fine. He just needs to heal now."

She stared at me, taking it in, her eyes going glassy.

The feeling of spirit being manipulated tore my focus away. This wasn't the same feeling as a spirit moving through the space, however. No, this was the feeling of something entering, like the other night at the house.

I turned, brow furrowed, stepping away a little. Daisy and I could hug it out later. We weren't out of the woods yet.

"What is it?" Daisy asked, sagging against the wall.

"Something's…" Another soul blipped onto my radar, faint at first, as though it was manifesting. It seemed to be overlaying Zorn's, sharing the same space.

Dawning understanding made my stomach drop. Before I could turn, the door closed with a soft thump, and the lock clicked over.

"Kieran!" I rushed to the door and turned the handle. "Kieran!"

"What's happening?" Daisy asked, pushing off the wall.

I banged my shoulder into the door to bust it open. It didn't budge. This was well made, from an era that hadn't tried to skimp on such things, and I didn't have Zorn's physique.

"Zorn's compromised," I shouted as Kieran approached the door.

"Alexis?" His voice was badly muffled. I almost couldn't make out my name.

"Zorn is compromised!" I yelled as loudly as I could, magically digging into Zorn's chest so I could boot out the Possessor's soul. But it overlaid Zorn's soul perfectly, as if the two had been fused. I couldn't rip out one without ripping out the other.

"Not without seeing," I muttered to myself, feeling around the edges of the soul box, trying to find any differences in how they were rooted. How they connected. "I can't work on feeling the first time. I need to *see*—"

"I got it," Jack said, dashing for the wall. "I can tell him."

The handle jiggled, Kieran at the door, and suddenly Zorn's soul—souls—burst into action.

"Kieran, watch out!" I screeched, clutching Zorn's soul in my fist. It didn't stop him. I could feel him pushing through my hold.

Something slammed against the door. A blast of power rocked me backward. Intense pain and alarm poured through the soul link. More power pumped into the room beyond, bleeding into the storeroom.

"You gotta get in there," Daisy said, joining me at the door. "Force your way in!"

I slammed my shoulder against the door again. A third time. It was too strong and I wasn't heavy enough. I backed up and kicked. Nothing.

"Damn it." I shook Zorn's soul, battered it. A prong snapped. "What's happening?"

Jack ducked back in, his face ashen. "Zorn stabbed Kieran in the neck with a knife. Take Zorn down."

I relayed the info, needing a witness, needing courage, not wanting to do this.

"Wait. Wait." Daisy put her hand on the wall as another blast of power pumped into the room, singeing my skin. "Kieran is a Demigod. Zorn doesn't stand a chance."

"Kieran has to maintain pressure on his neck. He can't fight the way he needs to fight, and Zorn doesn't give in to pain," Jack said. "He's withstood days of torture. Not to mention *he's not in control.* It's either Zorn or Kieran, Alexis, and if Kieran goes, think what'll happen to everyone else. This whole territory. You have to step in. Drop Zorn."

"There has to be a way around this," Daisy said, not able to hear Jack. "That Possessor can't win again." She fisted her hand. "We gotta get in there. We have to get in there, Lexi."

My heart ached as I held Zorn's soul, as I felt Kieran's energy fading.

I shrugged out of my skin without a second thought. I didn't lie down. I didn't go into a trance. There wasn't time for fear. I pushed my body away like a coat in the summer.

It fell lifelessly to the ground. Daisy screamed and bent to me. I probably should've told her what I was doing.

The colors changed, intensified. Too bright. The Line pulsed, feeding me power. Ultraviolet color filled in the world around me, lining the cracks and pooling in the holes. Spirit held me in place, nearly floating but still grounded. Not a shadow.

In my peripheral vision, someone stood watching. I turned to look, but in a flash the shadowy being fled. Which was creepy.

Without another thought, I pushed through the wall, Jack at my side, warning me away from this, worried I'd go down with the ship.

It was possible, but damn it, if I couldn't use my magic to save the people I loved, what the hell was the point? It was time to embrace the good aspects of my magic, since I had already embraced the bad.

On the other side of the wall, Kieran staggered, his hand to his neck and blood squeezing out between his fingers. Another knife was embedded in the middle of his back, where he couldn't reach it to pull it out. That was probably a good thing. It would've let more blood escape.

Zorn threw another knife from the middle of the room, keeping his distance. Kieran moved, still fast, dodging out of the way. The knife stuck in the wall at his back.

"Didn't see it coming," Kieran said to me when I stopped next to him. "I knew there was a Possessor on the loose, and I didn't watch my back. Stu…pid." He dodged another knife that flew through me and hit the wall.

Blood oozed around his hand and down the center of his back. He was fast, but slowing. Soon Zorn's Possessor would find the gun Zorn had brought with the other weapons. We needed more time! I needed Zorn to stop moving so I could get a good look at those melded souls.

Something Harding had said tickled the back of my brain. It was a stupid idea. Really dumb. But…

I reached into Kieran through the soul link, into the very middle of him. He gasped.

And I pulled.

His spirit followed the thick thread that connected us, glittering with our combined souls. It oozed out of his body and manifested right next to me.

He froze for a moment, his Adam's apple bobbing

as he swallowed.

"Did you just kill me?" he asked in a level voice. I had to hand it to him: even now, he seemed completely confident.

"I hope I just fooled this guy into thinking you're dead."

"Hey, sir," Jack said, on my other side. "Not so good to have ya."

I took a moment to get closer, digging into Zorn's body with my hands, physically feeling with spirit, trying to focus on the colors holding the souls together. Each of the colors signified a different type of spirit. I could see them as clearly as I would with Bria's incense smoke.

I studied the combined souls as Zorn closed in on Kieran—as he bent, knife out, for the kill strike.

"Hurry, Lexi," Jack said through his teeth. "Now or never."

"Let her work," Kieran said, amazingly not struggling to get back into his body to fight back.

I sure hoped that was a good idea.

Zorn reached out his blade tentatively.

The souls didn't fit perfectly over each other. I'd been mistaken.

Steel kissed Kieran's neck.

One didn't even have prongs—it had merely fused itself to the edges of what I knew was Zorn's soul. It was like a suction cup. All I had to do was stick a fingernail between them and…

Pop.

It didn't make that sound, but in my head it did. I flung the soul away.

Zorn stopped right before he ripped the blade across Kieran's neck.

A middle-aged man with a comb-over and wide, watery eyes sprang from Zorn's body, skittering across the floor. I shoved Kieran, not thinking. He slammed back into his body, gasping for air. Zorn flinched as though burned.

I was already running.

Chapter 31

ALEXIS

"RUNNING ISN'T GOING to help you!" I hollered at the retreating spirit.

I punched my way through the wall, seeing the spirit around me sucking at the guy. It was pulling him back to his body, and I could see the path.

Bria, Red, and the guys were running up the street, hurrying for all they were worth.

"He's this way!" I yelled as I zipped past them.

Only Bria slowed, her body twisting, probably catching the strength of my soul. I turned as I mostly flew, pushing myself toward the spirit that was pulling itself toward its body. It was so easy when I just went with it. Like a trip on 'shrooms. Thank you, Mick, for talking me into a bad idea that one time at the bar.

Bria slowed further, then stopped altogether. Boman stopped with her, keeping an eye on her as she started moving in the opposite direction, walking first, then running.

Maybe she didn't know it was me and thought it

was the Possessor. Either way, great instincts.

The spirit I was following soaked into a body in a plain brown car. The body jerked as if waking up from sleep. I stopped beside the driver's-side window as Bria caught up, sprinting now.

He looked through the windshield, and I half wondered if he could feel souls like Bria could and knew I was beside him.

Either way, he must've seen Bria, because he suddenly burst into action, reaching for the ignition, popping his seat up to normal.

I dug into his chest, knowing my body was really close, that my soul mate was right beside it. If I needed an escape hatch, I had it. I could use all the energy I needed. Probably.

I gripped his soul and tried to straight-up rip it out.

He sucked in a breath and clutched at his chest. My energy dimmed significantly. No soul popped out.

He reached for the keys again, and I went to work on his prongs. Something showed up in the corner of my vision. I glanced over, hoping it was Bria. A black shape skittered away. That was getting annoying.

The first prong broke, easier than it had been earlier that day when I'd tried this with Daisy's kidnapper. The second broke, too, but not as easily. The third I struggled with, bending it, then twisting it, pulling. Each movement elicited a grunt. Each time he paused.

Loud footsteps preceded Bria slamming her hands down on the side of the car door.

"Alexis? That has got to be you. You're like a damn strobe light right now." She straightened up and stepped closer to the driver's-side window opened a crack in the warm day. "Well hello, what have we here?"

The man reached again for his keys. He shrugged, then shrugged again, as though it wasn't intentional. "I'm just on my way home from work."

Bria's eyes flicked across his face, then to a collection of items he'd laid out on his passenger seat.

"Nope. You're—"

His spirit hopped, right in front of me. It jumped from his person to hers.

Immediately I was on it—digging into her chest, finding his suction-cupped soul, and popping it off. He slammed back into his body, and she fell against the car, breathing deeply.

"What are you?" he asked, his voice quavering.

She laughed and wiped her brow. "Part of the spirit police, asshole. And guess what? I play the bad guy." She curled her fingers through the opening and ripped backward, shattering the window. The next moment she slammed her fist into his face, pulled back, and did it again. She ripped the door open and grabbed his shirt front, ready to batter him a third time. His head lolled and a bruise was already forming. She had this well under control.

Thinking of the others, I turned back toward my body, only then realizing how exhausted I felt. My eyes drooped and my limbs felt like lead. My energy was nearly depleted, had to be.

Moving by sheer force of will, I pushed through the space, something that was harder now that I wasn't reeling myself in, like I was trudging through waist-high snow.

"Uh-oh." A strong arm wound around my waist, supporting me. "I think we overdid it a little, huh?" Harding winked at me, his side touching mine. "Sorry I'm late. What'd I miss?"

"Something isn't right with you," I said, trying to stand on my own and finding it difficult. "Why do you always disappear for our battles?"

"A lot isn't right with me, and because I can't get too involved or I'll be noticed. Trust me, when you have a magic like mine, like yours, the big dogs take notice. As you can attest, or have you been asleep for the last few months? I'd prefer those big dogs to not notice I'm around again. With that watch you have, it'll be two Spirit Walkers for the price of one, know what I mean?"

We drifted through increasingly shadowy fog, our path unclear, my comfort with him at an all-time high. I was happy to be shepherded this one time. To take a break.

"You handled all that well," he said, and midway through the sentence his voice broke off, replaced by the thought-speak of the spirit realm. "Some things were…extreme, but you mixed your limited training with your logical brain and acted accordingly. You saved the day. I'm proud of you."

I did the equivalent of huffing out a laugh. Deep, soothing spirit wrapped around us now. Except I didn't know how Kieran was, if they'd stopped the bleeding. And I needed to make sure Bria brought that guy in.

"Whoa, whoa, whoa." Harding covered my hand with his. "Calm. We're working our way back there. Your people are handling things, don't worry. But you need to rejuvenate. Your Demigod does it by swimming in the ocean, and you and I can do it by walking through deep spirit. It's cleansing. Refreshing. Tell me if I'm lying."

He wasn't. I could tell from the way I was soaking in our surroundings.

"It seems like Hades has the most dangerous, sneaky types of magics," I said, thinking back. "How could a normal person handle a Possessor?"

"How could a normal person handle a bolt of lightning dropping out of the clear blue sky, straight for their head? Magic is messy. It's brutal. You always have to be prepared, and to do that, you have to amass people around you that can handle the different facets of the various gods. It's the only way to stay on top, because each of the gods, mighty and not so much, have some sneaky, cunning magics. To combat them, you need something in your arsenal that speaks the same language, that can see through the ruse, as you can do with most Hades magics. Your Demigod expanded his protection base when he met you and then brought on the exceptional Necromancer. But if he hopes to make it in the magical world, he must find more people like you—those who can expose the secrets of other magics."

It sounded as though he thought that would be a simple thing to do. As though people that important in their magical discipline were hanging around on street corners, waiting to get picked up. As I was seeing firsthand, people like me were collected. Stolen, sometimes.

My mood soured. "We won't be kidnapping anyone, if that's what you had in mind."

He chuckled. "I figured. Your Demigod walks a fine line of morality, thanks to dear old dad, right? I doubt he'd want to tempt his dark side. Luckily, he probably won't need to. He's got...a way about him. People seem to like him. Want to hang around him. That Kraken is still working for him, for example. Most Demigod staffers, like the woman your kid killed, escape in death like they were afraid to escape in life. But not that

Kraken. He's just hanging around, hoping to be useful. It's pretty…strange."

"Jack is a good guy," I said, sadness trickling through me. I'd been so focused on finding Daisy that I hadn't gotten a chance to grieve. "He was dealt a bad hand."

He paused for a moment, letting silence cradle us as we walked. I closed my eyes, taking in the comfort of the spirit around us. I'd much rather do that than let my brain focus on the fact that there was zero visibility, the colors were disco-style crazy, and I had no idea how to get back to reality. All I had right now was my potentially stupid trust in this guy.

"What I am saying is, if he hopes to guard you and keep his territory, he will need to expand. He probably already sees this, but if he doesn't, you'll need to prod him toward it. Maybe amass your own people, and the two of you can lead them together."

"Why are you telling me this? Why not tell him?"

"Because I am of Hades, and he doesn't trust me. I'm not sure if the former caused the latter, or if the two are unrelated, but there we are." He paused again, and I felt a little hesitation in the air between us, a little resistance, as if he was debating how much to say.

"Out with it. No more clues. I always realize what they mean too late."

"I don't know about that, but you certainly do read

clues where there weren't any. Pulling your Demigod out of his body was an extremely risky thing to do, given your experience level. I'm not even sure the situation called for it."

"You were watching and you didn't help?"

"Yup. I'm a trainer, not your real-life training wheels."

I nearly pushed him away in frustration, but fear kept me from doing it. I didn't want to get stuck here—wherever this was—if I wasn't touching him in some way. So I settled for a scowl he hopefully sensed.

"Well," he said, and the feeling of his voice lowered to a whisper, "you didn't hear this from me, because I really shouldn't get involved unless I want to be dragged into this with you, but your Demigod will wish to react to this treachery, and he absolutely must not. He'll know this, but if he needs guidance, you must give it. His strength is in the long game. His survival is in the long game. And your survival is with him. Unless you are a Demigod, you are exposed. Sad but true. And *you* are exposed most of all. You must seek shelter with him. Aid him, so that he might aid you. Protect him so that he might protect you. You are his armor. He is your future."

I blew out a breath I hadn't known I was holding. "I was hoping for some light chatter and maybe a massage."

"I can give you a massage. Which area were you thinking?"

I felt myself leaning on Harding less. Worry crept in. I needed to make sure everything worked out all right with Kieran, that his soul was soundly in his body and his body was mending. I needed to make sure Zorn didn't have any damage, Daisy was seen to, and that Bria had that guy subdued.

Without realizing it, I was drifting, feeling my body now and letting its natural suction guide me. The feeling was faint, almost nonexistent compared to the soul link, which I didn't want to tug for fear it might harm Kieran. Then I noticed the little silver string connected to my soul, strobing light. Hadn't Bria told me that I reminded her of a strobe light?

I tugged on it and felt the anchor on the other end. My spirit drifted faster. This little string was the way home.

"Amazing." Harding drifted with me, letting me lead. "You're such a natural. I wonder...what is helping you through all this chaos?"

"My upbringing. Nothing has ever been normal. All you can do is adapt."

Chapter 32

KIERAN

KIERAN SAT BESIDE Alexis's still body, laid out on the couch. The bleeding from her head had stopped, and if she'd had a concussion from falling, it was likely healed by now thanks to the blood connection.

"Still feel her?" Bria asked, sitting on the couch arm with the Possessor knocked out on the floor at her feet. She didn't feel he deserved to be comfortable, and Kieran couldn't agree more. If it weren't for the information Kieran wanted, the man would be dead already.

"Yes," Kieran said as Boman finished stitching up his neck. "She never fully disappeared this time. Nearly—she was a wisp for a while—but I could still feel her. It wasn't like the other times." He couldn't know for sure, and likely Alexis wouldn't either, but he had a feeling he'd developed a keener sensitivity to spirit after being fully immersed in it.

"She needs to go to the hospital." Zorn stood next to Daisy, who was sitting on the floor against the couch, her eyes so heavily lidded that Kieran didn't know how she hadn't fallen asleep by now. Boman had fashioned a sling for her arm, but her wrist was broken, there was no doubt about it. She needed to have it professionally seen to.

"Not until Lexi is back," Daisy said, lifting her head a little. "I want to make sure she comes back."

Kieran checked his phone, seeing a new text from Mordecai, checking on Lexi's status. He handed it off to Daisy to answer.

She'd kept her emotions bottled good and tight until it was clear they were out of danger. And then, for the first time Kieran could remember, he'd seen Daisy cry. She'd curled up in a ball and sobbed. Shortly thereafter, when she'd gotten hold of herself, she'd demanded to be taken to Mordecai right after Lexi returned.

After the hospital.

Lexi's presence grew stronger within him. Her spirit drew nearer. She was almost back now, pulsing brighter than before. Wherever she'd gone had revived her.

"What are your plans with this shithead?" Thane prodded the Possessor with his toe.

"You wondering how soon we can kill him?" Bria asked with a grin.

"Yup," Thane answered. "And I would like to volunteer for that honor."

"Get in line." Donovan turned from the window, his arms crossed. All the guys were close, but Jack had been Donovan's cooking buddy. They'd been a little closer with each other than the others.

Alexis opened her eyes and sucked in a breath. Her chest rose and fell before her focus zeroed in on Kieran. A smile crossed her beautiful face. "You're sitting upright."

Daisy jolted and turned, grimacing as she pushed to her knees.

Alexis's smile grew. "Hey. How's your arm?"

"She won't go to the hospital because of you," Zorn said.

"Kieran almost went to the morgue because of *you*, so maybe a little less grumpiness would be awesome," Daisy replied.

Bria huffed out a laugh, spraying the edge of the couch in spit. "*Burn!*"

Zorn's face closed down. He didn't voice that it hadn't been his fault. Knowing him, he was beating himself up for it anyway.

Alexis sat up stiffly. She rolled her head and then her shoulders. She stretched, yawned, then noticed Jack, standing in the far corner, his hands at his sides and his face drawn. Kieran had noticed him but hadn't known what to say. How to make it better.

Alexis had no such qualms. "What's your story?

Why are you hiding in the corner?"

The guys stiffened. All looked at the spot she was focused on. Longing crossed their faces. They wanted Alexis's gift so they could see their brother in arms again. Their friend.

"He's probably so used to stinking up the place that he forgot he doesn't have to put distance between us before taking a shower anymore," Bria said, her eyes sad but her smile thawing the room.

Thane chuckled and then shook his head. "It wasn't the stink from working out, it was blowing ass. That guy was lethal."

A lopsided grin worked up Jack's face.

"It's because he liked everything spicy, but his gut couldn't handle it," Boman said, laughing. "He'd always steal my peppers, remember? Then he'd bitch about shooting flames out his hole."

"Gross," Alexis said, motioning Jack closer. "You don't have a virus or anything. You can hang around."

"Doesn't have a virus that she knows about, anyway," Donovan murmured.

Thane guffawed. "I remember that! I told him to stay away from that chick, but did he listen? Nope. Went and got himself a case of the clap."

"Oh, that curly-haired girl?" Boman asked, tying off the last stitch in Kieran's neck. In a few hours he'd rip the stitches out. It was an annoying wound. The Possessor really had it coming to him. "She was a looker."

"She came with baggage," Donovan said, shaking his head.

"She should've come with penicillin," Boman added.

They all started laughing, and Jack's smile intensified. Kieran felt himself relax a little, and Lexi put her hand in his.

"It'll be okay," she said softly as the guys continued reminiscing and Zorn helped Daisy to her feet. "We'll either make Jack's spirit welcome, or I'll help him cross over. He's not gone, just different."

By the time she was done, the room had gone silent again.

"He helped me today," she went on, speaking loudly enough that everyone could hear her. "He was my eyes when I couldn't see. He brought me information I couldn't get myself. He was my spirit watchdog whenever things got iffy with the other Spirit Walker. His role was different than it would have been before, but he still helped the team. He stuck around and finished the job. He made right something that wasn't his fault to start with." She nodded with tears in her eyes, her gaze shifting to Jack. "You did good. You'll need to decide what you want to do—hang around or go—but whichever you decide, I'll help, okay? I'll make it work for you. Don't be scared. Be at home."

Tears dripped down Thane's face. The guy had never been concerned with crying in public—he'd always figured that if someone had a problem with it, he'd change into a Berserker and teach them to mind their own business. The other guys looked down at their feet or stared off at nothing while nodding. Even Zorn.

"Thank you," Donovan said. He sniffed, and it was clear he was trying to hold back emotion. "Thank you for doing this, Alexis. I'm glad Kieran stalked you like a creeper and brought you into the fold."

Just like that, the tension and emotion popped.

Boman chuckled with glassy eyes. "Why'd you need to ruin that moment, you dick?"

"Why'd you ruin those stitches?" Donovan pointed at Kieran's neck. "Are zigzags all the rage now?"

Kieran stood and brought Alexis with him. They needed to tie everything up, then hit the books and figure out who was who, what was what, and some future plans to deal with them. Two people had declared war, and Kieran would need to answer. But he'd do it the modern way, the way his father had taught him—in stealth. In secret. Behind the scenes. He'd lay all the plans, map everything out, and slowly back his prey into a corner. Then, at the last moment, he'd pull the pin. Together, he and Alexis and the rest of their crew would watch their enemies blow sky high.

Someone had challenged him to a game of chess, and he would answer that challenge in a way that made them regret ever having brought out the game board.

Chapter 33

ALEXIS

"WAIT…" AUBRI STEPPED in front of me, her face as serious as a heart attack. "Do you want a selfie to post to social media?"

I tried not to roll my eyes. And failed.

"No, I'm good," I said, checking my newly finished face and hair in a handheld mirror while sitting off to the side in the kitchen. Normal people had their hair and makeup done in a bedroom or bathroom, or somewhere out of the way. But I hated being isolated from the others. I'd commit to looking good for the paparazzi as much as possible, but I drew the line at missing out on the fun—or pandemonium—while I did it.

Daisy and Mordecai slouched at the kitchen table. Daisy's arm had been in a cast for the last four weeks, with two to go, and Mordecai was right as rain. With Harding's help to show me how, I'd re-created and attached Mordecai's crumbled soul prongs. They weren't as good as the originals, but they would last a lifetime if he stayed away from more close calls of the head-crushing variety. They were like prosthetic limbs for the soul.

"Okay, but are you sure?" She stepped back, surveying me. "Because you. Look. *Fabulous.*"

Red, staring out the window, turned to look. Unimpressed, she turned back, watching the street. She would remain with me for the foreseeable future. No one could tell if she was particularly grumpy about that fact, or just the normal amount of grumpy. Donovan suspected driving a pink car was the cause of her habitually bad mood. It would be enough to drag anyone down, he reckoned.

Bria entered the kitchen with an apple in one hand and a phone in the other. She paused between me and the table before jutting out a hip. "Yeah, good. Well done. No one will be able to talk shit about that look."

Aubri beamed.

"What am I getting all dressed up for?" I asked, carefully sliding off the stool in my swirly black dress. It was a Saturday and we didn't have any plans; usually I'd just hang around in self-chosen attire, my hair in a pony and no makeup. It wasn't until Kieran left with all the guys, including Jack, that Bria had told me to get ready. Aubri arrived shortly thereafter.

We'd had a memorial for Jack and paid our respects the traditional way, but he'd chosen to stick around.

Given he could be seen and heard by a couple of us, and help guard the spirit realm, he figured there was plenty to do. I also had a sneaking suspicion that he was afraid of what awaited in the Beyond.

"You are a kept woman. You do what you are told without asking questions," Bria responded before taking a bite of her apple.

Daisy huffed. "I'd like to see someone *try* to treat my girl like that. I would slit them from neck to navel."

"Oh my God, wow." Aubri dramatically looked at Daisy. "That's psycho."

"Yeah, she's right," I said, my tone brooking no argument.

Daisy had dealt with trauma a little differently than most fourteen-year-old girls. Her confidence had flowered. Her hunger for learning to protect herself and her family had intensified. And the amount she was stealing from Kieran to secretly put away had grown. Zorn still couldn't figure out what she was doing with the money or where she was stashing it. It was her nest egg. Her escape hatch.

She was even teaching Mordecai to be better about stealing. It had turned into a game, and even though it didn't seem right, Kieran wasn't beat up about it. I'd decided to turn a blind eye.

"You need to chill out," I said. "No swearing, and no overt and gruesome threats."

Daisy shrugged, and Mordecai leaned toward her and whispered, "I could just maul them. If we dragged them out to the forest in the non-mag zone, no one would even question it."

Daisy nodded. "You're onto something."

"You guys, stop. Please." I nearly ran my hands through my newly styled hair. Aubri would've then threatened to slice me from neck to navel. "That's too violent, even for magical people. You need to pull way back."

They both shrugged. Mordecai wasn't so sweet and levelheaded since his near-death experience. He'd gotten more ruthless in training, more vicious. He clearly didn't want to end up in that situation again, and as a powerful shifter, he'd be challenged often.

Bria's phone chimed. She glanced at the screen. "Okey-dokey, here we go. Load up, kids and dolls. Time to go. Except for you, Aubri—we're good."

Red pushed back from the window, and when I passed by her, she filed in behind me. "He got you a limo for the occasion."

"Yeah, but what's the occasion? Should I not have eaten? Are we having dinner?" I asked, passing through the open door and into the front yard. Sure enough, a stretch limo awaited us.

"It's only two o'clock. It's an awkward time to eat," Daisy said, following us out.

"Wait, wait, wait!" Aubri ran out holding a large jewelry box. "I almost forgot this!"

She gingerly took out the necklace Kieran had designed for me. Butterflies filled my stomach as she put it around my neck. It wasn't just the beauty of the piece, or the way it made me feel—it was the meaning behind it. It was our two magics, intertwined. His life and mine.

"Even better." Bria looked down the street as Frank emerged from the bushes to the right. That was his new hangout. Apparently I'd had one too many visits from a Demigod hellbent on messing with my life. He'd lost faith in the safety of the open grass.

Thankfully, no Demigods—that I knew of—had traipsed by since the battle. None that had made contact, anyway, in spirit or in reality. They weren't done with me, Kieran firmly believed that, but they'd realized we were stronger than they'd anticipated. And so they'd taken a step back to reassess. Or so he said. I was still training like mad anyway, trusting Harding to show me new stuff when he came by (which wasn't as often now) and constantly practicing on the stuff I did know. I was making great strides in my magical reach, my abilities, and my comfort level with the spirit world. I still didn't travel in the Beyond without Harding, but I knew someday soon I would.

"We're clear." Bria nodded at the man holding the limo door open for us.

He nodded at me and put out a hand to help me in. Red followed, and Frank tried to climb in after that.

"No." I put out my hand.

He paused with his hands on the sides of the door. "What?"

Daisy's face pushed through his center, and she paused, her nose scrunching, before scurrying in. "Ew! Did I just pass through...something?"

"Frank, you can't come," I said as Mordecai stalled at the entrance.

"Gross! Lexi, banish him!" Daisy said.

"I concur," Bria murmured.

"He's fine, you guys. He's just doing his own thing." I pointed. "But do it somewhere else, Frank. You're not riding in here."

"But how will I know how to get to the new house? You can't leave me here," he whined. "I need to look out for you. Your mom said so."

I shoved him away with my magic, then motioned Mordecai in. "The new house?"

Bria froze before nonchalantly looking at her phone. The conversation with Kieran about moving in together pushed to the forefront of my memory.

"Oh my God, did he get us a new house?" I asked, trying to contain myself as the limo got moving.

"Why would we need a new house?" Mordecai asked. "Ours is plenty big."

"Whatever happens, make sure that house stays ours," Daisy said. "Just in case he gets grabby. We can flip it."

"It doesn't need to be flipped. It's in perfect condition," Mordecai said. "It's just in a bad part of town."

"No, it's just up against a bad part of town. I bet we can put in some legislature to get the border moved."

Mordecai frowned at her. "*We* can't do anything, and I doubt the non-magical government will let us claim part of the dual-society zone. That zone is for everyone. You sound like Valens."

Her eyebrows pinched together. "Low blow."

"Well?"

"Fine. We can trade. Maybe just extend that bit out—"

"Enough," I said, really wanting to run my hand across my face in annoyance. Trying to keep a perfect face was difficult. "We're not selling the house, and we're certainly not going to try changing the boundary lines to selfishly inflate our selling price."

"Just saying. It's a wasteland on the other side. I doubt they even want it."

"Daisy," I said as we drove along Ocean Beach, which was clear and beautiful. I looked at the clean white sands, which had been fixed up nicely since our big battle with Valens. Half-nude bodies stretched out on their beach towels, taking in the sun Kieran was ensuring continued to shine. Streams of gray smoke rose from barbecues. No one was crazy enough to swim in the frigid waters.

The limo quieted as we drove up the hill, higher and higher. My heart beat faster. Each turn made the butterflies in my stomach flutter harder. The increasingly beautiful view made my heart climb up into my throat.

Finally, we pulled onto a road I recognized. Bria, Mordecai, and I had once parked down the way in order to break into Valens's house.

And then, finally, we parked right in front of that house. That enormous house on the cliff, with arguably the best view in magical San Francisco.

"Out we get," Bria said, still nonchalant.

Daisy's eyes rounded as she looked at me, her eyebrows at her hairline. She was a kid from nothing, and she'd never been to this place before. She wasn't inside and already it was blowing her mind.

Mordecai climbed out first. "That weird fountain of Kieran's mom is gone."

"It was disturbing, at best," Bria said. "It was the first thing Kieran tore down."

I exited the limo with numb feet. A flash made me flinch, a paparazzo standing next to a car across the way. I tried to play it cool as I walked around the car with my kids. We stopped on the walkway as the front door swung open.

Kieran stepped out, his tailored suit perfectly showing off his broad shoulders and powerful body. Nervousness fluttered through the soul link as he walked toward me, his eyes soft and deep.

"Hi, beautiful," he said, sliding a hand around my waist. He pulled me closer. Everyone around us might not have been there for all he seemed to notice. He kissed me gently. "I was wondering..." He paused for a second, and I held my breath. Was he going to pop the question? Was this it? Was this forever? "Will you move in with me?"

He turned a little and looked back at the house. I slowly released a breath, and he looked back at me, eyes glimmering, as if he realized what I'd thought he would ask.

"You know that it was my dad's, so it's absolutely fine if you say no," he went on, dropping his hand so he could clasp mine. "But I've changed it a lot. Had it completely redone."

"Do we still get our own rooms?" Daisy asked, tilting her head back to look up at the third story.

Kieran smiled. He glanced at Daisy, but his focus came right back to me, his eyes intense and hopeful. "Of course. It now has seven bedrooms. There's plenty of room for us and a few leftover rooms if someone wants to stay over."

"Or is forced to stay," Red murmured, watching the paparazzo snapping pictures across the street. "Hey, kid, why don't you go sneak up behind that guy and break his camera?" She looked at Daisy. "Think you can do that with your broken arm?"

Daisy's smug grin was short-lived. She looked at a straight-faced Mordecai. "I notice you didn't pipe up to help."

"She asked you, not me," Mordecai said.

"She calls you kid, too. You just wanted me to run off so you could get the first pick of the rooms."

"Yeah." Mordecai crossed his arms across his chest. "So?"

Daisy took off running, but not toward the paparazzo.

Kieran's smile spread. "So I guess that's a yes."

I laughed and let him lead me into the house. The interior was painted a modern gray and all the floors had been changed out to hardwood. No more white carpet. My smile stretched as I took in the beautiful chandeliers that fit the rooms just right, and the shabby *chic* furniture that apparently matched my whole *look*. It was perfect. It was all perfect.

"Did you take out the hidden passageways?" I asked, leaning against him.

"Of course not. Zorn is wondering how long it will take Daisy to find them, map them all out, and get grounded for whatever she gets up to in them." He pulled me toward the wall at the corner of the sitting room, where I'd seen the ghost of the old butler on my last visit to this house. Kieran knelt beside the fireplace, stuck his finger in a groove, and popped open a little hatch to the side. The entryway was small, but even Kieran could get in if he stooped.

Light from the now-open doorway illuminated a slowly moving, furry white creature. On top of a furry black creature.

"Oh my God, what the hell? Harding, are you in there?" I gasped.

The cat kept at it. "Yup."

"That's... Dude, that's not right."

"It's not *me* trying to procreate with this other cat. I'm just along for the ride. I think he's a virgin, though, because he doesn't seem to be figuring this out. Hole confusion, maybe."

My mouth dropped open. "Why are you in there? Why is *it* in there?"

"Apparently this other cat is in heat, and someone must've missed it slipping in here when they were working on these tunnels. Your Demigod thinks of everything, Lexi, except chummy cats sneaking into his home. So my stallion of a cat meets this cat, and ba-da-bing. Here we are."

I averted my eyes. "But why didn't you *leave* the cat

body? There's no repellent up yet. You don't need it."

"I'm not gonna lie: I wanted to see how all this played out. When in Rome…"

"You're not in Rome. You're in a cat!"

"Right, well…when in cat."

"Ugh!" Valens's old butler stopped amid strolling through, peering into the passageway with disgust. "What is…" He gave Kieran a condescending look. "I wondered how you would change things, but allowing *this*?" His nose curled. "Times have certainly changed. It's true what they say—youth ruins everything. What are you doing to my house?" He shook his head and resumed his slow walk out of the room.

I slammed the door shut and stared at a blank-faced Kieran. There were no words.

We moved away as a howl from the hidden passages made me grimace. "That is so gross," I said, shivering.

"It's nature."

"Not when a human spirit is in on it. That guy is absolutely cracked!"

He led me to the back living room, and we came to a stop in front of the view that had stolen my breath the first time I'd seen it. Blue ocean, graced by fingers of light. The orange of the Golden Gate contrasted the surrounding gold and green hillsides.

"This is so beautiful," I said, tears in my eyes. "Everything. What you've done with this place, the view…"

"You," he said softly, nuzzling my neck. "I love you, Alexis. I'll sign your name to this house, right beside mine, if you'll let me. Anything you want to change or redecorate is totally up to you. I don't care what you do with it, as long as you're happy. As long as you and the kids are living under the same roof I am. There's plenty of space in the garage if you want a different car. You can pick out whatever you want. My father had an extensive collection if you'd rather pick out one of those. He has a hangar full of them." He turned me so he was looking down into my eyes. "I know my life is crazy, which has made your life crazy, but if I can ease that for you in any way, I will."

"You think a life of luxury is going to make up for showing my magic to the world?" I asked, my expression not selling my words, largely due to the way my tears were wreaking hell on my makeup.

"I sure hope so, or I'm screwed." His smile took my breath away. His handsome face was better than any scenic view. "But there is one thing." He grazed his lips across mine. "The butler comes with the house...and he's not overly fond of me or change."

I laughed, deepening our kiss. "Just wait until you meet the spirits in the secret passages. When they aren't...occupied. Speaking of which, did you get rid of the sex room? And that gross trophy room library?"

"Both, definitely. The sex room is a stylish guest

room now. I figure Jack can hang out there until he figures out what he wants to do. The library was revamped."

I smiled and let my hands trail down his body, letting everything else—the danger, the uncertainty, the animal kingdom situation I'd unfortunately stumbled upon—fall away.

I cupped his massive erection. "Where's our room?"

He groaned against my lips. "I gutted my father's old room. I didn't grow up here, so it isn't weird for me, and it has a fantastic view. I figured you'd be happiest with that. We can always change to—"

I stroked him through his pants. "That's perfect. Maybe we could see that now and tour the rest of the house later?"

"With pleasure." He whisked me up into his arms. "So living here is a yes, then?"

"Yes." I caressed his soul through our connection. "It will always be a yes."

Chapter 34

MAGNUS

"SIR, A PACKAGE for you."

Magnus glanced up, annoyed by the distraction from his work. Why had an import he'd been buying for years suddenly doubled in cost? Gracie held a square box, its size about that of her chest. She set it on his desk.

"It was delivered to your decompression chamber."

Magnus dropped his pen slowly and sat back, his hands on the chair arms.

His decompression chamber was where he sat when he went into the spirit world. It was fortified to protect his vulnerable body while he was away. Only a select few people knew about it, and he'd trusted those people for hundreds of years. He had a blood oath to keep their silence.

"We've tested the package for explosives or anything dangerous." She looked down at the top. It didn't say who it was from. "We couldn't determine what exactly was in it from an ultrasound."

He read her face and knew she wasn't lying. He checked their blood link to confirm it. She was anxious and curious and unsettled. Good. So was he.

He pulled the coarse brown string at the top. The thick brown paper reminded him of an old-timey parcel. The plain cardboard box inside wasn't taped shut.

Gracie scooped out the packing peanuts, letting them bounce across his desk and onto the floor. She looked in and paused before stepping back. "Looks like a chessboard, sir."

Bewildered, he stood and leaned over the package, hovering his hands at the top of the box. A strange feeling seeped down through his middle.

He delicately removed what was, indeed, a chessboard. The squares were translucent gray and clear. They overlaid a picture of Amos's severed head.

Magnus hadn't been able to track Amos down, either in life or in spirit. Now he knew why. The child knew of Magnus's involvement.

Underneath the board was a plain white envelope. A few carefully folded papers were tucked inside. He skimmed the contents. His stomach dropped to his feet.

He held a list of the various export items from the greater San Francisco Bay Area, a few select trade agreements recently secured by San Francisco that gave Magnus the import answer he'd been looking for, and more information on Magnus's operation than had ever, *ever* been made public. To get his records, someone would've had to hack into his systems. Except no breaches had been reported. No breaches had *ever* been reported. How could this have happened?

Magnus glanced back at his computer and the unexplained cost discrepancy he'd noticed earlier. The child was sitting on top of a healthy exporting territory. Vegetables, fruits, tech—their goods were plentiful. Clearly the child knew it, and he was hitting Magnus in a place that made him financially helpless—one of the *only* places Magnus was helpless.

Valens had always boasted about his son's knack for the job, about how easily he took to training. Valens had been absolutely right. He had created a nightmare worse than he had ever been.

One last sheet fluttered back into the box as Magnus sifted through the papers. He picked it up and read. Fire rose through his middle, and he gritted his teeth.

He held his private DNA records. With them were the findings that Alexis Price was his biological daughter.

The child had known all along.

And he'd taken Magnus's involvement in this last skirmish personally. He also must've known about Magnus's propensity for killing his kids. That would make him more territorial toward Alexis, and more dangerous.

And now the child was preparing for war.

Good. Magnus would be more than ready.

THE END.

About the Author

K.F. Breene is a Wall Street Journal, USA Today, Washington Post, Amazon Most Sold Charts and #1 Kindle Store bestselling author of paranormal romance, urban fantasy and fantasy novels. With over three million books sold, when she's not penning stories about magic and what goes bump in the night, she's sipping wine and planning shenanigans. She lives in Northern California with her husband, two children and out of work treadmill.

Sign up for her newsletter to hear about the latest news and receive free bonus content.

www.kfbreene.com

Printed in Great Britain
by Amazon

27584990R00219